# ROSES
# AND
# RED HERRINGS

## RAY HOBBS

Wingspan Press

Published in the United States and the United Kingdom
by WingSpan Press, Livermore, CA

The WingSpan name, logo and colophon are the trademarks
of WingSpan Publishing.

ISBN 978-1-59594-647-8 (pbk.)
ISBN 978-1-59594-959-2 (ebk.)

First edition 2020

Printed in the United States of America

www.wingspanpress.com

1 2 3 4 5 6 7 8 9 10

This book is dedicated to those whose fertile and inventive minds hoodwinked the enemy throughout the Second World War, thereby playing a significant part in the eventual Allied victory.

## Sources and Acknowledgements

Macintyre, B., *Double Cross* (London, Bloomsbury, 2016)

Macintyre, B., *Operation Mincemeat* (London, Bloomsbury, 2016)

Masterman, J. C., *The Double Cross System* (London, Sphere Books Ltd., 1973)

Stevenson, W., *A Man Called Intrepid* (New York, Ballantine, 1977)

Lycett, A., *Ian Fleming* (London, Phoenix, 1996)

Wheatley, D., *Stranger Than Fiction* (London, Arrow, 1976)

Hughes, R., *Through The Waters* (London, Kimber, 1956)

Mann, J., *Out of Harm's Way* (London, Headline Book Publishing, 2005)

Thanks are due, as ever, to my brother Chris, whose academic approach, ideas and arguments were invaluable in formulating the plot of this story.

# Glossary for Readers Outside the UK

Note: n denotes naval terminology or slang.

| | |
|---|---|
| Morphia: | (then) name for morphine, now archaic |
| Writer [n]: | clerk |
| Flag officer [n]: | commodore or above |
| 'Set' (of whiskers) [n]: | moustache and beard, the only facial hair allowed |
| Dispensing chemist: | pharmacist, druggist |
| RNVR: | Royal Naval Volunteer Reserve |
| Gieves: | naval tailors and outfitters |
| Wren: | member of the Women's Royal Naval Service |
| Flat: | apartment |
| Bowler hat: | derby |
| Music hall: | British equivalent of vaudeville |
| First Lord: | political head of the Admiralty |
| BEF: | British Expeditionary Force |
| *Kriegsmarine*: | German navy |
| Dartmouth: | home of the Royal Naval College |
| ATS: | Auxiliary Territorial Service, women's army |
| Women's Land Army: | agricultural workers |
| WAAF: | Women's Auxiliary Air Force |
| WTC: | Women's Timber Corps |
| Lisle: | fine, woven cotton |
| Biscuit: | cookie |
| Chemist's shop: | pharmacy |
| RAF: | Royal Air Force |
| 'Quid': | pound sterling |
| 'Tanner': | six old pence |
| Jelly: | Jell-O |
| Postman's knock: | a children's party game |
| 'Poodle faker': | womaniser |

| | |
|---|---|
| Blitz: | the nightly bombing of Britain 1940-41 |
| RNR: | Royal Naval Reserve, then drawn from Merchant Navy |
| 'Pusser' [n]: | [1] anything officially naval [2] strictly according to naval regulations |
| Home Guard: | civilian home defence force |
| NCO: | non-commissioned officer (e.g. corporal, sergeant etc) |
| QM: | quartermaster |
| Special Branch: | branch of Scotland Yard dealing with national security |
| *Luftwaffe*: | German air force |
| (walk-in) Cupboard: | closet |
| Wardroom [n]: | Royal Navy officers' mess |
| (Battle of)Trafalgar: | defeat of the French and Spanish fleets in 1805 |
| Mess Undress [n]: | uniform for wardroom social functions |
| Chip: | fried potato |
| Keeping 'mum': | observing secrecy |
| Rugby: | English forerunner of American football |
| 'Secure' [n]: | leave one's place of work at the end of a watch |
| 'Civvies': | civilian clothing |
| Pram: | stroller, baby carriage |
| Lord Woolton: | wartime Minister of Food |
| Woolton pie: | vegetable pie (meat being strictly rationed) |
| Bar (of music): | measure |
| 'Randy': | 'horny' |
| Try (rugby): | touch-down |
| 'Pongo' [n]: | soldier |

## Author's Note

It would have been impossible for me to have told this story without referring to everyday details of life in the early years of the Second World War, many of which have become generally forgotten and which are therefore a mystery to most young people today. Here are a few fragments of information that I hope will be helpful.

Although the Munich agreement of 1938 was hailed by Prime Minister Neville Chamberlain as a guarantee of 'peace in our time', plans were already in place for the large-scale evacuation of children from vulnerable cities to safer locations. The events of the Spanish Civil War had demonstrated that the civilian population would be in no way immune from air attack in the event of war, and evacuation was the most logical precaution. Consequently, in 1939, 1,500,000 children as well as expectant mothers and other vulnerable people were directed to arranged destinations, where they would be placed, for good or ill, with local families. Some were fortunate in their hosts, and many children grew up in a healthy, happy environment. Others were less fortunate and had to endure hunger and sometimes ill-treatment at the hands of their 'carers'. It must have been a desperate time, also, for parents, handing over their young children, to be re-united with them several years later as strangers.

Another change came with the National Registration Act of 1939, whereby every citizen was required by law to register at a government office and carry an identity card. Bureaucracy went on to flourish, as rationing made further registration necessary, firstly so that everyone could be supplied with ration coupons, which they could use only in shops where they were registered as customers.

The ubiquitous gas mask became, at first, a nuisance and then a fact of life. Poison gas had been a dreadful feature of the previous war, and the nation had to prepare for its anticipated deployment. Everyone had to carry a gas mask, and that included children, for whom a special version was created in the form of a truly awful 'likeness' to Mickey Mouse. A baby could be placed inside a canvas shroud into which air would be pumped, and we can only imagine the baby's response and its parents' feelings. Happily, the gas mask in its various forms was never needed and could eventually be discarded and forgotten, although examples still turn up occasionally in junk shops.

The National Service Act of 1939 conscripted men initially over the age of 20 into the armed forces, and young women without children were later conscripted into the women's services, the Women's Land Army, the Women's Timber Corps, or the factories.

Because so much of the nation's food was imported, people were encouraged by the slogan 'Dig For Victory', to bid farewell to their roses and dahlias, and grow vegetables instead. Certain foods were popularised via information posters on the basis that they were both health-giving, and plentiful if grown at home. These included 'Potato Pete' and 'Dr Carrot, the Children's Friend', who appears later in this story. Other posters warned against waste, while others urged anyone in possession of sensitive information to 'Be like Dad and keep "Mum".'

Everyone was therefore kept very busy, and it is perhaps interesting to note that Mr Winston Churchill had three jobs: those of Prime Minister, Minister of Defence, and First Lord of the Admiralty.

Wartime life had its lighter side, too, and a popular feature of *The Daily Mirror* was the strip cartoon *Jane*. It's eponymous character was a beautiful and alluring young woman who became involved in adventures that inevitably involved her losing most of her clothing, so that she would usually be found in the final frame clad only in her underwear.

The subject of life in wartime Britain is too vast to be covered in these pages, but it has been ably and widely chronicled elsewhere, and I recommend its study, if only to appreciate the efforts of the truly remarkable generation that experienced it.

RH

# 1

## ASHFORD, KENT
## 1940

'You're doing ever so well.' Miss Ridley, the physiotherapist, walked with William down the ward amid raucous encouragement from the other patients. She was a young woman, with neat, short hair and a professional manner. 'Have you used crutches before?'

'Only once.'

'There's nothing about it in your medical notes.'

'There won't be. It was when I played Long John Silver in the school play.'

She must have thought he was an unlikely pirate, with his short, medium-brown hair and gentle, aesthetic features, marred though they were by the recently-sustained scar on his left cheek. She made no comment, however, being more concerned with his crutch technique. 'Push down with your hands,' she reminded him. 'Don't hang from your shoulders.'

'Why not? That's how I did it in the play.'

'Because this is real life, and it will damage the tendons under your arms.' She checked for daylight between his armpits and the crutches. Then, satisfied that he was using them correctly, said, 'Presumably, the play only ran for a few nights. That would limit the damage.'

'Only one night, as far as I was concerned.' He narrowed his eyes, as if the recollection still caused him pain.

'Oh?'

He went on wretchedly. 'Then they took me off and gave the part to someone else.'

She touched his arm in sympathy. 'What an awful thing to happen.'

'Yes, and it was all the fault of the bloody parrot. It wouldn't stop talking to me, so I was always late on stage.'

She breathed the sigh of the long-suffering. 'Honestly, Sub-Lieutenant Stamford, you really are the limit with your silly stories.'

He stopped and sat on an empty bed, resting his hand on the carved oak wainscoting that embellished the ward. 'My silly stories, as you call them, Miss Ridley, keep my spirits up, and they do as much for my fellow patients. This ward isn't the happiest of places, you know.' He patted the bed where he was sitting and said, 'Take the poor devil who went home this morning. His was a horror story on its own.'

She looked at him blankly. 'He wasn't one of my patients. What was wrong with him?'

'He was the end of his family line.'

'What do you mean?'

'Simply that he would never know the joys and trials of fatherhood, Miss Ridley, owing to a tragic encounter with a steel splinter.'

'Oh, how awful.'

'You can say that again.' William had been kept awake repeatedly by the wretched litany of Midshipman Shaw mourning his lost manhood. There were no words capable of consoling him; the other patients could only give their silent sympathy tempered to some extent with the irrational but inevitable sensation of guilt at having avoided a similar fate.

Possibly to distract him from brooding, Miss Ridley asked, 'Are you ready for the return journey?'

'Raring to go, Miss Ridley.' Using his crutches to lever himself up, he squared his shoulders and set a course for the far corner of the ward, where his bed was situated.

'Your mother's coming this afternoon,' she reminded him somewhat unnecessarily. 'I believe she lives in Ashford. It's very convenient for you both.'

'That's right, in Beaver Road.' On reflection, he said, 'It's convenient, I agree, but I could live cheerfully without the inconvenience of having my leg broken in three separate places.'

'Your leg will mend. You had a lucky escape.' She helped him off with his dressing gown and then turned down the bedclothes for him.

'Thank you, Miss Ridley. Do I get a reward for doing well?'

She eyed him with suspicion and asked, 'What kind of reward have you in mind?'

'Would a kiss be in order?'

'It most certainly would not.'

'My nanny always gave me a kiss when I'd done something special, like the time I shinned up a drainpipe to the rooftop to save a wounded robin.'

'Well, I'm not your nanny, and I don't believe your story anyway.'

'You really know how to hurt a chap, Miss Ridley.'

'Nonsense.' She took the crutches and stacked them in the corner. 'Have you ever heard the story of the boy who cried "Wolf"?'

'No, was he one of your patients?'

'Of course not. It's a fictional story, like most of yours.'

'The robin never existed,' he confessed, looking suitably humble.

'I thought not.'

'Neither did the nanny.' He tried to look humbler still.

'You don't surprise me.'

'It's just the effect you have on me. One kiss would make such a difference to my recovery.'

'No.' She was insistent.

'Just a tiny one.'

'No, you're very naughty.'

'I can't help it when you're around, Miss Ridley.'

She blushed and said, 'Just remember your mother's coming to see you.'

'You're not going to tell her I've misbehaved, are you?' His face became a study in alarm. 'You wouldn't do that.'

'I've a good mind to do exactly that.'

'You're a hard, cruel woman, Miss Ridley, but thank you for the promenade. It was all the more enjoyable for being unexpected.'

'Good day to you, Sub-Lieutenant Stamford.' She smiled in spite of herself, so he blew her a kiss.

The officer in the next bed waited until she was gone, before saying, 'You'd be all right there, William. She's a vicar's daughter.'

'Is that good? It would be a new experience for me.'

'They have a lot to rebel against. Take it from me.' He emphasised his point with a lascivious chuckle.

William didn't know whether or not to believe him. In any case, his main concern was that he'd been laid up far too long and he was impatient to be on his feet again.

Three months had elapsed since he was lifted from the after gunnery director tower, bleeding copiously and with his left leg horribly broken. His rescuers had wrapped him securely in a Neil Robertson stretcher and taken him down a succession of ladders to the sick bay, to be treated along with what seemed to be half the ship's company.

*HMS Exeter* had received a terrible mauling and was ordered to steam to the Falkland Islands to undergo urgent repairs.

For three days, William lay in indescribable pain relieved periodically by injections of morphia, until *Exeter* eventually berthed in Stanley Harbour, and he and the other wounded could be transferred to the hospital ashore. There, he underwent an operation to plate and pin his shattered bones.

The voyage home to Plymouth the next month was infinitely more comfortable for William, and his brief stay at Stonehouse Hospital in Devonport was brightened by a visit from Captain Bell of *HMS Exeter* and Flag Officer Plymouth. For remaining at his action station despite severe injuries, and continuing to direct gunfire on the battleship *Admiral Graf Spee*, William was awarded the Distinguished Service Cross, which, for want of a more suitable home, the admiral pinned on his pyjama jacket.

His transfer to the home in Ashford was purely for convalescence, and William felt that he'd convalesced long enough.

His mother came on to the ward at a little after two-thirty, bearing carefully-stored apples and pears and a tin of John Player cigarettes.

After a joyous reunion, as they'd not seen each other since the previous September, William said apologetically, 'It's good of you to bring cigarettes, Mum, but I stopped smoking when I was in hospital.'

'Oh, did you? Jane sent you all she had.'

'That was good of her.'

'Mind you, she's given up too. She thought it would be better for the children if the house wasn't filled with smoke.'

'She's probably right. How is she, by the way? And George and the kids?'

'They're fine. I'm going to have the children on Sunday, so Jane can visit you. George is on a course at RAF Somewhere-or-other. He's a flying officer now.'

'Is he, by Jove? The cheek of it. Outranked by my brother-in-law.'

His mother ignored his outburst, thrilled as she was at seeing her son again. 'Oh, William,' she said, 'it's lovely to have you back.' She took his hands and clasped them between hers. 'It's an awful shame about that scar.'

'Don't you think it gives me a kind of roguish, devil-may-care appearance?'

'Frankly, no, but listen, William. I don't usually like facial whiskers, but have you thought of growing a beard?'

'Grow a set? No, Mum. Any hair I grow on my face comes out ginger.'

'You're not ginger. You just have natural reddish lights.'

'It's the same thing.'

'No, it's not. How's your leg?'

'Getting better all the time. At least, the pain's gone. They stopped the morphia at Stanley Hospital, and that was a bugg... a nuisance.'

'I should think so. You'd be surprised if you knew how addictive it is.'

'I suppose so.' His mother was a dispensing chemist and she knew best. To move the conversation on, he said, 'I'm on crutches now.'

'Are you? Maybe they'll let you come home soon.'

'And pigs might fly. They say I'll be here at least 'til April, and I've been laid up three months already.'

'I know, darling, but they were horrible fractures, and they've got to get you fit again. I don't know what they've got in store for you, but you won't be able to do it on crutches.' She added, 'Mind you, if it were up to me, they'd discharge you on medical grounds.'

'Not that, Mum. I've done nothing yet.'

'You've done plenty,' she protested, 'and all of it in the first four months of the war.' The thought seemed to lead to another, because she said, 'Anyway, where's your medal? I haven't seen it yet.'

'It's not the "done" thing to get excited about medals, Mum.'

'I don't care. We're all very proud of you, William. Let me see it.'

'All right.' He opened his bedside drawer and took out his medal in its case. His mother watched him open it.

'Oh, William,' she said, 'isn't it magnificent?'

He smiled at the pleasure it gave her, but said nothing. It was better to let her enjoy it.

After a while, she remembered something. 'There was a telephone call, yesterday, from someone at the Admiralty,' she said. 'I told the man you were still in hospital, and he said he'd probably see you here. I don't know what it was about.'

'I can't imagine either.'

'The man said he knew you at Thames Division RNVR, before the war. He probably told me his name, but it didn't register. Anyway, I've no doubt he'll be in touch if he needs to speak to you.'

⚓

In the light of his immediate frustration, William dismissed the matter, so he was surprised when, a week or so later, he was told he had a visitor. He could see the day sister talking to an RNVR lieutenant, and then, as they approached his bed, he recognised Nicholas Rogers from Thames Division before the war. His visitor offered his hand with a broad smile.

'William, how are you, apart from the obvious?'

'Quite well, thank you, sir, and you?'

'I'm fine, but let's not be stuffy. I'm still "Nick".' He took the seat beside William's bed and said, 'I asked Sister if there was somewhere private where we could talk, and she said I might take you on to the lawn in a wheelchair. She's gone to fetch one.' He peered towards the entrance, but seeing neither Sister nor a wheelchair, returned his attention to William. 'By the way, old chap, congratulations on your DSC. Well-deserved, I'd say.'

'Thank you. How did you know?'

'I made it my business to find out.' He looked behind him again and saw Sister with another nurse, who was pushing a wheelchair. 'Ah,' he said, 'your transport has arrived.'

'Right, Sub-Lieutenant Stamford,' said Sister, 'let's get your dressing gown on and then you can have a nice, healthy outing in the garden.' She held his dressing gown while he pushed his arms into the sleeves.

'Thank you, Sister.' He fastened the sash for himself, and she and the nurse helped him into the wheelchair with its horizontal support for his left leg.

'I'll look after him, Sister,' said Nick, taking the handlebars. 'Which way is out?'

'Back to the ward entrance, then left down the passage, Lieutenant.'

'Of course. Thank you, Sister.' Picking up his cap, he pushed William out of the ward and across the lawn as far as the nearest of several wooden tables. He parked the wheelchair on one side of the table and took one of the chairs.

Around the borders, daffodils and crocuses had defied the national exhortation to 'Dig for Victory', and now stood proud and colourful. It was the first time William had left the confines of the ward and, curious though he was about the need for reticence, he allowed himself to enjoy the luxury.

Presently, he asked, 'What is all this about, Nick?'

'An appointment. When you're fit, that is.'

'Where? Doing what?' He was a gunnery officer, and his duty was at sea with the fleet.

'It's come about because of your *penchant* for telling bloody silly stories and making people believe them. It's something everyone remembers about you at Thames Division, and there are those at the Admiralty who feel they can make use of that facility.'

It sounded too ridiculous for words. 'But no one at the Admiralty has ever heard of me,' he protested.

'Yes, they have. I've been extremely vocal about your ability to talk convincing bollocks, and most of those I've spoken to are very impressed, believe me.'

William shook his head in bewilderment. 'I only ever do it in fun.'

'But just think of it, William. It's a well-known fact that our not-so-worthy adversaries have absolutely no sense of humour, and even if they had, they'd see it as something to be taken bloody seriously.' He leaned forward to make his point. 'Deception could be instrumental in winning this war, and we need you on board.'

'This is sheer fantasy, Nick. I'm expecting to be joined at this table by a mad hatter and a march hare; in fact, I shouldn't be surprised by anything after what you've just told me.'

Nick waved his objection aside. 'I'll be in touch again, William, and I'll tell you where and when to report. In the meantime, remember that this is absolutely hush-hush. Not a word to anyone.'

'Of course not. In any case, I'd feel a complete idiot repeating what you've told me this morning.'

'Well, see that you don't. Oh, and before you report, you need to pay a visit to Gieves.'

'Why?'

'Because you need them to sew a full lieutenant's rings on to your uniform. You've been promoted ahead of your new appointment. You'll receive confirmation in due course, and then I'll look forward to seeing you at the Admiralty.'

# 2

## MAY 1940

Everything was new; the jacket and trousers, the shoes, and the white shirt and starched collar. His old uniform had been so badly damaged by smoke, and then by water pumped into the ship's burning compartments, that it had been discarded along with the ripped and bloodstained tropical whites he was wearing when he was wounded.

He was also awkwardly conscious of his walking stick, which had already prompted numerous people to step sympathetically out of his path even before he'd boarded the train at Ashford. It must have seemed wrong for a young man to be walking with assistance. He would be twenty-five in a few weeks' time, but they weren't to know that. In any case, he would still seem young to many of them.

And now he was on his way to London, to take up the bizarre-sounding appointment Nick Rogers had told him about. His long stay at the convalescent annexe in Ashford seemed an age ago, although he still winced at the memory of his last day there, when he'd called at Physiotherapy to speak to Miss Ridley, ostensibly to thank her for her efforts, but actually with a view to prolonging their association. That was when he noticed the engagement ring and he knew his cause was hopeless. He could cope with it, however, and now he was *en route* for London, his old hunting ground.

Cheered by the thought, he settled into his corner seat with a copy of *The Inimitable Jeeves*. He'd read it many times, but it had never lost any of its appeal.

He was so engrossed in the trials and misfortunes of Bertie Wooster, that the train was almost at Charing Cross before he looked up, and he hastily put away his book and reached up to the luggage rack for his case.

'Let me help you with that.' A grey-haired civilian seized the case and lifted it down for him. 'I could see you were struggling,' he explained.

'Not really struggling, but thank you anyway.' Again, he felt awkward at being helped by an elderly man.

'You're welcome. Where did you get the injury?'

'Oh, I'm just accident prone. I tripped over the ship's cat and fell down a ladder.'

'Nasty.'

'Not all that bad, really. I had a soft landing.'

'Really?'

'Yes, the cook was at the bottom of the ladder, and he was a man of generous proportions. He felt a bit flat for a while, but he's all right now.'

The old man shook his head in wonder. He asked, 'What ship was that?'

'I'm afraid I'm not allowed to say.'

The train jolted into the station and came to a halt, emitting a cloud of steam. William stepped down, good leg first, on to the platform.

'Can I help you at all?' The elderly man was at his elbow.

'No, thank you. I'm all right now.' He walked on, hoping the man would leave him alone as they both approached the barrier and surrendered their tickets.

'Good luck, then.'

'Thank you. Goodbye.' He crossed the ticket hall and made for the exit. The morning was mild and pleasant, and he walked steadily towards the familiar sight of Trafalgar Square.

It was impossible to make out Lord Nelson's expression, perched as he was 170 feet above London, but the sandbag-shielded lions that bordered the Square simply looked sleepy, as if they were emerging from their wartime bedding for the first time that day. It might have been Landseer's intention for them to be fierce and challenging, but to William's eye, they appeared to be yawning and, after more than 70 years, who could blame them?

Crossing Whitehall, he continued to Spring Gardens, arriving eventually at the address he'd been given. He passed the Royal Marine sentry and entered the building, where he found a neat, dark-haired Wren writer at the Quartermaster's Desk.

'Good morning,' he said.

'Good morning, sir.'

'I have to report to Rear Admiral Davies.' He showed her his identity card.

'I see, sir. Please take a seat.' She indicated a row of leather-upholstered chairs before picking up the telephone.

From his seat, William studied the panelled lobby, with its portraits and ornate mouldings. It was his first visit to the seat of power, and he felt very much like a small boy on his first day at a new school.

Presently, the Wren said, 'An officer from the Naval Intelligence Department is on his way, sir. He shouldn't be long.'

'Thank you.'

He waited for maybe two minutes and heard approaching footsteps on the corridor. The officer appeared.

'William,' he said, 'how are you?' It was Nick Rogers.

'Hello, Nick. I'm well, thank you. And you?'

'Very much in demand, old boy, and about to disappear up my own stern gland if I'm not careful, but otherwise in good health.' He watched William pick up his walking stick and asked, 'How's the leg?'

'Improving all the time.'

'Good. It's only a short walk to the Department. I'll introduce you to Admiral Davies and then I'll have to leave you. I'm being moved to another appointment. That's why I'm out of breath.'

'You conceal it well, Nick.'

'Am I walking too quickly for you?'

'No, I can manage, and I need the exercise.'

'Let me carry your case. It's no trouble.' Without waiting for a response, he took it out of William's hand.

'I'll need to find accommodation,' William told him.

'It's easy enough to find in London nowadays. So many people have moved out to so-called safe places ahead of the bombing that's expected, those of us who have to stay can almost pick and choose.'

'Good grief.'

'Yes, if you grab me later today, when, hopefully, I shan't be as busy, I should be able to put my finger on a place for you.'

'That would be very good of you. Thanks.'

'You'll be RA, I presume?'

'That's right.' The Ration Allowance was paid to officers and ratings obliged to live out, and therefore take on the responsibility for feeding themselves.

Nick came to a halt outside a door with a frosted glass window marked with the rear admiral's name and an indecipherable group of letters that presumably described his function. He knocked on the door.

A woman's voice said, 'Come in.'

Nick opened the door and said, 'Lieutenant Stamford is here to see Rear Admiral Davies, Bea.'

The lady named Bea was a Wren third officer. She was dark, slim and rather pretty.

'I'll tell him, sir,' she said, flicking up a switch on the desk intercom. A man's voice answered, and the third officer informed him of William's arrival.

The voice said, 'Send him in, Bea.'

'Aye-aye, sir.' Turning to William, she said, 'The admiral will see you now, sir.'

'Thank you.'

Nick touched his arm. 'I'll see you later, old man.'

William stepped inside the office and came to attention.

'Hello, Stamford.' The admiral offered his hand. 'How are you after your long stay in hospital?'

'Very much better, thank you, sir.'

'Good. Congratulations on your DSC. That was a splendid effort.' Even seated, he appeared tall. He was also lean, with dark, thinning hair.

'Thank you, sir. The whole operation was superbly carried out, if I may say so.'

'You may, and I agree with you, but I was referring to your individual effort, Stamford.' He held up his hand to forestall objection. 'There's no need for coyness. Let's leave it at that.'

'Thank you, sir.' William was a modest man, easily embarrassed by the attention his decoration had attracted, so he was grateful to the admiral.

'Now, take a seat, and I'll tell you what this is all about. First of all, though, I'll organise some coffee. Is coffee acceptable?'

'Yes, please, sir.' It was the first time he'd been entertained by an officer of flag rank, and he felt awkward.

The admiral flicked up the switch on his intercom, spoke affably to Bea and requested coffee for two.

'There,' he said, 'coffee should be with us shortly.' He sat back in his chair and said, 'The first thing I have to tell you is that the work of this department carries the highest security classification, and it is of the utmost importance that not even a hint of what we do is noised abroad.'

'I understand that, sir.'

'Good.' Something else occurred to him, because he said, 'Just while we're waiting for the coffee, I'd better explain that everyone's in a state of nervous expectation. Have you seen a newspaper recently?'

'Not today, sir. Are you referring to Norway?'

'No, although things are bad enough over there. The first thing is that Hitler has invaded France and the Low Countries.'

'Oh, good Lord.'

'Quite, and the second is that Parliament is in turmoil. The Labour Party has refused to serve under Chamberlain in a coalition. I can't say as I blame them, actually. The man's a clot. But the question is, who is going to take his place?'

It was news to William, who'd had other matters on his mind. 'Who do you think, sir? Lord Halifax?'

'Let's hope not. He's as big a ninny as Chamberlain. No, the main contender is Churchill. He's buggered up a few things in his career, but he has something in abundance that the others lack, and that's fighting spirit.'

'Do you think he stands a chance, sir?'

'Yes, and by Jove, this country needs him. Hopefully, we should hear something soon.'

There was a knock at the door, and the admiral put a finger to his lips.

'Come in.'

'Bea entered with a tray. 'I didn't have a girl to spare, sir, so I brought the coffee myself.'

'Bless you, Bea,' said the admiral. 'This is Lieutenant Stamford. Stamford, this is Third Officer Dean.'

The two shook hands and exchanged greetings.

Miss Dean asked, 'Would you like me to pour, sir?'

'No, thank you, Bea. We'll manage. Carry on.'

'Aye-aye, sir.'

'Oh, Bea?'

'Yes, sir?'

'Has there been any news?'

'Not yet, sir.' She opened the door to leave. 'I'll keep you informed, sir.'

He waited for the door to close behind her. Then he poured the coffee and said, 'The purpose of this department, Stamford, is deception. We have to deceive the enemy in any way we can. It may be by making him believe we are stronger than we actually are, that we have weaponry he's never heard of, or even that we use trained monkeys to handle ammunition because they do it so much quicker than a party of matelots, and they don't expect rum and duty-free tobacco. In short, if it helps our cause, we have to bamboozle the bugger in any way we can.'

'And you believe I can make a contribution to this work, sir?'

The admiral nodded confidently. 'Your reputation goes before you, Stamford, like a lurid trailer. Tell me, what kind of work did you do before the war?'

'I was a copywriter, sir. I worked for Groves and Holmes Advertising in Camden Town.'

'Ah.' The admiral smiled briefly. 'So you were a professional liar.'

'It seemed so at times, sir.'

'But an honest liar, or you wouldn't admit it.'

The occasion called for honesty. 'I think everyone knows the truth about advertising, sir.'

'In that case, Stamford, why do people fall for it? They obviously do.'

'Most people believe what they want to believe, sir. If we tell them that Satinesse stockings will make them look like Betty Grable, there'll be those who'll dash immediately to the nearest store to buy a pair. Similarly, if we tell men that smoking Colonial tobacco gives them an air of rugged authority that women find irresistible, it will disappear from the shelves like sou'westers in a monsoon.'

The admiral chuckled quietly before saying, 'That's the kind of thinking we're looking for, and also the reason we recruited you.' He opened a box of cigarettes and offered it to William, who shook his head.

'No, thank you, sir. I don't.'

'Very sensible, Stamford. I should know better, being a martyr to bronchitis.' He closed the lid and asked, 'Have you any questions so far?'

'Yes, sir. Is this a long-term appointment?'

'That depends on how long the war will go on.'

'So it will be, then.'

'Does that disappoint you?'

'Well, sir, I was trained in gunnery, and I rather see my place in a director tower.'

The admiral raised an eyebrow. 'I, too, was a gunnery officer, Stamford, and I served as such in the last war, but now my place is here, doing a very important job.' He took a cigarette from the box and lit it. 'In Naval Intelligence, you'll be hitting the enemy much harder than you ever could as a gunnery officer. Do you hear what I'm saying?'

'Yes, sir. Of course, I'll serve wherever I'm appointed.'

'Good man. Now, you're possibly wondering how we communicate disinformation to the enemy.'

'The question has crossed my mind, sir.'

'Quite. The fact is, we are in touch with a small number of enemy agents, although that number is growing steadily.'

'*Enemy* agents, sir?' William wondered if he'd misheard the admiral.

'Yes. One such agent, codenamed "Snow" is being particularly helpful. It's our policy, you see, to turn captured agents if we can, and employ them as double agents.'

'What if they refuse to co-operate, sir?'

'We extract whatever details we can from them, such as their identification and background information, so that we can keep them "alive and transmitting" as far as Berlin is concerned, and then we shoot them.'

'So the disinformation you were talking about is sent to Berlin via these double agents?' It all sounded like a tale from a boys' adventure paper.

'Exactly so. In a few minutes, I'm going to take you to Security, where you'll be given the necessary identification to enter the most sensitive areas, and then I'll leave you with some files I want you to read.'

There was a knock on the door. The admiral looked up and, recognising a familiar outline through the frosted glass, said, 'Come in, Bea.'

Third Officer Dean entered the office with an air of barely-suppressed excitement. 'There's been a development, sir,' she said. 'It's just been announced by the BBC that His Majesty has asked Mr Churchill to form a government.'

⬦⊶⊰⊱⊷⬦

Later that afternoon, Nick Rogers called at William's new office, where he had been trying to digest information from the files Rear Admiral Davies had left with him.

'Hello, old man. How's it going?'

'This is difficult to take in, Nick, chiefly because it seems so... I don't know.' He tried to think of an appropriate description.

'Mata Hari? *The Spy in Black*?'

'Exactly.'

'It's only because you're new to it. It'll all seem quite normal before long.' He looked at his watch and said, 'I've been released from my duties to help you find accommodation and, as it happens, I know the very place.'

'Already?'

'Yes, I'll explain as we go. First of all, you need to return those files to the Records Department.'

On the way, they encountered several people in civilian dress, and William remarked on it.

'Civil servants, old man. You'll find them everywhere. It's my belief they get together in enclosed places and breed like bowler-hatted rabbits, but regard that as classified information.'

'I'm the very soul of discretion.'

'Working here, you'll need to be.'

They delivered the files to Records and continued on their way.

'Nick?'

'Yes, old man?'

'What's the situation with Third Officer Dean?'

'The fair Beatrice? Availability, do you mean?'

Somewhat embarrassed, William mumbled, 'That sort of thing.'

'Handle with great care, old man. She's the admiral's niece.'

'Good heavens.' He resolved to resist the temptation.

'The flat is on the north side of Clapham Common,' explained Nick. 'We have to walk to Charing Cross, but then we can get the tube to Clapham.'

'How do you know about this place?'

'It's been my abode until now, but things have moved on rather quickly. I received orders today to report to my new appointment tomorrow morning.'

'Where's that?'

'A place in the wilds of bloody Cornwall, and I have to travel down there tonight.'

'Bad luck.' William knew better than to enquire into Nick's new appointment. Instead, he said, 'Tell me about the flat.'

'Okay. It's a furnished flat, a lovely, comfortable town residence with two bedrooms, a kitchen and a sitting room *cum* dining room. Not only that, it's a basement flat. It'll be safer, I imagine, when the *Luftwaffe* makes its appearance. I spoke with the letting agent today, and he was more than happy that I'd found a new tenant. I told him we'd meet him at the flat at five o'clock.'

Twenty minutes later, they reached the flat, and William could see at once that it was as Nick had described it. The letting agent arrived with the necessary papers, and the arrangements were put into place. It would be the perfect bolthole after the bizarre world of Naval Intelligence.

# 3

William wished he'd been present in the House of Commons on the 13th, when Mr Churchill made his maiden speech as Prime Minister. It must have been a magnificent occasion, with Clement Attlee, Leader of the Labour Party, leading the deafening applause. William hardly ever read a newspaper but, exceptionally and like most people, he'd read about it in the press. It was second-best, but it still made stirring reading.

The newspapers were also full of reports of the latest Nazi advances, which were seemingly unstoppable. Everything rested on the French and British forces in France, because it was clear that Norway was now as good as lost.

As he was thinking about it, there was a brief courtesy knock on the door, and Rear Admiral Davies entered, followed by an army officer bearing the crown and two pips of a full colonel. William rose to attention.

'Good morning, Stamford. Stand easy.'

'Good morning, sir.'

'I've brought Colonel Loxton to meet you.' Turning to the colonel, he said, 'Lieutenant Stamford is our latest recruit.'

'How do you do?' Loxton offered his hand. He was extremely tall and powerfully built, but his most noticeable feature, as William saw it, was a downturned mouth that gave him a grim and determined expression.

'How do you do, sir?' The two men shook hands. Loxton's handshake was brief but extremely strong.

'And what did you do before the war, Stamford?'

'I was a copywriter, sir.'

Loxton frowned and looked to the admiral.

'Advertising,' explained the admiral.

Loxton's eyes narrowed, but he made no comment. The admiral appeared not to notice. He asked, 'Have you everything you need, Stamford?'

'I have one request, sir. I wonder if there's any possibility of my being given an assistant.'

'An assistant?' The admiral looked surprised, whilst the colonel appeared faintly amused.

'I need a sounding board,' William explained. 'I need to put ideas to someone capable of questioning them, or maybe making suggestions. It's the best way I know of arriving at a coherent plan.'

'I don't know, Stamford. I can't let you have another officer. We're hard pressed as things stand.'

'Maybe a rating, sir?'

Before the admiral could reply, the colonel said, 'I have an idea, sir. We have just the person for such a role. She has Ultra Clearance and is available.'

<hr />

William had printed *Lt. W. J. Stamford, D.S.C., R.N.V.R.* on a rectangle of thin card, and had just attached it with gum to the glass pane of his door. It was his second attempt, as he had abandoned the first when the admiral insisted that he must dispense with humility and include his DSC in the title.

He was casting a critical eye over his handiwork, when he heard approaching feminine footsteps on the corridor. Purely out of curiosity, he waited to find out whose footsteps they were.

A few seconds later, the mystery woman appeared, looking a little anxious, but no less fetching for that, in a dark-grey worsted skirt and a white, short-sleeved blouse.

'Good afternoon,' she said. 'I'm looking for Lieutenant... Stanforth.' She seemed unsure of his name, which was understandable.

'I think you mean *Stamford*, in which case I can help you.' He wanted to help her, because she had the kind of smooth and flawless complexion he'd associated with northern Britain ever since the advertising campaign for Hill's Cold Cream. Also, dark-brown hair cut expertly in a long bob framed an appealing face, and her gentle brown eyes suggested vulnerability. It was an engaging ensemble.

She read his name on the glass pane and asked, 'Are you Lieutenant Stamford?'

'I am. Come inside and tell me why you were looking for me.'

'Oh, weren't you expecting me?' The look of concern returned.

'Should I be expecting you?'

'I'm Lucinda Pendleton. I thought they'd told you I was coming.'

'Come in and take a seat, Miss Pendleton. Then you can tell me who "they" are.' He unhooked his walking stick from the doorknob and stood aside for her to enter.

'Oh, gosh, you're injured,' she said. 'Can you manage, or do you need help?'

'I'm all right, thank you. I hope I shan't be needing this thing much longer.' By explanation, he added, 'I had a broken leg, but it's much improved now.'

'Oh, good.'

He removed his steel helmet, gasmask haversack, webbing belt and revolver holster from the chair in front of his desk. 'Take a seat, Miss Pendleton, and please excuse the artillery. It's a precaution against a sudden influx of German visitors.'

'Oh, I'm used to that.' She took the vacated seat and said, 'Colonel Loxton, one of the Deception Planners, sent me. He said you wanted someone to help you.'

'Ah.' It was falling into place. 'You must be the person he mentioned.'

'Probably. Do you mind?'

'Not in the least.' Remembering his manners, he said, 'I'd offer you a cigarette, but I don't smoke.'

'That's all right. Neither do I.'

'Would you like a cup of tea? I can organise that.'

'Oh, let me do that,' she said, standing up eagerly.

'All right.' He sat back to take stock as she disappeared in the direction of the small galley that served the floor. If she hung around long enough, he would get to know her better, but at a first glance, she seemed unsure of herself, and that was odd, considering her neat and well-groomed appearance, not to mention her looks.

She returned after a few minutes with a tray loaded with a teapot, hot water, a strainer, cups and saucers, milk and sugar.

'I didn't know how you take tea, Lieutenant Stamford, so I brought everything,' she said, setting the tray down on his desk.

'Good thinking. I have milk, but not sugar.'

'Right.' She lifted the teapot lid and gave the contents a stir. 'Shall I pour?' She seemed eager to please him.

'Please go ahead.' He let her pour the tea. 'I must say, a china cup and saucer is a luxury in this place. I usually have to make do with a mug.'

'Oh, there are lots in the galley, and I always think tea tastes better in a china cup. Don't you?'

'I do. Tell me, though, what is your function in this organisation? Are you a civil servant?'

'I suppose I am. At least, the Admiralty pay me as a junior clerical assistant.'

'And what's your main job?'

'I don't really know.' She looked caught-out, as if he'd asked the one question she was hoping to avoid. 'I've had so many, it's difficult to say. My last placing was a disaster, and when they said you needed an assistant, I leapt at the chance. I didn't know what the job entailed, but it was a way out. I thought, *Noli equi dentes*, I suppose. I hope you don't mind.'

'What?'

'*Noli equi dentes inspicere donati*,' she said. 'It means, "Never look a gift horse in the—" '

'I know what it means. I was just wondering if you do all your thinking in Latin.'

'No, it's a bad habit. I'm sorry.' She seemed deflated, and he wished he hadn't mentioned it.

'Please don't be sorry. I get the impression you spend your life apologising.'

'I seem to,' she agreed, 'nowadays.'

'So, "nowadays" is not the happiest period of your life. Why don't you tell me your story from the beginning, Miss Pendleton? Tell me how you came to be here and why.'

'All right.' She took a sip of her tea, possibly to fortify herself.

'When war seemed imminent, I wanted to do something useful, such as joining one of the women's services, but my father wouldn't hear of it. He said I was too scatter-brained for that kind of thing.' She shrugged helplessly. 'I couldn't really blame him for thinking that after the awful mess I made of running the Sports and Social Club.'

William had to interrupt her flow. 'Tell me about the Sports and Social Club,' he said.

'All right. My family own Pendleton Engineering in Manchester.'

'I've heard of them. Don't they make gears?'

'That's right. Well, my grandfather, who started the company, is what I believe they call a "benevolent employer", rather like the cocoa manufacturers, except he's not a Quaker or anything like that. He's Congregationalist and a Liberal. Anyway, he started the club years ago for the benefit of his employees, because he believes that a happy worker is a loyal worker. There are football and cricket teams, a choral society, a chess circle, and they go on excursions and that sort of thing.'

'Good for your grandfather.'

'Yes, he's a sweetie. I love him dearly, but I let him down. You see....' Her voice faltered. It seemed the memory was still painful. 'My father put me in charge of the Club.' She hesitated again, and William thought she might give way to tears, but she recovered and continued. 'My brothers had to take over and clear up the mess I left behind.' It sounded like the ultimate disgrace.

'Evidently, you're not cut out for management.'

'That's putting it mildly, Lieutenant.'

'Did you receive any training?' As far as he knew, managers were usually trained up gradually until they were deemed capable of taking control.

'No, and it wouldn't have made any difference. I was just a complete dunce at the job.'

'It's not given to everyone, Miss Pendleton,' he said. Then, not wishing to dwell on the incident, he asked, 'How did you come to work at the Admiralty?'

Looking a little shamefaced, she said, 'My grandfather pulled strings. Well, just one string, actually.'

'He must have a lot of influence.'

She nodded. 'He and Mr Churchill are friends. They have been since the last war, when they were developing the tank. Pendleton Engineering made the parts that solved some of the problems at the time.'

'Really?'

She gave a matter-of-fact nod, as if she'd told the story many times.

'What have you done since you came here?'

'I've been through various departments, each with glaring lack of success. So far, I've made an absolute hash of typing, shorthand, and anything else they've set me to do. Colonel Loxton called me "Hitler's secret weapon." He couldn't wait to get rid of me, although he wasn't the worst.' She looked suddenly apprehensive and asked, 'Will I be expected to type reports, Lieutenant?'

'No, you can leave that to me.'

'Oh, can you type?'

'Can I type? I'll have you know I'm a two-finger Thibaud.'

'He plays the violin.'

'Not with two fingers, he doesn't. Anyway, I couldn't think of a pianist beginning with "T".'

She thought for a moment and said, 'There's Rosalyn Tureck.'

'Well done, Miss Pendleton. I'd forgotten about her.'

'I'm surprised, because she's amazing.'

'I've always thought so.'

'Neville Cardus says she makes interpretation an act of creativity, and I know just what he means.'

'You're musical, evidently.'

'I play the violin.' She hesitated. 'At least, I did. I left my fiddle behind in Carrbrook.' She explained, 'That's where we live, Carrbrook, Stalybridge. It's only the factory that's in Manchester.'

'Even so, that's not the end of the earth, Miss Pendleton. In any case, how do you rate your violin playing?'

'Oh, well, it's not for me to say, is it? I do have a diploma from the Guildhall School of Music.' She added shyly, 'I won a prize for music at school as well, but that's not much use here, is it?'

'Not directly, I suppose, but as well as calling for musical ability, playing an instrument to a high level requires skills of a more general nature.'

'I suppose it does. Do you play an instrument, Lieutenant?'

'I play the piano, but not as well, I imagine, as you play the violin. Tell me, what else did you do at school?'

'The usual things, I suppose. Gymnastics, hockey, lacrosse.... Sport was important at my school.'

'Fascinating, but what did you do academically?'

'Not much.' She wrinkled her nose in self-deprecation. I opted for classics because I couldn't cope with maths and science. Also, I was captivated by the characters and life of Ancient Greece and Rome, and I enjoyed learning their languages. I think language tells us a lot about people.' She shrugged wretchedly. 'But that kind of thing has no place in the modern world, has it?' In her distress, she clasped her hands so that her knuckles showed white.

'I'm not so sure about that.' It seemed to William that someone had made a thorough job of undermining the poor girl's self-confidence. 'You've had a rotten time at this place,' he told her, 'and all because certain people have discovered, and very likely exaggerated, your weaknesses without ever taking the trouble to look beyond them. You must have felt insulted, to put it mildly.'

It was evident that she couldn't trust herself to speak, because she merely nodded, causing a tear to fall on her folded hands.

'I'm sorry,' he said, offering her the handkerchief from his breast pocket. 'I didn't mean to upset you, but it really is time to leave all that behind you. We need to concentrate on what you *can* do and, in particular, what you do *well*.'

She bit her lip but said nothing.

'In the short time we've known each other,' he told her gently, 'you've demonstrated your ability to communicate ideas and to think analytically and intuitively.'

'Have I?' She stopped dabbing her eyes with his handkerchief to look at him in wary surprise.

'You certainly have, and those qualities are going to prove invaluable, believe me.' He waited for her to finish blowing her nose, and then said, 'Let's make a fresh start.'

'But how?'

'First of all, by saving "Lieutenant Stamford" and "Miss Pendleton" for when we're in the company of senior officers. My name is William. What do you want me to call you?'

'Mine's Lucinda.' She said apologetically, 'It wouldn't have been my choice, but I have to make the best of it.'

'It's an appealing name, but it's a bit of a mouthful, isn't it?'

'At school, my chums called me "Lucy".'

'Are you happy with that?'

'Yes.' She was smiling again.

'In that case, Lucy,' he told her confidently, 'this is where your real contribution to the war begins.' He sat back in his chair, pleased by the progress they'd made. 'Only one little job remains to be done before you and I can get on with the business of winning this war together.'

'What's that?' Her red-rimmed eyes were now wide with curiosity.

'I haven't yet told you what your duties actually are. It helps to know these things, doesn't it?'

# 4

Hitler's invasion of the Low Countries continued almost unabated. Queen Wilhelmina of the Netherlands accepted King George VI's offer of sanctuary, and the Dutch army finally surrendered to Germany.

Meanwhile, Rear Admiral Davies called William to his office. Another officer, a Commander, RN, was also present. He was a tall, angular man with curiously elongated features that created an impression of haughty condescension. William hoped he was wrong.

'Commander Bonnington,' said the admiral, 'Let me introduce Lieutenant Stamford, our latest recruit. He was seriously injured in the River Plate action but, happily, he's on the mend now.'

'I see.' Bonnington eyed William's DSC ribbon coldly, but offered his hand.

'Commander Bonnington is one of the Deception Planning Staff, Stamford. You'll be reporting to him, rather than to me.'

'How d' you do, sir?' William shook his hand.

Bonnington evidently thought some overture was necessary, because he asked with barely-concealed mischief, 'How is "Useless Eunice" getting on, Stamford? I believe you were the latest to draw the short straw.'

'I beg your pardon, sir?'

'I'm referring to that feather-brained typist Miss Lucinda Pendleton.'

'I think she's going to be a valuable member of the team, sir.'

Bonnington stared at him, perhaps searching for a suspicion of irony in his otherwise blank features. Then, failing in his quest, said, 'I can't believe you mean that.'

'I do, sir. You appear surprised, but I should explain that I have an unusual facility for identifying human potential. I'm not boasting; as far as I know, it's an innate gift that seems to run in my family's genes.'

'Good heavens.'

'I know it sounds implausible, sir, but let me give you an example. My grandfather was a theatrical agent when music hall was in its hey-day. He handled a multitude of performers who went on to attain immortality in the business, but there was one he refused to represent, and that person, believe it or not, was the great Charlie Chaplin.'

'You astound me, Stamford.' Bonnington looked at the admiral, who appeared similarly surprised.

'The young Chaplin – I believe he was nineteen or thereabouts at the time – stood before my grandfather, hoping he would prove to be the portal to the most prestigious theatres and music halls in the country, but my grandfather refused to accept him. Chaplin was almost tearful, but my grandfather, who, I should explain, was a plain-speaking Yorkshireman, said, "Listen, Charlie, your future's not in music hall, an' I'd be doing you a great disfavour if I were to offer you representation. Instead, I'm going to give you an introduction to Fred Kano, who'll send you to one of his contacts in America. Why? Because your future's in moving pictures. With a talent like yours, lad, you could easily become one of the greatest names in kinematographic comedy." '

'Astonishing.'

'He was an astute man, sir.' William shook his head in wonder at the prescience of his forebear.

'Oh, well.' Bonnington looked at his watch and then at the admiral. 'If you'll excuse me, sir, I should be at a planning meeting.'

'Of course, Bonnington.'

Bonnington turned to William and said, 'We can only wait to see if you can exercise your hereditary genius with Miss Pendleton. That *will* be a challenge.' He replaced his cap and left the office.

'Sit down, Stamford.' The admiral waved him in the direction of a chair. 'In Commander Bonnington's absence, I shall tell you about your assignment, and then, as I told you earlier, you will be required to report to him.'

'I understand, sir.'

'Good.' The admiral lit a cigarette and continued. 'The situation in France is not at all promising. Hopefully, the BEF and the French army will be able to contain the Nazis, but we know that the British army is lamentably ill-equipped. If Hitler manages to take France, his next move will be to invade Britain, and I need hardly tell you that defending this island would be a gigantic task.'

'But surely, we have command of the seas, sir.'

'We have,' agreed the admiral, 'and that is our best card. If the *Kriegsmarine* continues to warn Hitler against invasion, we may yet be spared, and this is where we come in. We have to convince the *Kriegsmarine* that the odds at sea would make an invasion suicidal for them.

'But wouldn't they, sir?'

'Convoy requirements and the need to guard against a break-out by surface raiders mean that the Home Fleet is dispersed far too thinly.' He stopped to light another cigarette. 'Any invasion is likely to be launched across the narrowest part of the Channel, the Straits of Dover. Basically, Stamford, your job is to make the *Kriegsmarine* believe that we have more warships in the Dover and Chatham areas than we actually have.'

'I'll get on to it immediately, sir.'

'Good man. I really don't care how you do it, but good luck to you.'

'Thank you, sir.' William rose from his seat.

'Just one thing, Stamford.'

'Yes, sir?'

'That was a remarkable story you told Commander Bonnington. I could scarcely believe it.'

'It is a remarkable story, sir,' agreed William.

'In fact, considering your reputation, Stamford, I found myself wondering a little about its veracity.'

'Really sir?' William looked hurt.

'Yes, but I'm prepared to give you the benefit of the doubt.'

William gave an innocent shrug. 'Thank you, sir.'

'I have a new superior officer,' William told Lucy. 'No more reporting directly to the admiral. I must say, the Navy is adept at keeping us temporary officers in our place.'

'Who is this new officer?' Her tone was wary.

'Commander Bonnington.'

'Oh, no.'

'I wasn't impressed either, but don't worry. We have a more immediate matter to attend to.'

'What do you want me to do?'

'I want you to help me dissuade the Nazis from invading, by conjuring warships out of fresh air.'

After a moment's thought, she asked, 'Do you mean we have to make the Nazis believe we have more battleships and things than we have?'

'That's the general idea.'

She thought again. 'Could messages be sent to non-existent ships?'

'Good thinking, Lucy. Messages are normally encrypted, but a few new callsigns might not come amiss. The idea's worth putting forward.' He wasn't prepared to dismiss any ideas at that stage. 'What we need, though, is something the enemy can actually see.'

'Something that looks like a warship?'

'That's right.'

'What looks like a warship, William?'

'Another warship, and they don't come cheap.' He returned to the half-conceived possibility he'd considered so far. There's one idea I've had,' he said.

'Go on.'

'It's not original. They used it in the last war.'

'Did it work?'

'Apparently.'

'Well, wouldn't it work again?' She was endearingly optimistic.

'I don't know.' He pondered it afresh.

'Bring it out in the open, William. Now you've given me this job, I need the practice, not that I feel at all confident.'

He couldn't resist smiling at the difference in her after only a few days. She still had some way to go, but he was nonetheless pleased with her progress. 'All right,' he said. 'They made merchant ships look like warships by building superstructure, guns and so on, with plywood.'

'What's plywood?' Given her background, it was a fair question.

'It's laminated board, thin slices of wood glued together with the grain running in opposite directions.'

She nodded. 'So what are your reservations?'

'In the last war, an enemy agent might have viewed a dummy ship through binoculars, and the whole artifice would probably stand up to that kind of scrutiny, but things have moved on since then. Nowadays, there's aerial reconnaissance, and I'm not sure a dummy warship of the kind I've described would fool those whose job it is to scrutinise the photographs. Viewed from above, an awful lot of detail would be missing.'

Lucy was evidently thinking hard. 'A painter and decorator working on the house once told me that a coat of paint could work wonders. I'm thinking now of a more skilful kind of brushwork.'

'What do they call the people who paint street scenes and countryside for backdrop in films?'

'Scenery artists, I suppose.'

'Yes, that sounds right. When you see something like that in a film, you stare at it for long enough before it dawns on you that it might be painted. It could look very convincing from the air.'

'Are we thinking of the same thing, William?'

'It was your idea, Lucy, and I think it would work.' He moved the blotter to one side of his desk and pulled the typewriter towards him.

Two days later, William received a note. It read: *I'm sorry, Stamford. The mock-up idea was basically sound, but time is too short for the construction work to be completed.*

*Your phantom signal idea is already in operation, and has been for some time.*

It was signed: *H. F. Bonnington, Cdr., R.N.*

It was disappointing, but Bonnington was probably right. Meanwhile, William had to think of something else.

'I really thought he'd buy the idea, Lucy. I mean, he believed my grandpa was responsible for furthering Charlie Chaplin's career, and the dummy ships idea was infinitely more plausible than that.'

'Why did you tell him that about your grandfather?'

'I couldn't resist it. He must have gone from school straight to Dartmouth. He's never known anything else, so he's quite gullible. I shouldn't do it, I know, but it's fun.'

'But what made you think of that story particularly?'

'I had to explain why I was able to see potential in a person, when he wasn't and, for obvious reasons, I didn't want to accuse him of being short-sighted and unimaginative, so I made up the story.'

She lowered her eyes. 'You were talking about me, weren't you?'

It was better to be honest. 'He asked me how you were faring, and I told him.'

'He wouldn't be impressed. He was horrible to me after I... you know, refused him.'

'You spurned his advances, did you?' Mindful of her embarrassment, William decided not to make a joke of it. 'I'd have thought he was rather old for you.'

She pulled a face, registering disgust. 'And he's married. He has two children.'

'Some men are just greedy.'

Returning to the main subject, she asked, 'How did you recognise the potential in me?'

'Oh, call it intuition.'

'No, I really want to know, and please don't tell me a silly story like the one you told Commander Bonnington.'

'All right, Your critical observations about Rosalyn Tureck and languages revealed insight and analytical thought. It was nothing more mysterious than that.'

'But not everyone would have known that.'

'True.' Once again, he opted for the truth. 'After leaving school,' he told her, 'I spent eight years in an advertising agency, writing copy, and you don't do that without learning something about human nature.'

'Don't you?'

'A copywriter has to know the minds of the people he's trying to reach,' he explained. 'Suppose he's advertising a shoe polish with a posh label. We'll call it "Urwins' Wax" because it's too posh to be called a shoe polish, even though that's what it is. Now, it's more expensive than most, so why would anyone want to buy Urwins' Wax? The answer is that they have to believe not only that it's better than the rest, but that they *should* use it. He aims his campaign at responsible owners, telling them that fine shoes *deserve* a fine polish, so what do they do? They're not going to ill-treat their shoes with just any polish, are they?'

She looked uncertain. 'It sounds cynical to me,' she said, 'but I suppose I've always known that.'

'It is cynical,' he agreed, 'and so is the job we're doing now.'

'Yes. Have you had any thoughts since the dummy ships idea capsized?'

'Only one.' He leaned forward to explain. 'The Navy has a number of coastal craft: motor anti-submarine boats, motor launches, and now motor gunboats and torpedo boats as well. They wouldn't need added superstructure, only dummy guns and torpedo tubes. The information could be leaked through the usual channels, that we have a large number of these things held in reserve against the possibility of invasion. If they are frequently moved around, and their pennant numbers are changed repeatedly, aerial reconnaissance will bear out our claim.'

'Do you think Commander Bonnington will shout, "Hoorah"?'

'That remains to be seen.'

# 5

William was surprised and disappointed when he received no response to his second suggestion. The situation in France had deteriorated to the extent that the British Expeditionary Force had fallen back on the port of Dunkirk, and its evacuation was already taking place. It seemed a strange time for inaction and, having failed several times to contact Commander Bonnington by telephone, he set off to find him.

After an abortive visit to the commander's empty office, William found him outside Room 40, centre of the Naval Intelligence Department. He was just leaving, and he was in a sour mood.

'Damn it, Stamford,' he said, returning William's salute, 'must you limp so obviously? What are you doing here anyway?'

'I came looking for you, sir, and I didn't realise my limp was so obvious.'

'Men have been injured before, you know. You're not the first.'

'I realise that, sir. I actually came to ask if you'd read my submission.'

'Of course I have.' Bonnington gestured impatiently to William to accompany him. 'We'll walk back to my office, and I'll give you my reaction on the way.' He set off at a pace that William kept with difficulty, hampered as he was with a leg not long out of plaster.

'Thank you, sir.'

'I don't think you've much to thank me for. Frankly, your submission was of no use to me whatsoever.'

'I'm sorry to hear that, sir,' said William, still struggling to keep up.

'It owed more to *Boys' Own Paper* than the mind of a naval officer.'

'I'm sorry, sir. I've only been a naval officer for two years, and only one of them full-time.'

'And it shows.' As they approached Bonnington's office, he relaxed his pace, much to William's relief.

'Coastal Forces are an ill-conceived venture manned by amateur yachtsmen. They cannot be relied upon to carry out a disciplined operation.'

'Really, sir?'

'Yes, really, Stamford. It's just one of the things you temporary people are not expected to know until they're pointed out to you.' He stopped outside his own office. 'Keep trying, Stamford,' he said, 'and try to keep your ideas within the bounds of realism.'

'Aye-aye, sir. I wonder if I might be allowed to read the report you sent to the Director of Naval Intelligence.'

'Why?'

'A detailed report might give me a clearer idea of how to frame future submissions, sir. I feel that I'm currently bowling at invisible stumps.'

'Oh, very well. I'll send it to you. I'm rather busy now, so you'll have to excuse me.'

William made his way back to his office, where Lucy was waiting for him. She asked, 'Did you find him?'

He nodded and took his seat behind his desk. 'It seems that coastal forces are unreliable. I don't know why he thinks that. Maybe it's because they're seen as an irregular force.' He smiled sadly. 'And we know how the regular services feel about irregulars.'

'Shall I make coffee?'

'Will you, please?'

She stopped at the door to say, 'Commander Bonnington never said, "Please".'

William wasn't surprised. Nothing Bonnington might do would surprise him. The man was a complete enigma. He brooded about that until Lucy returned with coffee and an extra luxury.

'Biscuits? How did you manage that, Lucy?'

'Sh.' She held a forefinger to her lips. 'They were destined for a conference,' she explained. 'I didn't think they'd miss a couple, or three, or four, and I know the Wren who was taking them to the conference. She's a sport.'

'You're a lucky find, Lucy.'

'I'm glad you think so.'

'I've been meaning to ask you, with your home being in Cheshire, where you're staying in London.'

'I'm with friends in West Kensington. They have lots of room, so they're happy enough to put me up, and my parents are happy with the arrangement. When all's said and done, the Nazis are not likely to bomb Kensington, are they?'

For her sake, William hoped they weren't.

<hr/>

He waited, but the report failed to materialise. After two days, he telephoned Commander Bonnington to remind him. Bonnington's response was terse and unhelpful.

'Damn it, Stamford, I do have other matters to occupy my time. I'll send you a copy when I can. You'll just have to be patient.'

'Yes, sir. There is one more thing I need to ask you about.'

'Well?'

'It occurs to me that I could be more useful in the short term, helping with the evacuation. Do you think I might be released temporarily from my present duties?'

'That's not up to me, Stamford. You'll have to take your quest for glory elsewhere.'

Incredulous but determined, William pressed on. 'I only want to contribute to a vital operation, sir,' he said, 'and, as you are my immediate superior, I'm asking you as a matter of courtesy.'

'And I've told you it's not up to me, Stamford. Now, stop wasting my time.'

'Aye-aye, sir.' William pressed the switch on the telephone cradle and asked to be connected with Rear Admiral Davies.

'Third Officer Dean. Who is calling?'

'Lieutenant Stamford. I wonder if I might speak to Rear Admiral Davies, please.'

'Hold the line, sir. I'll ask him.' There was a brief pause, and then she returned to say, 'The admiral wants to know what it's about, sir.'

'It's about a request to be released from my present duties.'

'I see, sir. I'll tell him.'

After a few seconds, the admiral came on the line, clearly displeased. What is this about, Stamford? You report to Commander Bonnington, not to me.'

'I've spoken to Commander Bonnington, sir, and he said it wasn't up to him. I should explain that I asked him to release me so that I could assist with the evacuation of the BEF. I gather they're calling on civilian operators and boat owners now, and I thought I might be useful.'

There was a pause, and then the admiral asked, 'And what about your duties here, Stamford? Don't you regard them as important?'

'I do, sir, but my last submission was severely criticised and rejected, and I've been given nothing further to do.'

'You can't take your bat home because of that. In any case, Stamford, your place is here. You can leave the evacuation to those already involved.' As if further argument were needed, he added, 'And, of course, you're not yet fully fit. Your request is refused.'

'Thank you, sir. Goodbye.'

'Goodbye, Stamford.'

Lucy waited until he'd replaced the receiver before giving him an inquiring look.

He shook his head. 'My place is here, and I'm not fully fit.'

'You're not,' she agreed, 'and I know it's frustrating, but I have to be honest and say I'm relieved.'

'Why?' It wasn't the response he'd expected.

'I've finally found a boss who treats me with respect, and who doesn't think I'm only fit for the second eleven. I don't want to lose you now.'

'I'd have been very careful, Lucy.' Her concern surprised him, but he found it no less pleasing.

'It's not always up to you, as you know,' she said, looking pointedly at his left leg.

'Hm.' He took a sheet of paper and began doodling. 'What did you do after school, Lucy?'

'I left at sixteen, and then I went to... a finishing school.' She spoke the words quietly, as if she were ashamed of the fact.

'There's no need to run for cover. I'm not going to poke fun at you.'

'I know you're not. It's just become a habit.'

'Those people have a lot to answer for.' The thought of her being needlessly hurt made him angry. 'You know, you're the first girl I've known who went to a finishing school, and I'm just curious. Were you a debutante?' He'd heard of them, but he'd never met one.

'No, my parents drew the line there, although I did become engaged when I was eighteen.'

'Did you? What happened?'

'I broke it off.' She peered across his desk and asked, 'What are you doing?'

'Just doodling.' Having sketched some large letters, he was shading them in so that the whole thing resembled an engraving.

'What are you writing, William?'

'Nothing important. What did you learn at finishing school?'

'Oh, how to run a household, how to organise a dinner party, how to choose a cigar for one's husband or *fiancée*—'

'What?'

'Yes, the lady is supposed to roll the cigar between her fingers so that she can feel the texture, and then she runs it beneath her nose to scent the aroma. I'd offer to do it for you some time, but you don't smoke.'

'I smoke a cigar occasionally, but never mind. What else did you learn?'

'Deportment. How to climb into and out of a low-slung sports car without creating a spectacle.'

'Fascinating.'

'Your turn,' she prompted.

'Mm?'

'It's your turn to tell me something about your past. Come on,' she urged, 'join in.'

He laid down his pen and gave her his full attention. 'You know what I did after school,' he said.

'Yes, I do, but tell me about your family.'

'All right.' He gave his work a final looking-over and sat back in his chair. 'My dad was killed shortly after I was born, so we never actually met.'

'Oh, I'm sorry.'

'That wasn't all. My mum was left to bring up my sister and me on very little money. When we were older, she got a job as a counter assistant in a chemist's shop, and that improved the situation, especially with my grandparents helping to look after my sister and me.'

'What's your sister's name?'

It occurred to William that, like most women, Lucy felt obliged to keep interrupting.

'Jane. She's a year older than me, she was a nurse until she had the children, and her husband George is in the RAF. Okay?'

'Yes, I just wanted to know.'

'Right. When we were older, my mum went to evening classes in pharmacy and eventually qualified as a dispensing chemist.'

'Gosh. How jolly clever, and what a plucky thing to do.'

'I suppose so.' He'd never thought of his mother as plucky, so much as determined, but he was inclined to agree, now he thought about it.

'Does your mum live in London?'

'No, she moved to my grandparents' house in Kent when my grandma died.'

'Ah.'

'Now you've heard the story of my life, it'll be your turn again tomorrow.'

'I don't think my story is half as fascinating as yours.'

'Fascinating?' He had to smile. 'You found my story fascinating?'

'A young woman widowed and left to bring up two young children, who studies in what little spare time she has to get a professional qualification? Yes, I find that fascinating. Your mother must be a remarkable woman.'

'Yes, you're right, Lucy. I admit it.'

She took the doodle from him and read it. It said:

**IT IS BETTER TO REMAIN SILENT AND BE THOUGHT A FOOL THAN TO SPEAK AND REMOVE ALL DOUBT**

'That's clever,' she said. 'How did you learn to do it?'

'When I was a junior at the agency, I used to watch the artists at work. Mine's a poor effort compared with theirs, but I haven't had their training.'

'You're very modest, William. That's another quality Commander Bonnington lacks.'

Mention of Bonnington came as a reminder. William had been thinking, and he decided to try out his idea on Lucy.

'If you were an enemy spy,' he said, 'and you knew that a certain harbour was too shallow for capital ships, but you learned that dredgers had been moved in and they were working round the clock, what would it tell you?'

'I don't know. Aren't dredgers those things that dig up the seabed?'

'That's right.'

'I suppose I'd wonder if they were going to use the place for a special purpose.'

'Good.'

'Does that help?'

'It certainly does, especially if the same thing were to happen in more than one harbour, say Dover and Harwich. It might tell the enemy spy that battleships and so on, were being based in secondary harbours, as well as in Portsmouth and Chatham, to prepare against invasion.'

'I like your idea.'

'Thank you, Lucy.' He reached for the typewriter. 'Let's hope Commander Bonnington does.'

⚜

The next day, a Wren writer came to the office with a sealed folder.

'It's from Lieutenant Hughes, sir,' she said.

'Thank you.' He signed the receipt. 'Carry on.'

'Aye-aye, sir.' She went on her way, leaving him to open the folder.

It was the report he'd requested, and he began reading with

interest. Much of it concerned other branches of the armed forces and, whilst he found it interesting, he was keen to find the responses to his suggestions.

After some sifting, he finally located them.

*A suggestion that merchant ships might be disguised as capital ships by adding dummy superstructure was rejected because of the time constraint.*

That was fair enough. He read on.

*Another suggestion by Cdr H. F. Bonnington, R.N., that coastal craft might receive extra, dummy, armaments and be presented as an anti-invasion force, and that those ships might be moved frequently so as to create the illusion of greater numbers, is under consideration.*

'The duplicitous bast...! I'm sorry, Lucy.'

'Don't mind me. What's the matter?'

'Bonnington told me my idea of using coastal forces was of no use to him. Now I find,' he said, tapping the offending report with his forefinger, 'that he's passing it off as his own.'

'Surely not.'

'It's here in black and white.'

'Now I think of it, I don't know why I'm surprised. He's the kind of man who'd cheat at a charity cricket match.'

'There's no prize for guessing what he'll do with the dredger idea.'

William continued to turn the matter over in his mind. Eventually, he took another sheet of paper and set to with pen and ink. Lucy left him to work.

After a short time, he wiped his pen and put it away. His doodle read:

**THERE IS NO LIMIT TO WHAT MAN CAN ACHIEVE AS LONG AS HE DOESN'T MIND WHO TAKES THE CREDIT**

'It's just a bit of nonsense, Lucy,' he said. 'We're all in this war together, and it really doesn't matter who bags the kudos.'

'That's a noble stance, but don't let Commander Bonnington see your handiwork, because I don't think he would be as magnanimous as you.'

# 6

William had intended to destroy the doodles; they had been no more than a whim and they'd served no useful purpose, so it was unfortunate that, on leaving the office, he was so involved in formulating his next idea, he forgot all about them. His reminder came early the following morning, when Bonnington called to see him.

'Good morning, Stamford,' he said. 'Where is the file Hughes sent you?'

'Good morning, sir. I returned it to your office just before I left. Lieutenant Hughes signed for it in your absence.'

'I see. Of course, I haven't seen him yet.' His eye fell on the second chair in the room. He said, 'I notice your assistant's not here yet.'

'She's a civil servant, sir. They work office hours.'

'I know that. I simply thought that if she's as valuable as you claim she is, she might also be keen.'

'I can't fault her enthusiasm, sir.'

'No, I don't suppose you can. Maybe you should set higher standards.' Bonnington was looking through the window, and William used the opportunity to remove the second of his doodles. He was about to place it in his desk drawer, when Bonnington turned away from the window.

'What are you doing, Stamford?'

'Just removing my rough working, sir.'

'Let me see it.'

'It really is of no importance, sir.'

Bonnington held out his hand. 'Give it to me.'

'It was a harmless joke, sir, no more than that.' William handed it over.

Bonnington read it, screwed it into a tight ball, and dropped it contemptuously into the bin marked 'Non-Classified Waste'. He was silent for a moment, and then he spoke. 'So that was your idea of a harmless joke,' he said, scarcely controlling his anger. 'I suppose it was prompted by what you read in the report.'

'I really don't care who takes the credit, sir.'

'Don't you though? Then why did you indulge in a childish joke at my expense?' Instead of waiting for a reply, he went on. 'It may interest you to know that ideas are listed officially in the name of the committee member, and not those of the individuals in his team. Damn it, Stamford, I knew you had no background to speak of, but I never thought you would stoop to disloyalty on this scale!'

'What can I say, sir? I apologise unreservedly for any offence I've caused, but I must insist that it was wholly unintentional.'

'It's too late for that, Stamford. You've proved yourself to be disloyal, and I no longer want you in my team. I'm going to recommend that you are returned to the fleet.' He seized the doorknob and wrenched the door open. 'At least, then, you'll be someone else's problem!' He left, slamming the door behind him.

William sat, berating himself for an irresponsible fool. His childish doodlings were reprehensible enough, but to leave them on his desk for Bonnington to see was an act of careless stupidity.

He was emptying his desk drawer when Lucy arrived.

'Good morning, William.'

'Good morning, Lucy.'

'What's the matter? You look as if you've lost a quid and found a tanner.' She took her usual seat and gave him her whole attention.

'What?'

'It's something my grandfather says. What's the matter, William?' Reflecting quickly, she said, 'I suppose, if I'm going to sound like a proper Lancastrian, as I was born there, I should say, 'What's to do?' It sounded strange in her cultured accent, but William's attention was centred elsewhere.

'Bonnington came in this morning and saw my doodle about taking the credit,' he told her.

Her expression changed immediately. 'Oh, no.'

'It was my own stupid fault. I forgot to destroy it last night.'

44

'What did he say?'

'I shan't trouble you with all of it, but he's going to have me returned to the fleet. That's if he hasn't already done so.'

'Oh, William. Can he really do that?'

'Yes, he can, and he will. He's vindictive enough.' He looked down at the desk he'd been emptying and said, 'You know, I didn't want this job at first. I thought it was a ridiculous appointment for a gunnery specialist but in the short time you and I have been working here, I've changed my mind. I've developed a passion for plotting and scheming and, whatever Bonnington says, we thought up some pretty good ruses, you and I.'

'We did, although it was mainly you.'

'No, fair's fair, Lucy. I'd have struggled without you, and that's another thing.'

'What is?'

'I don't know what they'll do with you when I'm gone. That's something else I've got on my conscience.'

'Nonsense, and I'll tell you something else. Commander Bonnington needn't think he's going to get away with this.' She sat at her desk and took out a sheet of paper. 'When I've done this job,' she said, 'I'll have to ask you to excuse me for a few minutes. Then, when I return, I'll make us both some coffee. I daresay you need it.'

Preoccupied as he was with his own misfortune, William only half heard her. He saw her remove the cap from her fountain pen and begin writing.

'What are you doing, Lucy?'

'Writing a note. I shan't be long.' She continued to write, finally signing, blotting, folding and placing the note in an Admiralty envelope, which she marked 'Private and Personal.'

'Where are you going, Lucy?'

'I'm taking this to the internal mail.' She dropped the envelope into her shoulder bag and left the office.

William could only wonder, but only until the telephone interrupted his thoughts. He picked it up, expecting another broadside from Commander Bonnington.

'Good morning, sir. Third Officer Dean here. Rear Admiral Davies wishes to see you in his office.'

'Now?'

'Er, yes, he would like to see you now.'

'Very good.' He put the telephone down, reached for his cap and set off to the admiral's office, telling himself that the situation couldn't possibly deteriorate further. He continued to reassure himself until he reached his destination, when he concluded that his plight was as hopeless as ever.

'Good morning, sir.' Third Officer Dean greeted him more cheerfully than the occasion seemed to merit. She spoke into the intercom, informing the admiral of William's arrival, and he heard the admiral say in a surprisingly equable tone, 'Send him in.'

William pushed open the adjoining door and stepped inside.

'Come in, Stamford. Commander Bonnington has been baying for your blood, and I'd like to hear what you have to say for yourself.'

Humbly, William stated his case. 'I made a childish and ill-considered attempt at humour, sir. I intended no disrespect and I apologised for any unintentional slight Commander Bonnington might have felt, but he refused to accept my apology.'

'Surely there's more to it than that,' the admiral insisted. 'What persuaded you to perform this silly prank in the first place?'

'I read the report on an idea I'd advanced, sir.'

'What was the idea, Stamford?'

'It was to add dummy armaments to coastal forces craft to present a force equipped to tackle an attempted invasion, sir.' He went on to describe the plan in more detail. 'Commander Bonnington dismissed the idea, sir, on the basis that it was ill-conceived and that coastal forces were incompetent and therefore incapable of disciplined action.'

The admiral nodded. 'You mentioned a report.'

'Yes, sir. The official report said that an identical idea, proposed by Commander Bonnington, was under consideration. My mistake, sir, was to leave a bit of silliness I'd been doodling where he could find it.'

'Doodling?'

'Sketching, lettering and that kind of thing, sir. I do it when I'm thinking.' His eye fell on the admiral's blotter, where pencilled hieroglyphics betrayed a similar habit.

'And how, exactly, was Commander Bonnington offended by this doodle?'

William took a deep breath. 'It was a paraphrase of an aphorism, sir, basically, to the effect that there is no limit to what man can achieve as long as he doesn't mind who takes the credit.'

The admiral closed his eyes, holding them like that for several seconds. 'I can see,' he said. 'how that might have caused offence.' He opened the cigarette box on his desk, and was about to offer it to William, but then he remembered. 'Of course. You don't smoke, do you?'

'No, thank you, sir.'

'No, but you're not above creating a bloody silly piece of graffiti that appears, on the face of it, to lampoon a senior officer at a time when our destroyer fleet aided by the biggest assortment of odds and sods is struggling to evacuate the BEF. There are more important matters afoot than this ridiculous business, Stamford, and I resent having to deal with it.'

'I really am most awfully sorry, sir.'

'Oh, I'm sure you've seen the error of your ways by this time.'

'Yes, sir. Commander Bonnington told me he was going to arrange for me to re-join the fleet.' He thought it was worth mentioning that the punishment was already in progress.

The admiral raised his eyebrows briefly and said, 'Actually, that's not up to Commander Bonnington. It's my decision and I've yet to make it.' He lit a cigarette before going on. 'I'll let you know what I've decided, probably tomorrow. Meanwhile, Stamford, do try to stay out of trouble.'

⊕⊦⧉⊸⟩⊧⟨⊱⟩⊕

For the rest of the day, William took great care to avoid trouble. He tried to be creative but, in its current state, his mind refused to co-operate. Eventually, he allowed Lucy to engage him in conversation.

'Honestly, William, now that Rear Admiral Davies is involved, you can remove the blotting paper from your trousers. You're no longer at Commander Bonnington's mercy.'

'That's true, Lucy. You're a source of real comfort to me, even though I don't deserve it.'

'I wish you wouldn't berate yourself. If you'll just step out of the sack cloth and ashes – I mean metaphorically, not starkers or anything like that – you'll realise how much you've done for me.'

For the first time that day, William smiled. 'If I've done anything at all for you, Lucy,' he said, 'then I'm heartily glad.'

'Good, because—' She was interrupted when the telephone rang.

William picked it up, wondering if the admiral had already made his decision, but the voice belonged to someone else.

'This is the First Lord's Office. I should like to speak to Miss Lucinda Pendleton, please.'

William held out the telephone. 'The First Lord of the Admiralty's Office for you, Lucy,' he said, adding wearily, 'Put a word in for me, will you?'

'I'll try.' She took the receiver from him while he stepped outside to respect her privacy.

❦

It occurred to him that evening that, preoccupied as he'd been with the new job and its attendant frustrations, he'd not fully appreciated the flat. As he looked around him at its cosy friendliness and the six-foot grand piano that he simply lacked the heart to play now, it seemed the greatest shame that he had to leave it all behind, probably for a shared cabin in a warship.

On the other hand, as a gunnery officer he knew his duties, which came down largely to a matter of drill, unlike his present situation, which seemed to throw up an ever-changing diversity of demands. Most of that, he was convinced, had been the work of Commander Bonnington, for whatever reason, but the fact remained that Bonnington was staying and he was leaving.

❦

At 11:00 the next day, Lucy reported to the Secretary to the Prime Minister and First Lord of the Admiralty, who checked her appointment and offered her a seat.

A pair of solid oak doors led to the inner *sanctum*, but Lucy could still hear a voice raised, it seemed, in raucous approval. A moment later, the doors opened, and Lucy recognised the familiar wide forehead and pugnacious jawline of Mr Winston Churchill. He was in a celebratory mood.

'Listen, everyone,' he announced. 'The First Sea Lord tells me that the British Expeditionary Force has been evacuated! More than a third of a million men have been returned to our shores! I have just spoken with Vice-Admiral Ramsay and congratulated him on a magnificent achievement!'

Lucy joined in with the general applause until Mr Churchill called everyone to order and spoke to his secretary.

'What am I doing now, Colville? I have to address the House at mid-day, but there is something else.'

'Miss Pendleton is here to see you, sir.'

'Of course.' He looked around him. 'Where is she?'

'I'm here, sir.' Lucy stepped forward so that he could see her.

For a moment, he looked at her without recognition, but then he realised who she was.

'Lucinda, my dear, come into my office. The last time I saw you, you must have been....'

'About four years old, sir,' she prompted, following him into a huge office that reeked of cigar smoke.

'And how is your dear grandpapa? In fact, how is your family?' He shook her hand warmly and showed her to a comfortably upholstered chair.

---

'It'll be all right, William, honestly.' Lucy was brushing his uniform in response to a call from Rear Admiral Davies. More than an hour had passed since her mysterious absence from William's office.

'Thank you, Lucy. Wish me luck.'

'Of course, but you won't need it.'

He paused in the doorway to ask, 'By the way, where were you this morning?'

'I was visiting a family friend, as I told you. Now, you'd better cut along or you *will* be in trouble.'

William made his way to the admiral's office, prepared for anything. When he arrived, however, he was surprised to see its occupant in a cheerful mood. He had a visitor with him, a commander, RN, who seemed to share his good humour. He looked young for a commander, and he gave the impression that he might be quite approachable. It had just been rotten luck for William to have drawn Bonnington.

Still affable, the admiral said, 'Come in, Stamford. Commander Challock, this is Lieutenant Stamford, the officer I spoke to you about.'

The two shook hands.

'Now, sit down, both of you. First of all, Stamford, the BEF has been evacuated. We've just heard that more than a third of a million men have been embarked.'

'Thank goodness for that, sir. What an achievement!'

'It certainly was.' He gave William a meaningful look and said, 'Now, regarding your own situation, you already know, of course, that you're off the hook.'

'Am I, sir?'

'Didn't you know?'

'No, sir.' The news baffled him.

'Well, surely you know that influence has been brought to bear on your behalf. You seem to have friends in high places, or at least one friend in a very high place.'

'Do I, sir?'

The admiral stared at him impatiently. 'Well,' he said, 'someone went out to bat for you, someone who has the ear of the Prime Minister.'

Things began to fall into place. 'I can only imagine, sir, that my assistant Miss Pendleton has been busy on my behalf.' He thought about her mysterious absences, and everything came together. 'Her grandfather, sir, is a close friend of the Prime Minister.'

'I see. Well, for what it's worth, the PM agrees with me that leaving incriminating evidence loafing in your office was bloody silly, but he likes the suggestions you've put forward, and he wants you to continue thinking up "ruses and red herrings", as he called them.'

'I really had no idea about this, sir. Miss Pendleton never said a word to me.'

'Be that as it may, you'll be working under the direction of Commander Challock, who has taken Commander Bonnington's place on the Deception Committee.'

'Thank you, sir. I'm most grateful.'

'All I ask is that you keep your nose clean.'

'Oh, I shall, sir.'

The admiral merely smiled and said, 'Carry on, Lieutenant Stamford.'

'Aye-aye, sir.'

'Come and see me in about an hour, Stamford,' said Commander Challock. 'You'll find me in Commander Bonnington's old office.'

'Aye-aye, sir.'

William made the return journey in the highest of spirits. He found Lucy waiting for him.

'I told you everything would be all right,' she said.

'Lucy, it was embarrassing at first, as I hadn't a clue what the admiral was talking about, but you got me off the hook, and I can't begin to tell you how grateful I am.'

'I thought Mr Churchill would be as good as his word. You know, I wouldn't have had the nerve to do it a few weeks ago, but I felt that, after all you'd done for me, I had to do what I could to help you.'

'Thank you, Lucy.' He leaned forward and kissed her cheek. 'I feel a celebration coming on. Have you anything arranged for this evening?'

'What do you have in mind?'

'I thought I'd stand you dinner.'

'That's a lovely idea, but can we make it another evening?'

'Of course. You must have things to do.'

'Not really, but I've nothing here to change into, and I don't want to dine out in my office clothes.'

'I should have thought about that. When you do suggest?'

'Tomorrow?'

'Fine.'

# 7

'That was a lovely meal. Thank you, William.'

'I enjoyed it too.' He'd also enjoyed seeing Lucy in a halter-neck evening gown. The colour, she told him, was sage green, and a touch of that other scarcity, make-up, completed the ensemble, which he found captivating.

'It's good that they remembered you here after so long.'

'I used to come here often, and it's been less than a year.'

'Of course. So much has happened since last September, it feels much longer.'

'Much, much longer.' He put the money on the plate with the bill and asked, 'Where shall we go? Do you like dancing? I still have a membership card for the Glass Slipper.'

'I love it, but can you dance with your leg?'

'Yes, but I'm better on two.'

'You know what I mean. I noticed you weren't using your walking stick.'

'I'm trying to give it up.'

'Goody. In that case, let's go to the place you mentioned.'

'We should, because, as well as being our celebration, today is my birthday.'

'I don't believe you.'

He sighed. 'That's the price of crying "wolf", but today really is my birthday.'

'I wish I'd known earlier.'

'Do you mean we could have had jelly and cake and played Postman's Knock at the office?'

'You know what I mean.'

An elderly waiter stopped at their table to collect the bill and the payment.

'That's fine,' William told him.

The waiter glanced at the bill, recognising a generous tip. 'Thank you, sir. I trust you enjoyed your meal?'

'It was excellent, thank you. Do you think someone could organise a taxi?'

'I'll arrange that, sir.' He left them and returned with their hats and coats. 'Someone is hailing a taxi for you now, sir,' he said.

'Thank you.'

They made their way to the exit and reached the door as a taxi pulled into the kerbside.

'The Glass Slipper in Soho, please.' William tipped the doorkeeper and opened the taxi door for Lucy.

'Right away, sir.'

Lucy settled into the back seat. 'I haven't danced for ever such a long time,' she said. 'I imagine you did it frequently before the war.'

Before he could answer, the driver asked in a loud voice, 'Just back from the sea, are you, sir?'

'Yes.' It was easier to go along with it.

'Good for you, sir. See much action?'

'Yes.'

'Marvellous about Dunkirk, wasn't it, sir?'

'Yes.'

'It was good to see our lads on the newsreel.'

'Yes.'

The driver took the hint and lapsed into silence.

Lucy asked, 'Did you go to lots of night clubs before the war?'

'Just a few.'

'It must have been wonderful, living the London night life before the blackout and everything.'

'I did work sometimes, you know. I had to, to pay for the night life.'

'You know what I meant.'

'That was where I worked,' he said, pointing through the window. 'The Groves and Holmes Advertising Agency.'

'It sounds very grand.'

'It's quite ordinary, really. The proprietor is called David Waldheim, and the name of the firm is a play on the words *Wald* and *Heim*. When war seemed likely, Mr Waldheim was worried that his German-Jewish ancestry might be held against him, as it was at the start of the last war, but he needn't have concerned himself. Everyone knew he'd served in Flanders.'

'How did they know?'

'He never stopped talking about it.'

The driver interrupted him. 'Here we are, sir, the Glass Slipper.'

'Thank you.' He stepped out, opened the door for Lucy, and paid the driver.

'Much obliged, sir. Enjoy your leave.'

'Thank you.' He lent Lucy his arm and led her to the entrance, where a man in formal dress greeted them.

'Are you a member, sir?'

'Yes.' He showed his card.

The man glanced at it and said, 'Please come through, sir.'

They accepted his invitation and encountered another member of the club's staff, who asked the doorman to take their hats and coats, before opening a door and inviting them into a large, softly-lit room furnished principally in wine red. Beyond the tables, which were set discreetly apart, were a small dance floor and a band consisting of a piano, bass, drums, alto saxophone and clarinet. They were playing 'South of the Border', a song released the previous year to widespread acclaim.

Their host showed them to a table in a discreet alcove and said, 'Perhaps you would care to see the wine list, sir.'

'Yes, please.' William turned to Lucy to ask, 'What do you think? Shall we have some more of the wine we had at the restaurant?'

'Only if it's not too expensive.'

'Don't worry, Lucy. If you remember, this is my way of thanking you.'

'If you say so, but I didn't do all that much.'

'You did plenty. How many invaluable assistants do you know, who've asked a prime minister to get their stupid boss out of a mess he'd created for himself?'

'That does rather narrow the field, I admit, but you're not at all stupid. I can't imagine that Groves and Holmes employ stupid people.'

'You'd be surprised.' He looked up as a brightly-dressed waitress came to the table.

'Have you decided, sir?'

'Yes, we'd like a bottle of the 'thirty-seven *Saint Emilion* red, please.'

'Very good, sir.' She closed the wine list and left them.

'As a matter of fact, I'm thinking of trying something different after the war,' he said. 'I've always been keen on writing; I had some short stories published in a magazine a few years ago, and I'd like to try my hand at writing a novel.'

'Would you really?'

'Well, it's not all that different from advertising. The lies are just longer and more complex, that's all.'

Lucy shook her head in disbelief. 'You're almost self-defeatingly honest, William,' she said.

'It's necessary to recognise dishonesty and not be carried along with it.'

'So that we never fall into the trap of believing our own lies?'

He nodded. 'That's the idea.'

'Do you believe that "A Nightingale Sang in Berkeley Square"?'

'Not for one moment.'

'They're playing it. Are you going to ask me to dance?'

'Of course.' He rose to his feet and asked, 'May I have the pleasure?'

'Consider it yours.'

※

In writing her next letter home, Lucy decided to abandon family tradition. Instead of addressing it to 'Mummy, Daddy and Grandpapa', she followed William's example.

*6th June, 1940.*

*Dear Mum, Dad and Grandpa,*
*I hope you're all in the best of health and good spirits, despite rationing, rotten news and beastly bureaucracy.*

*I can tell you now that I wasn't at all happy at first, working at the Admiralty; in fact I almost reached the point of leaving and coming home. Somehow, I found the work impossible to do to anyone's satisfaction. I realise it's been the story of my life, but they didn't have to be so horrible to me. But – I know I shouldn't start a sentence with 'but' because it's bad form and all that, but, dash it all, there's a war on and some things are more important than grammar – anyway, I can tell you now that everything is fine. I'm working for an officer in the R.N.V.R. For reasons of national security, I can't tell you what we do, but I can say that working with him is a delight.*

*His name is William, and he used to write advertisements before the war, but he told me recently that when things return to normal, he wants to write novels. I think he'll be jolly good at it, too.*

*He was in trouble recently, but only because a rotten egg of a senior officer had a down on him. It was serious stuff, though, and William thought he was going to be sent back to sea. Well, I wasn't going to stand for that, so I wrote to Mr Churchill and asked to see him. He was quite busy with Dunkirk and various things, but he agreed to see me. He was very nice about it and sent his best regards to you all, and I'm glad I did it, because he sent the horrible senior officer to do a miserable job somewhere else, and told the admiral to keep William in his job. William was so pleased, he took me out to dinner last evening to celebrate. He also gave me what must be the last dozen red roses in existence, now that everyone's Digging For Victory. He said he'd bought red ones because I'm a Lancashire lass, even though I was only born there, but I suspect they were the only ones available. Anyway, they're lovely, and it was a smashing gesture.*

*The Cohen family all send their best regards. I do enjoy staying with them. Take care.*

*Lots and lots of love,*

*Lucy XXX*

*P.S. I'm only "Lucinda" on formal occasions now.*

There was a confident knock on the door and, when it opened, it was to admit Lieutenant David 'Dai' Hughes, an officer, whose lungs had been affected by chlorine inhalation when his submarine was damaged in the Bay of Biscay. He was now recovering from the condition whilst serving as Communications Officer to the Deception Committee. He was carrying a manila file, which he handed to William with a flourish.

'Read and enjoy, William. It's hot off the press.'

'Thank you, Dai.' William placed the file on his desk. 'Lucy,' he asked, 'do you know Dai Hughes? You'd do well to avoid him He's the most awful poodle-faker.'

'It's because I'm a Celt,' explained Dai. 'All Celts are romantic souls.'

'I know him as "Lieutenant Hughes",' said Lucy. 'Only Commander Bonnington was allowed to be romantic when I worked for him. At least, I suppose that was what he would call it.'

'Call me "Dai",' he told her. 'We can relax now he's gone.'

'It must have been worse for you,' said William. 'You saw more of him than I did.'

'Oh, he was an embittered man.' Dai sat down to reminisce. 'He'd been passed over more times than Westminster Bridge and he knew he'd be put out to grass after the war.'

Lucy asked, 'What does "passed over" mean?'

'Officers with less seniority had been promoted to captain,' explained William. 'He knew he would never be promoted.'

Dai continued. 'He despised the RNVR, the RNR and anything that wasn't strictly pusser.'

'Coastal Forces too,' added William, recalling his plagiarised suggestion.

'That's true. He called them "costly farces", not that he was alone in that. There's no shortage of dinosaurs in this building.'

'What I couldn't stomach,' said William, 'was the way he looked pointedly at my medal ribbon when he was giving me a dressing-down. It was as if he wanted to take it from me.'

'That was Bonnington all right. He joined the service shortly after the last war, which meant he would never receive an award for gallantry. It rankled with him to see a young chap like you, and a reservist to boot, with a shiny, new DSC. He was a miserable failure.' He got up to leave. 'I'd read the report if I were you, William,' he said. 'You'll enjoy it.'

As the door closed, William opened the file and was surprised to find a brief, one-page report on his three ideas so far.

*A suggestion by Lt. William Stamford, R.N.V.R., that merchant ships might be disguised as warships, and particularly as capital ships, by adding dummy superstructure has been noted for future implementation.*

He read on.

*Another suggestion made by Lt. Stamford, that coastal forces craft might receive extra, dummy, armaments and be presented as a fast-moving anti-invasion force, and that those ships might be moved frequently so as to create the illusion of greater numbers, is strongly recommended.*

The final report read:

*A subsequent suggestion by Lt. Stamford, that overt dredging activity, particularly in the entrances and exits of secondary harbours, such as those of Dover and Harwich, might give rise to the belief that those harbours are to be used by capital ships, is also strongly recommended.*

He showed them to Lucy, who read them and said, 'That's wonderful, William. Do you think this is all down to Commander Challock?'

'Yes, the signs were good at Tuesday's meeting, although it's anybody's guess what impression I made on him. Naturally, he knows about the row with Bonnington, and I did myself no favours with that.'

'*Errare humanum est.*'

'As the Ancient Romans said.'

She looked down, embarrassed. 'I've done it again, haven't I? I only meant that he's probably put it out of his mind, as you jolly well should.'

'Don't apologise, Lucy. It's just one of your endearing characteristics, but it may be some time before I can stop kicking myself over that episode.'

'Oh, you'll recover.'

# 8

## July

When William was called to Commander Challock's office, he was surprised to see Colonel Loxton with him.

'Take a seat,' said the commander.

William sat and waited for him to speak.

'Colonel Loxton is here because the army has asked for our help. The Colonel will give you the details.'

Loxton fixed William with his usual grim stare. 'Stamford,' he said, 'what do you know about the Home Guard?'

'Absolutely nothing, sir. Who are they?'

Loxton blinked impatiently. 'They were known as the "Local Defence Volunteers", but they've been renamed the "Home Guard." '

'I see, sir. I didn't know about the change of name.'

'Damn it, Stamford, don't you ever read the newspapers?'

William felt that the interview was going less well than he might have wished. 'Not very often, sir,' he admitted.

'Don't you want to know how the war is going?'

'Well, as I see it, sir, I do get regular updates and, in any case, the war will go on just the same, whether I read the papers or not.'

Commander Challock fought to suppress a smile, whereas Loxton appeared to be controlling his impatience with difficulty.

'Right,' he said, 'I'll bring you up to date. Hitherto, the volunteers have paraded in civilian clothing and have been armed with shotguns, pikes, and even carving knives tied to broom handles. They've also had to suffer the taunts, insults and mockery of those whose lives they've pledged to protect.'

'Poor devils. How unfair.'

'Agreed, but now they have denim uniforms, and the first consignment of rifles and automatic weapons has arrived from Canada and the USA. Morale is greatly improved.'

'Good. I'm glad.' William allowed himself a glance at Commander Challock, who was watching him with obvious interest.

'What we're concerned about now,' said Loxton, 'is how the Germans feel about the Home Guard.'

'How do they feel about it, sir?'

'We don't know, Stamford, but it's your job to promote it so that the enemy sees it as a viable deterrent.'

'How many have enlisted so far, sir?'

'More than one-and-a-half million.'

William nodded slowly. That kind of commitment was impressive. 'And what backgrounds do they come from, sir?'

'Most of them are veterans of the last war, as you might imagine. There are also young men awaiting conscription, and men of all ages in reserved occupations.'

'I see, sir.' An idea was already forming, but he needed to find out more about the Home Guard. 'Is there any possibility of my visiting a Home Guard unit, sir?'

'You want to speak to the troops on the ground, I imagine. I'll speak to someone and let you know.' He stood up. 'I think that just about wraps things up. I must leave you now. I'll be in touch when I've arranged a visit for you, Stamford.'

'Thank you, sir.' William came to attention, but Loxton was clearly in a hurry.

'Goodbye, Challock. Goodbye, Stamford.' He let himself out.

Challock waved William back to his seat and asked, 'Have you any ideas yet, Stamford?'

'Yes, sir. I need to do some work on them, but I have something in mind. It shouldn't be any more difficult than writing copy, really.'

'Oh, well, you're the expert on that.' He appeared to have something else on his mind. He asked, 'Stamford. If you don't read the newspapers, how do you spend your evenings?'

'I find that, as well as relaxing, sir, I need to do something that allows the unconscious mind to work on ideas that occur to me in the course of my work. Do you remember the Sherlock Holmes stories, sir?'

'Yes, he played the violin to aid thought, didn't he?'

'He did, sir, but I play the piano.'

Challock studied him gravely. 'Well, blow me down,' he said.

The conference ended, and William was almost out of the door when Challock called him back.

'Sir?'

'Stamford, that wasn't one of your silly stories, was it?'

William looked hurt. 'No, sir,' he said, 'I take music seriously.'

---

Two evenings later, he arrived at an elementary school in Lambeth. Now, with its children evacuated to safer parts of the country, it served as a drill hall and home to the local Home Guard platoon. Captain Morris, the unofficial platoon commander, welcomed him to the platoon office, formerly the headmaster's room.

'My rank is also unofficial,' he explained. 'I wear the pips simply because that was my rank in nineteen-twenty, when I was demobbed. No officers have been appointed yet, so I have to play it by ear.'

William reckoned he must be at least in his mid-forties. His hair was largely grey, and he had a protuberant vein at the side of his forehead.

'They must surely take previous war service into account,' said William.

'Who knows? The army did some strange things in the last war, and I'm not convinced it's learned its lesson, particularly after the Battle of France *debacle*. Anyway, what's behind all this? I was just told an officer was coming on a fact-finding visit. I certainly wasn't expecting a naval officer.'

'Being as yet unfit for active service,' William told him, 'I'm involved in public information, basically propaganda.'

'Some things never change,' commented Morris. 'What were you doing to become unfit?'

'I believe they're now calling it the "Battle of the River Plate",' said William. 'I was serving in *HMS Exeter*.'

Morris was suddenly contrite. 'I'm sorry, old chap,' he said. 'I should have trodden more warily.' His eye had fallen on William's medal ribbon.

'There's no need for apology. Let me tell you about this visit. I want to find out how you and your men feel about being in the first line of defence.'

'I can tell you now how I feel, Lieutenant. I think the politicians have made a total bugger of things so far. The BEF was half-trained and ill-equipped when it left for France, and now it's left for everyone else to pull the irons out of the fire.' The surface vein in his forehead was throbbing. 'Well, so be it. Let the buggers come and they'll find us ready. We have rifles and tommy guns, and we'll use them.'

'I believe you will, sir.'

The captain looked at his watch. 'The men should be assembled now. I'm just waiting for my NCO to report. He'll be here any minute. In fact, I can hear his footsteps outside. They're quite unmistakable.'

'Have you just one NCO, sir?'

'Yes, he retired as a company sergeant-major in the Gordon Highlanders.'

William remembered some of the senior ratings he'd known. 'I imagine he's worth his weight in gold at a time like this,' he said.

'He's worth at least that.'

There was a knock on the door, and Morris called, 'Come in.'

A sergeant-major, smart as he could be in shapeless denims, stepped inside, came to attention, saluted and said, 'Number Three Platoon are fallen in, sir.'

'Thank you, Sergeant-Major.' He motioned to William to follow him across the parqueted corridor to what must have been the assembly hall, where two dozen or more men were lined up in threes. The NCO stood in front of them and ordered, 'Platoon, 'toon, shun!'

William winced as their boots hit the maple floor in a ramshackle chorus, reminding him of his first drill at *HMS President* in London.

The captain said, 'I've never seen anything so shameful in all my life. Try again, Sergeant-Major.'

The NCO eyed his men with smouldering anger. 'Platoon, stand at ease! Platoon, 'toon, shun!'

This time, the welter of boots was much more together. The captain nodded and said, 'Stand the men at ease, Sergeant-Major.'

'Platoon, stand at... ease!'

The result was promising. The captain took his place before them and ordered them to stand easy.

'We have a visitor tonight,' he told them. 'He is Lieutenant Stamford of the Royal Naval Volunteer Reserve, and he's going to speak to some of you individually about how you feel now you're in the first line of defence. Treat him with respect. Not only is he a commissioned officer, but he was wounded in the Battle of the River Plate and was awarded the Distinguished Service Cross.'

William wished he'd left the last sentence unspoken, but he carried on in spite of it, and spent the rest of the drill speaking with randomly-chosen members of the platoon, most of whom were clearly new recruits and unused to military procedures, but who nevertheless shared their officer's defiant attitude.

Eventually, he was able to speak with the sergeant-major, who had been occupied for most of the evening with his NCO's duties. His name was Wallace, and he bore it proudly, pointing out to William that an earlier Wallace had been a Scottish hero and martyr.

'Sergeant-Major Wallace, where did you serve in the last war?'

'At Third Wipers, sir, and *Cambrai*, where I was wounded. I served later in India, sir, on the North-West Frontier.'

William nodded, recognising the soldiers' anglicisation of *Ypres*. 'My father and uncle were killed at Third *Ypres*,' he told him.

'I'm sorry to hear that, sir.'

'Thank you. How do you feel this platoon's coming on after such a short time?'

'They're good lads, sir, and they'll get there if they're allowed.'

'Do you mean if the enemy doesn't invade us first?'

Wallace gave him a direct look. 'If the enemy come,' he said, 'I'll expect these lads to follow me and give a good account of themselves, but it would be better if they had more time to train.'

'Quite. What makes a good infantryman, Sergeant-Major?'

'It takes marksmanship, discipline, loyalty and pride, sir, and when an infantryman goes into action, he has to have it in him to kill, because if he doesn't kill, make no mistake, he will *be* killed. He has to go forward and use his bayonet without flinching. If he can do that, he'll put the fear of God into the Hun.' Wallace's voice had risen toward the end of his last sentence, so that the captain and several others looked anxiously in his direction, but William made a calming motion with his hand to set them at ease.

Afterwards, he spoke to the platoon commander.

'Sergeant-Major Wallace has told me what I needed to know, sir. As you said earlier, you have an excellent NCO there. I'd pity any paratrooper that got in his way.'

***

William reported to Commander Challock the next morning. The commander was keen to know what progress had been made.

'It was a useful night, sir. I can see my way forward. I just need to spend an hour or so working on the detail.'

'Can I tell Colonel Loxton that you'll have something for him by tomorrow?'

'Yes, sir.'

'Just out of interest, what was your general impression?'

'They reminded me of my earliest days at *HMS President* seven years ago, sir. There's a hardcore of experienced soldiers and a lot of naïve, eager recruits. Best of all, though, the one NCO, an ex-company sergeant-major, is a soldier to the very core, and I think my conversation with him will enable me to rekindle memories that the enemy would much rather forget.'

***

When he arrived at Commander Challock's office the next day, he found Colonel Loxton keen to begin but surprised to see William empty-handed.

'What, no display, no presentation, Stamford?'

'Only my notes, sir,' said William, taking a single, folded sheet of paper from his pocket, 'and your imagination.'

'My what?'

'Your imagination, sir, because the enemy will be using his.'

Loxton gave way grudgingly. 'Oh, very well. Carry on.'

'Aye-aye, sir. The message for the enemy is this:

' "Have you heard about *Die Damen vom Hölle*? The Women from Hell? Your fathers and uncles may have told you about them. Maybe they still suffer nightmares about the army of battle-hardened Highlanders charging towards them across No-Man's-Land, shrieking Gaelic battle cries and curses, bagpipes wailing, kilts flying, and each man with undiluted hatred in his eyes. They last confronted a German army in nineteen-eighteen, and they have not changed. They're just a few years older, and as fearsome as ever. They are now the backbone of the Home Guard, two million men, who have sworn to deny you even one square millimetre of their homeland. You have been warned!" '

Loxton blinked several times. 'By Jove, Stamford,' he said, 'I think you have something there, something to make the blighters think again. What do you think, Challock?'

'I'm most impressed, sir.'

'One thing puzzles me, Stamford.' Loxton scratched his chin. 'How on earth did you come by this idea?'

William's mind returned to his conversation with Sergeant-Major Wallace. He recalled the venom in the Highlander's eyes and the ferocious timbre of his voice. 'I met someone last night, sir,' he said, 'a retired CSM in the Gordon Highlanders, who'd faced the Kaiser's army and who is now sharpening his bayonet to confront the next generation.' He closed his eyes, recapturing the image of Wallace's bellicose features. 'That, as we know, is yet to happen, but I have to confess, sir, that he scared me half to death.'

# 9

'There's a gap in the middle of the Atlantic that is beyond the range of land-based aircraft, and we simply haven't enough aircraft carriers to escort every convoy. For that reason, it's proving to be a popular hunting ground for U-boats.' Commander Challock's expression was particularly grim. 'Until we can complete the carriers under construction, the problem remains insurmountable. In the meantime, we have to rely on our destroyers and corvettes, and we're woefully short of both.' He paused to light a cigarette, and then continued. 'There is a glimmer of light on the horizon. Escort vessels are being routinely fitted with ASDIC, and that's a step in the right direction.'

'ASDIC, sir?' The term was new to William.

'Anti-Submarine Detection Equipment, Stamford. It transmits a note at the high end of the human hearing range, which bounces off whatever it meets, hopefully a U-boat with malicious intent, and forms a crude image of it on a glass screen, giving its range and bearing.'

'I see, sir, like Radio Direction Finding, but with sound?'

'Correct. Now, there's another device that is only available as yet to shore establishments. It's called High Frequency/Direction Finding, short title: "Huffduff", usually expressed in print as HF/DF, and it's proving very useful in home waters.'

'Why isn't it carried in ships, sir?'

'Because it's too big and bulky. We're waiting for the experts to develop a more compact version before that can happen.'

'I see, sir.'

'But it's not all gloom.' The commander allowed himself a half-smile. 'As I told you earlier, shore-based HF/DF has enjoyed a measure of success in intercepting U-boat transmissions and calculating the enemy's position, to the extent that they're wondering how their U-boats are being detected so readily in British home waters.'

'Don't they have a similar system of their own, sir?'

'They have, and they've had it for some time, but it's not as good as ours, although they don't know that, and it's vitally important that they don't find that out.' He spread his hands like an indulgent parent about to announce a treat. 'That, Stamford, is why you're here.'

'What do want me to do, sir?' The technicalities of wireless telegraphy were beyond him, and he was intrigued that Challock wanted to involve him in the esoteric world of science.

'I want you to produce a credible explanation for our success, Stamford. I think this one will really tax your powers of invention.'

❦

'I can't even begin to think of a scientific explanation,' he told Lucy. 'I don't know what he's expecting.'

'Didn't he give you a clue?'

'Not even a hint.'

'Oh dear.'

They lapsed into an anxious silence, which occupied a good five minutes, until William said, 'This calls for a dose of Mozart.'

'Who?'

'Mozart. Wolfgang Amadeus,' he prompted, 'a musical genius, but otherwise an insufferable, precocious little horror with an ambitious father.'

'I know who Mozart was,' she protested, 'but why bring him into this?'

'The owner of the flat I'm renting,' he said, 'moved out in a hurry and left behind his Bechstein grand.'

'Gosh. Aren't you lucky?'

'Yes, because I produce some of my better ideas when I've ploughed through a sonata, or maybe two.' Seeing that her shoulders were shaking, he asked, 'All right, what do you do when you have a problem?'

68

She shrugged, still trying to contain her laughter. 'Not much. It's my normal state of mind.'

'I recommend Mozart. Bach is quite good for stimulating the mind, too.'

'He would be.'

They resumed their silent contemplation until Lucy said, 'Things were easier at one time.'

'What time was that?' He couldn't remember a time when things were easier.

'Roman times.'

'Not if you were a slave.'

'No, but slaves have always had a rotten time. A free man, on the other hand, always had someone to ask about things. For example, if you were organising a get-together with your chums on a certain date, and you didn't want it to come an awful cropper, you'd take the advice of an *auspex*.'

'A *what*-specs?'

'An *auspex*, a soothsayer, who would observe birds in flight, and ascertain from their behaviour whether or not the date was *auspicatus*. Auspicious, that is.'

William was impressed. 'I could have used the services of an *auspex* when I was planning my twenty-first birthday party,' he told her.

'What went wrong?'

'I'd rather not talk about it, if you don't mind. The memory is still too painful.'

'And most likely fictional, knowing you.'

'Lucy, that was below the belt.' He would have said more had a pigeon not distracted him by landing on the window ledge beside him, balancing perfectly on its one remaining foot. The whereabouts of the other was a mystery, but the pigeon looked remarkably carefree in spite of its incompleteness. He wondered if stoic acceptance of pain, frustration and disability were a pigeon characteristic, or if it applied to most creatures. What, for example, passed through the mind of a red mullet the moment before being devoured by a shark? Fish, as well as birds, might have untold properties. He explored the possibility briefly, and it gave him the germ of an idea.

'Lucy?'

'Yes?'

'I've been thinking about those *auspex* characters you told me about.'

She smiled indulgently. 'They were charlatans, William,' she said. 'It was only Roman superstition.'

'Yes, but just suppose it were possible to interpret bird flight, or maybe the behaviour of fish or marine mammals. I mean, I don't know what scientists know about the subject; I suspect very little, and that might give us the opportunity we're looking for.'

She regarded him with a bewildered expression. 'Please start at the beginning, William,' she said. 'I haven't understood a word so far.'

'All right. We know that marine mammals transmit sounds, very likely to communicate with one another.'

'Yes.'

'If they can hear those sounds, chances are they can hear the noise of a submarine's electric motor and propellers as it runs submerged, or its diesel engine when it's on the surface.'

'All right.' Her look of bafflement was gone. She was becoming involved in his hypothesis.

'If they are attracted by those sounds, it should be possible, by plotting the converging courses taken by schools, or whatever the group is called, of porpoises, to determine the position of a U-boat.'

'Why porpoises, particularly?'

'Because they're found in coastal areas.'

'If you say so.'

'It's true, and it sounds feasible to me. Always supposing I can sell the idea to the Deception Committee, it'll be interesting to hear what the scientific chaps make of it.'

⊷⊱⊰⊹⊱⊰⊹⊱⊷

Commander Challock was sceptical. 'On the face of it, it sounds like a *Boys' Own* story, Stamford,' he said. 'Are you sure it's the best you can manage?'

'Absolutely, sir. I think there's a great deal of scope in this war for zoological warfare.' He wished senior officers would stop maligning *Boys' Own Paper*. It had provided him with many an hour's enjoyment in his youth.

'Zoological warfare, Stamford? You make it sound like an official department.'

'Why not, sir? They used homing pigeons in the last war, and canaries to check for gas in the trenches, or so I'm told. They used elephants on the North-West Frontier, mules in South Africa and camels in Mesopotamia. To use a less exotic example, what was cavalry but zoological warfare? What is zoological warfare itself but the harnessing, if you'll allow the pun, of animals because of their special characteristics? What, then, is the study of porpoise behaviour in this case but an example of zoological warfare?'

'Stop.' Challock held up his hands. 'Rather than putting your idea to the Deception Committee myself, I'm going to ask them to consider calling on you to make the presentation. Do you feel equal to it?'

William had presented advertising campaigns to some of the most powerful leaders of industry and commerce. The Deception Committee held no terrors for him. 'Yes, sir,' he said. 'I'll do it.'

# 10

The faces at the table might have been those of a poker school for all the reaction William could detect. They were a representative gathering comprising Rear Admiral Davies, Colonel Loxton and Commander Challock, plus three officers William had not yet met: a brigadier, an air vice-marshal and a wing commander.

He had delivered the idea in principle, and now he needed reaction.

'If you have questions, gentlemen, I shall do my best to answer them.'

The air vice-marshal was the first to speak.

'How did you first arrive at this remarkable supposition, Stamford?'

'I have to confess that it was largely serendipitous, sir. My assistant made a remark about the Ancient Romans and their reliance on *auspicare*, the practice of reading omens in bird flight. One thought led to another, and I found myself considering the properties of sea mammals.'

'And you believe that the animal kingdom is a largely untapped resource, albeit a fictitious one?'

'It has been genuinely exploited for centuries, sir, as I've already pointed out, but I do believe it has more to offer us in the field of deception, and I'm thinking in terms of birds and reptiles as well as mammals.'

The air vice-marshal smiled mischievously. 'One might almost be tempted to say, "All things bright and dutiful".'

'One might, sir,' agreed William, acknowledging the obligatory comedian in the gathering.

A burst of polite laughter died away, and Rear Admiral Davies spoke.

'Lieutenant Stamford,' he said, 'how might your department of zoological warfare be made to appear authentic in the eyes of the enemy, given that, by it's very nature, it sounds incredible?'

The question was a gift, and William welcomed it.

'To be credible, sir, the department has to exist, if only on paper. It must have a senior officer as its head, it must have a staff, an address, stationery, and links with scientific bodies and underwater weapons establishments. Only by treating it as an authentic department can we convince the enemy of its existence and make it impervious to espionage.'

'Thank you, Stamford.' Turning to the other members, he asked, 'Has anyone else a question to put to Lieutenant Stamford?' He waited. 'No? It remains for me to thank Lieutenant Stamford for the work he's put into this project and for this morning's presentation. We shall retire to consider our response.'

⇒⊷३⊶∺∹⊱३⊷⇐

Lucy was waiting for him in the office. Sensitive to his needs, however, she brewed coffee and poured it for him before sitting opposite him with an excited and questioning look.

'Well? How did it go?'

'It's difficult to say. They're an inscrutable lot, so it's impossible to gauge a reaction. We'll have to wait and see.'

'Did they question you about it?'

'Yes, an air vice-marshal asked me how I came by the idea. Naturally, I gave you full credit for the *auspicare* thing.'

She put her cup down, almost choking on her coffee. 'I can't imagine Colonel Loxton being impressed by that,' she managed to say, coughing into her handkerchief.

'Are you all right?'

'Yes, thank you. I'm breathing again.'

'That's a relief.' Returning to the presentation, he said, 'Rear Admiral Davies asked me how I proposed to make the department

73

appear authentic to the enemy, and he seemed satisfied with my answer.'

Her mouth fell open. 'You did well to answer that. I must admit, it would have floored me.'

'I'm not so sure it would, Lucy. I think Commander Bonnington and the others have a lot to answer for.'

She smiled faintly. 'It wasn't just them. I wasn't exactly full of myself when I first came here.'

'But you're more confident now.'

'Thanks to you.'

'Lucy,' he said, touched by her gratitude but reluctant to take the full credit, 'I didn't give you any of those qualities. They were there all along, just waiting to be tapped.'

'Well, I'm grateful to you, anyway.' She smiled, lightening the atmosphere. 'I'll take the coffee things and wash them up,' she said.

There was a knock on the door, and Dai Hughes peered in.

'Hello, William. Hello, Lucy. Here, let me hold the door for you.'

'Thank you, Dai.'

Closing the door after her, he said eagerly. 'You've got the top brass talking, William. They've been at it continuously since you left them, and there's some pretty hectic argument going on. I'm staying out of the way. I don't want to be caught in the crossfire.'

'You're doing the right thing, Dai, although I'm glad they're still arguing.'

'Mm.' Dai was looking nervously through the glass window in the door. 'While I'm here, mun, and I hope you don't mind my asking, but are you and Lucy... you know?'

'Are she and I what?'

'You know.'

'Not until you tell me.'

With an effort, Dai managed to ask, 'Are you seeing her... *on shore?*'

'Ah, I see, and no, I'm not.'

Dai's expression brightened. 'Do you intend to, at some stage?'

'No.'

'Why not, mun? She's a peach.'

William nodded. 'A lovely girl in every respect, but I have to work with her, and I'm pretty sure that an out-of-hours relationship would pose a serious distraction. I took her out to dinner once as a way of thanking her after she dug me out of the dirt with Bonnington, but that was as far as it went.'

Dai looked unsure for a moment, as if considering how to phrase his next question. 'If you're really not interested,' he began tentatively, 'would you mind if I... you know?'

'For all I know, guessing games may be popular during the long, winter evenings in *Llanelli*, Dai, but I have to confess I'm not much of a hand at them. It's prosaic of me, I know, but could we try that question again in English?'

Dai looked hurt for a second. 'My home,' he said with dignity, 'is in *Rhuddlan*, as a matter of fact, and we play civilised games, such as bridge and pontoon. I was enquiring if you'd mind my asking the fair Lucy to accompany me on a run ashore.'

'I'm not her keeper, Dai. You must follow the dictates of your libido.'

'I'll have you know that my intentions are strictly honourable.'

'Good.' William got to his feet. 'I'm about to heed a call of nature. Lucy should be back anytime now, so you can ask her. I shan't hurry back.'

'Thanks, mun.'

William walked slowly to the heads, regretful that he'd found it necessary to take the line he had. He was well aware of Lucy's charms and attributes, but working with her would be impossible under those circumstances. Also, there was another reason why she was out of bounds where he was concerned, and that was Pendleton Engineering or, more precisely, the wealth created by it, and what that wealth meant to her family. Their worlds were as different as champagne and best bitter.

---

Two days later, Commander Challock called William to his office.

'Good morning, Stamford.' He sounded in good humour. 'The Department of Maritime Zoological Warfare now exists. It has a home here at the Admiralty, in Room Thirty-Three, and it answers to Vice-Admiral Davies.'

William hesitated, wondering if there were maybe two flag officers of the same name, 'Do you mean Rear Admiral Davies, sir?'

'No, Stamford, I do not. The officer in question was promoted yesterday to vice-admiral and, as we speak, Gieves are making the necessary adjustments to his uniform.'

'That's excellent news, sir.'

'Quite. Now, you must get to work and produce a list of everything that's necessary to make the department a credible entity. Oh, and you and Miss Pendleton are to move into Room Thirty-Three. From now on, it's your permanent home.'

'Aye-aye, sir.'

'Well done, Stamford.'

# 11

## AUGUST

Dai swirled his beer into a vortex before draining his glass. 'An evening that began with such promise,' he said bleakly, 'ended in total frustration.'

He and William were at the Old Shades in Whitehall, where they had called for an end-of-watch drink, although William was distracted for the moment, engaged as he was in signalling the barmaid to refill their glasses.

'What was that, Dai?'

'I said I thought it was going to be the beginning of something splendid, but the whole thing tailed off into, "Thank you for a lovely evening", and when I suggested we might do it again, she said, "Maybe".' He reflected on the tragedy and said, 'You know, William, a woman can inflect that word with a whole lexicon of meanings, from, "You're on to a racing certainty, boyo" to "Not if you were the last man on earth".'

William paid for the drinks and took his change, asking, 'How did you interpret Lucy's version?'

'It sounded very much like, "I don't want to be blunt, but if you get any other offers, don't turn them down".'

'Bad luck, Dai.'

'I wouldn't have minded so much, but she spent half the evening telling me how good you'd been to her, how much she enjoys working with you, and how she'd most likely have buggered off home to Cheshire if it hadn't been for you.'

William nodded in sympathy. 'I'm sorry, Dai,' he said. 'It wasn't meant to happen.'

'Oh, I got that impression all right.' Then, possibly out of awkwardness because he'd been hogging the misery, he said, 'I'll survive, but what about you, William? You haven't been looking all that chipper.'

'Is it so obvious?'

'Not to an Englishman, maybe.'

'Are you telling me the Welsh have a special kind of intuition?'

'That's right. What's troubling you, William?'

William put his glass down. Unburdening himself never came easily, but Dai's was a safe pair of ears. 'I'm concerned about my mother and sister,' he said, adding, 'and my nephew and niece. They're in Kent, you see, where the bombing is. It was always reckoned that children would be safe in rural Kent, so they were never evacuated. I suppose the authorities forgot about the airfields.'

'Jerry's concentrating on the airfields, though, isn't he? I mean, he's not going after civilians. There's every chance they'll be all right.'

'I hope so.' He managed a smile. 'Like most kids, my nephew is collecting war souvenirs, bits of crashed Heinkel and Dornier.'

'Not Spitfires and Hurricanes?'

'No, he's very patriotic,' he said, grimacing, 'bloodthirstily so.'

'Good for him. Just keep telling yourself it's the airfields Jerry's after, William. It makes sense.'

'I suppose it does.'

※ ❦ ※ ❦ ※

A week later, William had more to occupy his thoughts. The department's identity had been carefully leaked through the usual channels to the *Abwehr*, the German secret service, and its naval wing, the *MND*, and he and Lucy had moved promptly into Room 33.

Because Lucy had not been present at any of the meetings, William had to brief her as they went along.

'They haven't leaked the porpoise idea yet,' he told her. 'They're waiting to see if the enemy accepts the existence of DMZW before they try that.'

Lucy raised a questioning eyebrow. 'DMZW?'

'Department of Maritime Zoological Warfare.'

'Of course.' She looked suitably caught-out. 'I'll get used to it.'

Quite unexpectedly, because they'd only recently moved in, the internal telephone rang. William picked it up, expecting the caller to be Commander Challock, as he could think of no one else who might wish to speak to him.

'Room Thirty-Three. Lieutenant Stamford speaking.'

'QM's Desk here, sir. There's a Lieutenant Commander McDowell here, from the Underwater Weapons Laboratory. He's asking to see someone from your department, sir.'

William was instantly wary. 'I'll come down,' he said.

Lucy raised an enquiring eyebrow.

'There's an unexpected visitor at the main entrance,' he told her. 'I'm going down to meet him.' He picked up the internal telephone again and spoke to the operator. 'Will you put me through to Commander Challock in Room Twelve, please?' He waited impatiently until someone came on the line.

'Room Twelve. Lieutenant Hughes speaking.'

'Dai, it's William. Is Commander Challock there?'

'He's in conference, William. He should be out soon, though.'

'Listen, Dai. When you see him, will you tell him I'm going down to the QM's Desk to see a visitor, a Lieutenant Commander McDowell? He says he's from the Underwater Weapons Laboratory. Frankly, I smell a rat, but if I don't bring him up here, he'll probably smell one too.'

'Okay, I've got that.'

'Thanks, Dai. I'm going to see him now.' He replaced the telephone and said to Lucy, 'When I bring him up here, if he asks you anything, stonewall him.'

'I'm only a junior civil servant,' she said. 'What do I know?'

'Good girl.' He picked up his cap. 'See you later.'

He walked slowly, hoping Commander Challock would get the message in time to join him in Room 33. He had grave doubts about Lieutenant Commander McDowell and the Underwater Weapons Laboratory, but he was reluctant to challenge a senior officer on his own.

He found his visitor in the chair he'd occupied nearly four months earlier. He was dark-haired, possibly in his mid-thirties, and he wore a neatly-groomed set.

'Lieutenant Commander McDowell, sir? My name's Stamford.'

The visitor returned William's salute before offering his hand.

'You'll have to forgive me for dropping in rather than telephoning,' said McDowell as they shook hands, 'but I was in town and, as I suspect our paths will cross sooner or later, I decided to pay a visit.' He showed William his Naval Identity Card.

'That's fine, sir.' William detected a suggestion of an accent in McDowell's otherwise carefully enunciated delivery. There was something odd about the way he pronounced the word 'town', but it was difficult to place. He asked, 'Would you like to come up to Room Thirty-Three, sir? It's the administrative centre of DMZW, so there's very little to see, but we can talk there.'

'Thank you, Stamford. That's an excellent idea, as long as I'm not interrupting normal activity.'

'Don't worry about that, sir.' William had heard that accent somewhere, and it continued to puzzle him until they'd almost reached their destination, and that was when he remembered the man in the next bed to his in the Falklands. He was from Belfast in Northern Ireland, and his accent, whilst heavier than McDowell's, was very similar.

Satisfied with his conclusion, he opened the door to his office and invited McDowell inside.

'We usually have coffee at about this time, sir. Won't you join us?'

McDowell's eyes betrayed a hint of momentary surprise at the mention of coffee. 'I will,' he said. 'Thank you.'

'Miss Pendleton,' said William, 'will you do the honours, please? Commander Challock may join us later.'

'Of course, Lieutenant.'

When Lucy had left the room, McDowell asked, 'Are there many civilian workers at this establishment?'

'Not all that many, but those we have do a splendid job.'

'Really?' His eyes flitted about the room, and then he asked, 'Where is the work of the department carried out?'

William thought quickly and said, 'That's mainly the province of *HMS Vernon*, although *HMS Dolphin* also has a part to play.'

'I see. Have you served on either of those ships?'

'No, sir. I'm much more familiar with *HMS Excellent.*' He'd attended several courses at the gunnery school before the war.

'I hope you don't mind my mentioning it, Lieutenant, but I notice you have a slight limp. Have you been wounded in action?'

'Yes, sir, at the River Plate.'

'Ah. Was *HMS Excellent* involved in that battle? I don't recall hearing about it.'

'Only indirectly, sir, and very much in spirit. I was serving in *HMS Exeter* when I was wounded.'

'*HMS Exeter*. Of course. I trust you're making a full recovery?'

'It's going well, thank you, sir.'

There was a gentle knock on the door. William said, 'That will be Miss Pendleton with the coffee, sir.' He opened the door to let her in.

As Lucy dispensed the coffee, there was another knock and Commander Challock walked in. William hoped his relief wasn't obvious to McDowell.

'Good morning, sir,' he said. 'May I introduce Lieutenant Commander McDowell of the Underwater Weapons Laboratory?' To McDowell, he said, 'Commander Challock is Executive Officer of the Department, sir.' The two officers shook hands.

Lucy poured a cup of coffee for Commander Challock.

'Thank you, my dear.' He turned again to McDowell and said, 'I've no doubt Lieutenant Stamford has been an excellent host, McDowell, but I must deprive you of his company.' He looked across at William and said, 'Vice-Admiral Davies wants to see you, Stamford. Don't keep him waiting.'

'No, sir.' William picked up his cap and took his leave of the two senior officers. Why the admiral should send for him was a mystery, but he didn't have to wonder for long.

Third Officer Dean welcomed him with a smile and notified the admiral by intercom that William had arrived.

'You're to go in, sir,' she said, opening the door for him.

William stepped inside.

'Good morning, Stamford.' The admiral seemed friendly, and William continued to wonder.

'Good morning, sir. May I congratulate you on your recent promotion?'

'You may, Stamford, and thank you.' He indicated the chair opposite him. 'Take a seat.'

'Thank you, sir.'

'I want you to tell me all you've learned about Lieutenant Commander McDowell.'

The mystery was lifted. 'Of course, sir. To begin with, he's certainly not an officer in the Royal Navy.'

'How do you know that?'

'My suspicion was aroused by a disguised but identifiable Northern Irish accent, sir.'

'And why do you think that would keep him out of Dartmouth?' The admiral seemed almost amused.

'To have reached his rank, sir, he would surely have entered the RN during the nineteen-twenties, when, if you'll permit the observation, the service attracted candidates of a certain social class.'

The admiral greeted the remark with half-raised eyebrows. 'In most cases, yes,' he conceded.

'He also referred to my service *on* a ship, when, as you know, sir, the preposition is frowned upon in that usage.'

Again, the admiral looked amused, but William hung on. 'Also, and more particularly, sir, he doesn't know that *Vernon*, *Dolphin* and *Excellent* are shore establishments. He asked me if HMS Excellent had been involved in the River Plate action. I told him she was indirectly involved, sir.'

The admiral gave way to hearty laughter. Eventually, he asked, 'Was there anything else?'

'Only that he claims to represent the Underwater Weapons Laboratory, sir. Unless there's been a change of name in the last few days, its correct name is the Admiralty Research Laboratory.' He thought again and said, 'Oh, and he seemed surprised that we drank coffee at the Admiralty. It was almost as if he'd come from a place where coffee was impossible to find.'

'In fact, as if he were a Nazi spy?'

'Yes, sir, and I do think we should have someone keep an eye on him.' It had been worrying him that time was running out.

'Don't worry, Stamford. Special Branch have someone waiting to follow him when he leaves the building. They'll know who he is as soon as Commander Challock escorts him to the exit.'

'What will happen to him then, sir?' William was conscious of being an innocent newcomer to the world of intelligence and espionage.

'They'll find out where he's working from. It's bound to be somewhere in London in case he's required to make another visit. Then, when he's had time to contact Berlin and tell them that DMZW is a genuine unit within the Admiralty, they'll arrest him. The next stage will be to try to turn him, to make him a double agent. Then, if he refuses, and few of them do, that's when he'll stand trial for espionage.'

It was heady stuff. Commander Bonnington had accused William of conceiving a plan fit for *Boys' Own Paper*, but this was a likelier candidate.

'Something troubles me, sir,' he said, 'something that doesn't seem right.'

'What's that, Stamford?'

'Just the appalling way McDowell has been prepared for this operation, sir. The enemy have always given the impression that they're highly professional and efficient, and now we see that they hadn't a clue when they created this spurious naval officer. If he has any sense at all, he'll grasp the first opportunity to throw in his lot with us.'

'I'd put a substantial wager on it, Stamford, and I agree with you. Happily for us, Nazi intelligence *is* extremely naïve. That's how we've managed to catch so many of their agents in the short time we've been at war.'

'Oh well, you know far more about it than I do, sir.'

'I do.' The admiral was smiling. 'I know enough, also, to congratulate you on holding the fort the way you did. Well done, Stamford.'

# 12

## SEPTEMBER

Third Officer Beatrice Dean's bedsitter in Pimlico was tiny but cosy, and Lucy imagined herself living in such a place. Staying as she did with friends, she had no immediate need to move out, but she fancied that if she ever did, a place of her own would give her a level of independence previously unimagined.

At the tiny stove in the corner, Bea scalded the tea.

Lucy said, 'I feel guilty, taking your precious tea ration.'

'Don't give it a second's thought.' Bea set the teapot on a cork mat on the table. 'It's pusser's tea. It fell quite accidentally into my bag.'

'I'm sure you'd no idea it was there, Bea.'

'Not until I got home,' she confirmed.

There were several explosions to the east, and Bea winced. 'They're bombing the docks again,' she said.

Lucy nodded glumly. 'I feel guilty when I think of the people living near the docks. They're getting it all the time.'

'We'll get our share soon enough.' Bea took the lid off the pot and stirred the tea.

'Do you think so?'

'My uncle says it's inevitable. It was how the Nazis subdued Holland.'

'Your uncle. Of course.'

'Had you forgotten? You're the only one who has.' She poured the tea and added milk.

'Is it such a problem, having Vice-Admiral Davies as your uncle?'

'Only that most of the time it's like wearing man-repellent.'

'Only most of the time?'

'As it happens.' She eyed Lucy playfully over her teacup. 'You went out with Dai Hughes, didn't you?'

'Only once.' She knew where the conversation was heading, but she also knew that Bea would prefer to tell the story herself.

'Why only once, Lucy?'

'My interest was elsewhere at the time.'

'I see.' Bea's eyes flickered with momentary interest, but it seemed she was keen to stay with the subject of Dai, because she asked, 'What was he like?'

'Attentive and courteous, but that's Dai. His manners are impeccable, although he does tend to be somewhat direct in his approach to women. At least, that was my experience. Also, he's not a very good dancer, but he could improve with careful tuition.'

'There was an explosion, louder than the rest, and Bea blinked several times before saying, 'I'll bear that in mind, Lucy. He's picking me up tomorrow evening.'

'Oh, you'll enjoy his company.'

'I hope so.' Then, in response to an earlier remark, she asked, 'Who was the object of your interest?'

'Mm?'

'The reason you went out only once with Dai.'

'Oh, well... I was quite keen on William at the time.'

'At the time, Lucy?' Bea's eyes teased her. 'I was under the impression you were still quite taken with him.'

'He's a hopeless case where I'm concerned, Bea. He took me out once, but that was to thank me for helping him out when he was in trouble with Commander Bonnington. No more than that.'

'That must have been....'

'Nearly four months ago.' Lucy supplied the information without hesitation, but not without a hint of embarrassment.

'Someone's been counting the months,' observed Bea.

'Not really.'

'I'll believe you, Lucy.' She picked up the teapot. 'More tea?'

'No, thanks. I'll have to go soon.'

'Don't take this the wrong way,' said Bea, pouring tea for herself, 'but I get the impression you're not very experienced in the world of work.'

'I've never been in any job for long,' confessed Lucy.

'That doesn't matter. All I'm saying is that you may not have considered that William is doing work of great importance. So are you, if it comes to that, but have you made allowance for it?'

'What do you mean?'

'Simply that he's not allowing himself to be distracted from what he's doing. Why else would he resist your charms?'

'I'm beginning to wonder if I have any.'

'Fiddlesticks.' Bea patted her hand encouragingly. 'You're very pretty, intelligent and jolly good company, and William is doing well to centre his attention on the job he's been given.'

'I'm not convinced.'

'Of course, there's something else you may not have considered.'

'Trot it out, Bea.' She wanted to hear something concrete.

'I don't know much about William's background, but do you think he may be in awe of your family, Pendleton Engineering and so on? Men can be like that, you know, the hunters and providers.'

Less than four miles away and oblivious to Lucy's dilemma, William was working on a prelude by Claude Debussy. It was called 'The Girl with the Flaxen Hair', and it was written in six flats, a key that he had found initially daunting, but he was beginning to get the hang of it, albeit with occasional excursions into wrong-note territory.

The picture Debussy had in mind was unclear, at least as far as William was aware, but he imagined a pretty girl with long, blonde, flowing hair. She was walking along a beach, possibly a private beach, where she could do as she pleased, and he imagined her enjoying the ultimate freedom that only total nudity could give her. As she journeyed across the warm sand, a mild zephyr would caress the whole of her body. William even fancied he could hear the breeze in the music.

He held the picture in his mind a little longer before returning to the task of learning the piece, although he was beginning to question its relevance to him. Being a gregarious man, he'd known for some time that he wasn't a born soloist. One of the advantages of manning a gunnery director tower was that he'd had the company of four ratings. It had been the ideal situation, at least until an eleven-inch shell had burst close to the tower, killing three ratings and leaving him and the fourth rating seriously injured. All right, company wasn't everything, but he valued it nonetheless, and it was equally important to him in music. Like sex, music was better when it was enjoyed by two people rather than one.

He wondered about the possibility of Lucy bringing her violin down from Carrbrook on her next visit. He would suggest it to her.

⊕◄╞╣╬╠►⊕

Home was very much in Lucy's mind when her mother's next letter arrived.

*Dearest Lucinda,*

*We hope you're still enjoying your work. Daddy says he's very pleased that you're making a success of it, and so am I. You will tell us if you're ever unhappy again, won't you?*

*Now for our news. Manchester was bombed last night, but don't worry – it wasn't anywhere near us. The Palace Cinema in Oxford Street was hit. Was that the one you used to go to? It's not there now, I'm afraid.*

*Grandpa, as he calls himself after your letter in May, says you're safer where you are for now. The Germans won't bomb south-west London. He says there are no military targets there, so why would they?*

*Is there anything you're short of, that we can send down to you? Maybe you'd like some more of your clothes. Let us know.*

*How are the Cohens? Has Joseph been called up yet? Give them all our love.*

*Daddy and Grandpa (it still sounds odd) both send their love. The house seems empty with you and the boys away. Eric and Francis are both stationed in Scotland, of all places. Still, at least they're together. It's important for twins to be together, even when they're twenty-three and grown up.*

*Take care and write soon.*
*Lots of love,*
*Mummy XXX*

William pressed the button and heard his coins fall. He'd made arrangements to take over the telephone account at the flat, but was obliged to use the kiosk for the time being.

'Hello, Mum.'

'William, are you all right? I mean with the bombing?' The line was crackling. It was impossible to hear her clearly.

'They're bombing the docks. Don't worry about me. How are you?'

'Oh, we're coping. It's very noisy here with aircraft overhead. We can see them circling each other and we can hear them firing their guns. It's been going on since August.'

William smiled to himself. 'I know, Mum,' he said. 'You'd think they'd show more consideration.'

'Don't be silly.'

'How are Jane and the kids?'

'They're coping.' It was strangely comforting that everyone was 'coping'.

'Are you still working nights at the First Aid Post?'

'Of course I am. It's my war work, not that we get to do very much, but we're there in case we're needed.'

'You're a tower of strength, Mum.'

'A flower of what? This line's terrible. When do you think you'll get leave?'

'That's anybody's guess. Unless the Germans invade, I expect it'll be Christmas.'

'Did you say you're expecting the Germans to invade at Christmas?'

'No. You're right about this line. You'll have to expect me when you see me, Mum.'

'All right. How's your leg?'

'It's fine. I've got a crutch and a parrot to go with it.'

'What was that about a Dutch carrot? This line is awful.'

'No, a parrot. I was joking. It's as right as rain.'

'Thank the Lord for that. I think we'd better ring off before there's a misunderstanding.'

''Bye, Mum.'

''Bye, darling. Take care.'

# 13

Commander Challock was clearly relieved to see William. 'Take a seat, Stamford. I'm glad you're here.'

'Thank you, sir.' William was guarded in his response. It was good to feel welcome, but he wanted to learn something about his next task before enjoying his new-found popularity.

'You acquitted yourself very well in the McDowell business.'

'Thank you, sir.'

'Our Nazi opposite number, the *MND*, have accepted the existence of DMZW, and we can now move on to the next stage. I'll naturally let you know when your services are required again.'

'Thank you, sir.' There was nothing else he could say.

Challock picked up a message form and considered it briefly. It was clearly causing him some consternation. 'I have a different kind of task for you this time, Stamford,' he said, 'completely unconnected with deception or intelligence in any form, but it's no less important.' He referred again to the message form and said, 'It's to do with recruitment.'

'Surely, sir, conscription and enlistment should give us the manpower we need.'

'I'm not talking about matelots, Stamford. 'This is an entirely different matter. It concerns... well, it concerns... the *female* of the species.'

'Wrens, sir?'

'In a word, Stamford, yes, and I have to say I'm at a loss.' He held up the message form as if it were the greatest nuisance to mankind. 'Their Lordships have charged us with a task that could, I'm sure, be better carried out by a Wren officer. It makes no sense at all.'

'In that case, sir, why don't you pass it to a Wren officer?'

'You may well ask, Stamford, but you're going to preen yourself in a moment.' He added, 'If, indeed, that is your habit.'

'As a rule, I try not to, sir.'

'Quite. But in this case, your name has been mentioned.'

'*My* name, sir?' William couldn't imagine that anyone in the corridors of power had heard of him.

'You have a certain reputation, Stamford, and that's a dangerous thing to have, because an officer with a reputation attracts bloody silly jobs. In this case, you've been given a particularly bloody silly job to do, principally because they can't trust anyone else with it.'

William hoped that the job would prove less monumental than the suspense Challock was creating. He asked, 'What is the task, sir?'

'The task is essentially to recruit more Wrens. You've seen the poster, haven't you?'

'Yes, sir.' He recalled the Wren with the hourglass figure executing a perfect salute, and the exhortation, *Join the Wrens and Free a Man for the Fleet.*

'They're actually doing a damned good job, you know.'

'I don't doubt it, sir.'

'Yes, they've freed a great many men for the fleet, but the problem is that the fleet needs yet more men, and that calls for more Wrens to do the freeing.' He sighed at the awfulness of the task. 'It calls for more Wrens than we're currently recruiting.'

'As I see it, sir, we have to persuade the girls to join the Wrens rather than the ATS, the WAAF or the other services.'

'In a word, yes.' He rose from his desk, bringing the meeting to its close. 'I don't know how you're going to do it, Stamford, but it's your problem now. Good luck.'

∞┉╋╬╋┅∞

Like most people in southern England, Lucy had been constantly distracted by aerial activity. The previous day, Sunday, had seen the greatest concentrations of enemy bombers since July, when the assault began, and the sky had been etched with circling, twisting vapour trails as the RAF's Hurricanes and Spitfires repeatedly intercepted the Heinkels, Dorniers, Junkers and Messerschmidts of the *Luftwaffe*.

'I can't believe that Commander Challock can get worked up about the recruitment of Wrens with all this going on,' she said, tearing herself away from the window. 'How can he concentrate on anything else?'

'He has a talent for delegation,' William told her gently. 'He's leaving it to the RAF.'

'I know, silly. You know what I mean.'

'Yes, but I need your help with this one, Lucy.'

'All right,' she said, giving him her full attention, 'but I can't see what's so difficult about it.'

'Can't you?' William had given it much thought since his meeting with Challock, and he was no further forward.

'You've had some excellent ideas in the past,' said Lucy, 'but you're struggling with this problem, and the answer's too obvious for words.'

'Take pity on me, Lucy. Share the secret.'

'All right. You want to persuade more girls to join the Wrens rather than the other services, so you have to ask yourself one question. What is important to girls of that age group?'

William didn't need to think for long. 'Men,' he suggested, 'but we can't use that. In any case, they'd meet men in any of the services.'

Lucy gave him a look of mock disapproval. 'There are other things in life, you know. I was thinking of clothes.'

'Clothes?'

'Yes, clothes are very important, and a uniform could be a big attraction. What we need to do is to get some Wrens together and ask them for their ideas. It should be interesting.'

---

The exigencies of war limited the number of available Wrens to three, and that might have created a problem, had Bea not intervened and ensured that they were a representative cross-section. They comprised Betty, a writer from the Paymaster's office, Iris, a telegraphist from the wireless station, and Ruth, a plotter from the Operations Room. Their respective departments released them for a generous half-hour the next morning.

'It's better if I don't take part,' said Bea. 'The girls might feel inhibited with a Wren officer present.'

Accordingly, the three girls reported to Room 33 at three bells of the forenoon watch, which William had translated earlier for Lucy's benefit, as 9:30 a.m.

'Come in, girls. Don't be shy.' William held the door and ushered them in. 'Now, sit down, all of you. We're just going to have an informal chat.'

The three Wrens sat, almost at attention, each with the same rigid expression. Clearly, none of them knew what to expect.

Lucy patted William on the shoulder before pushing him gently aside. 'There's nothing to worry about,' she told them. 'It's as simple as this. The Admiralty has asked us to find out how Wrens feel about their uniforms. That's why we arranged for some of you to come and talk to us. You can be absolutely honest, because we want to know just how you feel.'

Their faces relaxed a little, but they remained silent.

'Let's start at the top, shall we? What do you really think about your uniform hat?' She addressed the question to Iris, the telegraphist.

Iris said tentatively, 'Well, ma'am, they're what our mothers used to wear, aren't they?'

Now that one girl had broken her silence, the others nodded their agreement.

Betty, the writer, said, 'They call them "pudding basins", and that's what they look like. That's right, isn't it, girls?'

Her companions registered their unanimity.

'Thank you.' Lucy made a note on her pad. 'What would really help us now is if you could give us an idea of the kind of hat you'd rather have.'

'That's easy, ma'am.' Ruth, the plotter, joined the discussion. Whilst not strikingly attractive, she was tall, fair-haired and slim. 'We'd all rather have flat caps like the sailors wear.'

'That's interesting.' Lucy wrote that down. 'Now,' she said, moving on, 'What's next?'

'Collars, ma'am.' Betty ran a finger inside hers and grimaced. 'They come back from the laundry starched and stiff. They're awful next to the skin.'

'Okay. What about the tunic and skirt? Are you happy with them?'

The trio looked at each other and nodded. Then, rather as an afterthought, Betty said, 'We'd really like a bag, if that's possible, ma'am. A shoulder bag would be nice. As it is, we have nothing to carry things in, and it looks awful if we fill our pockets with odds and ends.'

Ruth added cryptically, 'And we have to carry things that sailors don't. A bag would be a good thing.

'A shoulder bag.' Lucy made a note. 'Now, stockings.'

'No, ma'am.' Ruth spoke for them all. 'Who invented woollen stockings, ma'am? If it comes to that, who would ever want to wear them?'

'They're every bit as bad as the lisle cotton stockings the WAAFs and ATS girls have to wear,' said Betty, encouraged by the nodding heads of her colleagues.

'Black, woollen stockings.' Lucy added the offending item to her list. 'What do you suggest in place of them?'

'Almost anything, ma'am.' She glanced furtively at Lucy's silken calves and said, 'Nothing posh, of course, but not wool.'

'Okay, that's noted.'

'There's something else,' said Ruth, 'except I hardly like to mention it in front of an officer.' She glanced awkwardly at William.

'Would it be easier if I asked Lieutenant Stamford to leave us for a minute?'

'Oh, no, ma'am,' said Ruth quickly. 'That won't be necessary.' Whether out of reluctance to inconvenience an officer or determination to make her point, it seemed she was about to introduce a matter of some sensitivity.

'All right. Go ahead, Ruth. Lieutenant Stamford is very understanding.' She smiled sweetly at him before returning her attention to Ruth.

'Well, ma'am, I'm a plotter. I work in the Operations Room, and it's part of my job to place markers on a huge wall chart.' She looked guiltily at William and corrected herself. 'I mean a *bulkhead* chart, ma'am.'

'That's all right. Go on.'

'You see, some of the markers have to go to positions in the North Atlantic, and anywhere north of Stornoway is a long way up the bulkhead. It means going up a ladder, ma'am.' She lowered her eyelashes and added, 'In a skirt.'

Lucy made a note. 'I see your difficulty, Ruth. You wouldn't feel quite so much the object of male scrutiny in trousers of some kind, would you?'

'No, ma'am.' Ruth wriggled self-consciously, still watching William out of the corner of her eye.

'What kind of trousers do you find most appealing?'

'Bell-bottoms, ma'am.' Ruth spoke with instant enthusiasm. 'Visual signallers wear them in cold places, like Scotland and Liverpool and Belfast, so I've heard.'

'That's right,' said Iris. 'The V/S girls I knew in training all had bell-bottoms issued for working out of doors.'

Lucy made a final note and said, 'I think that's a very comprehensive list. Do you agree, Lieutenant Stamford?'

William looked up from the document he'd been pretending to read. 'Yes, I do,' he said. 'If you're all happy, we'll call it a job well done.'

'Well, girls,' said Lucy, 'is there anything else you'd like to add to what you've told us?'

They looked at one another, hesitated, looked again and then shook their heads.

'In that case,' said William, 'let me thank you all for your help this morning. You've probably done your service and therefore your country a great deal of good.'

He closed the door after the Wrens had gone. 'Full marks, Lucy,' he said. 'I couldn't have got them to open up like that.'

'Of course not.' She smiled. 'They were shy because you're an officer and because you're male. They're not used to talking to men about clothes, and they wouldn't normally dream of criticising their uniform to an officer.'

'But the girl from the Operations Room declined your offer to kick me out so that she could tell you about her dilemma.'

She laughed. 'I think the opportunity to air the problem helped overcome her coyness. That,' she said, 'and a degree of resentment, I shouldn't wonder.'

'She's very young.'

'Maybe a year or so younger than me, but she showed a lot of pluck.' Reflecting briefly, she said, 'A few months ago, I probably wouldn't have said, "Boo" to a goose, but now, if I caught a man standing at the foot of my ladder with prurient intent, I'd soon tell him what was what.'

'Good for you, although I'm a little shocked that an innocent young thing such as you has even heard of prurient intent.'

'There's no reason to be shocked,' she told him, handing him her notes. 'It was that year at finishing school I told you about. Our teachers taught us all about prurience and how to avoid unwelcome advances.'

'I'm glad they did. As a matter of fact, I have an invitation for you, and I hope it won't be unwelcome.'

'I'm sure it won't.'

'I have to report to Commander Challock tomorrow morning, and I want you to come with me.'

'Me?' Her eyes betrayed the memory of earlier times. 'Why on earth do you want me there?'

'I'm going to tell him the truth about this job, how you did everything while I stood by in awe and confusion. It's time you got the credit you deserve.'

# 14

## OCTOBER

William knew he hadn't slept for long; even with sleep-blurred eyes, a glance at the clock confirmed that impression. It was only a quarter to midnight, and he must have slept through the warning siren, because an air raid was in full progress. The *Luftwaffe* were evidently extending their operations from the docks to other parts of London.

He listened to the explosions, which seemed to be approaching, like giant footsteps, from the south. Between each detonation, he heard the bells of the fire engines, ambulances and the rescue teams responsible for recovering survivors and casualties from the wreckage.

A stick of bombs fell much closer, causing the building to shake as if in response to a minor earthquake. Then, another series of explosions followed, all of them worryingly close, until the building shook violently. A fraction of a second later, there was a deafening blast.

For a moment, William was back in the after director tower of *HMS Exeter*. Shells were exploding around the ship; one had hit the after turret, putting it out of action. He heard shouted orders and the cries of injured men. Then he shook himself, closing the door on the past.

Determined not to be rendered homeless in his pyjamas, he dressed as quickly as he could in the grey, civilian flannels, shirt and jersey he'd worn the previous evening.

There was a commotion outside the flat. He couldn't work out what was happening, so he picked up his helmet and gasmask haversack, and went out to investigate.

Mercifully, at least for the immediate neighbourhood, the bombing was now taking place to the east, but the carnage it had left behind was too appalling for William to take in immediately. Only about three hundred yards from where he stood, a row of buildings was on fire; firemen were fighting the blaze, and one of several ambulances was now leaving the scene, its bell playing its part in the hideous symphony.

Without stopping to don his steel helmet, William ran to where a Heavy Rescue lorry stood beside a public shelter. An air raid warden saw him and shouted, 'Are you bleedin' daft or what? Get under cover!'

'I've come to help.' William fastened his helmet, and the warden saw the badge of rank painted on it.

'Sorry, sir. I didn't know you was an officer.'

'Never mind that. Just tell me what I can do to help.'

The warden looked relieved. 'There's a woman an' two kiddies trapped in number forty-nine, sir. Heavy Rescue are workin' on it but there's a lot of bricks and stuff in the way.'

William followed the man's pointing finger. An earlier fire had been extinguished, and men were sifting through the burnt and soaked detritus.

'Get some men to form a chain with me,' William told him, shouting above the noise from the fires further along the road. 'We'll dump the rubbish here on the Common.'

'Right, sir.' Again, the man's relief was evident. Opening the door of the air raid shelter, he called, 'We need five men to form a chain.'

Instead of five, six men emerged from the shelter, dazed by the fires and the devastated landscape, but ready to do what was necessary.

'Join this officer in a chain across the road,' he told them, 'and start shifting rubbish. We're going to pile it on the grass, there.' He pointed unnecessarily to the Common. Then, taking his place on the opposite side, he shouted to the rescue squad, 'Chuck the rubbish to us, lads. We'll get rid of it!'

The chain was soon in motion and, as the pile of bricks, charred timber and other mutilated remains grew at the roadside, the rescue squad broke through to the under-stair cupboard, where the family was trapped. Cries for help had begun to sound increasing optimistic as the scraping, levering and wrenching of the rescuers came ever closer and, when they pulled open the cupboard door, the two children were ecstatic. Their mother was speechless, but she hugged her rescuers.

After a welcome bath, William sank, exhausted, into bed. It was after two o'clock.

⊷⊷❧⊱•⊰❧⊷⊶

He returned, the next morning, from a meeting with Commander Challock. He brought good news.

'Those three Wrens we spoke to are going to be very grateful to you, Lucy,' he said, 'and the others would be if they only knew.'

'If they only knew what?'

'That you were responsible for their good fortune.'

She looked incredulous. 'Do you mean they're going to change the uniform?'

'Some of it. They're going to get flat caps similar to the ones worn by junior ratings.'

'Similar?'

'Well, sort of flatter, according to the picture he showed me, but similar.'

She asked eagerly, 'Is there anything else?'

'There certainly is. They're going to have shoulder bags, and black, artificial silk stockings instead of those horrible woollen things.'

'Lovely, but what about the stiff collars?'

'Oh, those things.' He felt his own collar in sympathy. 'Candles will be made available.'

'For what purpose?'

'They'll be able to rub their collars with them. The wax will make them less abrasive.'

'How generous.'

'Ah, but wait. I almost forgot. Wren plotters will be issued with bell-bottomed trousers. Personal privacy will be preserved.'

'Good. I find the idea of sailors neglecting to look the other way grubby, to say the least.'

He shook his head. 'Sailors never get a look-in,' he said, adding mischievously, 'or even a look-up. It's flag officers only. They won't allow anyone beneath the rank of commodore anywhere near the foot of a ladder.'

'That's awful.' She stared at him angrily and then closed her eyes. 'You made that up, didn't you? Tell me it's not true.'

He assumed a contrite expression. 'It's not true,' he said. 'I made it up.'

'You horror. If I could lay my hands on something soft, I'd throw it at you.'

'In that case,' he said, taking his greatcoat and cap from the coat stand, 'I'll make myself scarce. I have a lunch appointment.'

⊷⊷३⊶⊱⊰⊷⊷

His appointment was at a restaurant off the Strand that he'd noticed but never used. It offered kosher food and it looked expensive.

'I'm here to meet Mr Waldheim from Groves and Holmes,' he told the waiter.

'Very good, sir. Let me show you to Mr Waldheim's table.' He showed no surprise at the German name, and William imagined that the restaurant numbered several among their patrons. In any case, Mr Waldheim was probably a regular visitor.

The waiter took his coat and cap, leaving him with his gasmask and discreetly ignoring the holstered revolver.

'Perhaps you would care for a drink, sir, whilst you wait for Mr Waldheim?'

'Yes, gin, please.'

'Very good, sir.'

William had almost finished his gin by the time Waldheim arrived, rushed and apologetic.

'William, my boy, how good it is to see you again. I'm sorry to keep you waiting. A client telephoned as I was leaving the office, and it was a matter that couldn't wait.' He made a visible effort to

100

calm down, and asked, 'How are you keeping these days?'

'I'm all right, thank you, Mr Waldheim, and you?'

Waldheim shook his head. 'Don't ask.' His manner was guarded. 'Tell me, my boy, what do you think are the chances of invasion?'

'Rather less than they were, I'd say, now that the *Luftwaffe* has been given the hiding it deserved.' In fact, William knew that the invasion had been postponed until spring, but it was vital that the public and the Nazis themselves were kept unaware that British Intelligence had that information. The fact that the British were reading the *Enigma* code had to be the best-kept secret of all.

William's companion refused to be comforted. 'Oh, from your lips to God's ears! I'm thinking of changing my name by deed poll,' he said.

'Are you really?' William recalled the time the Waldheim Advertising Agency claimed to have 'merged' with Groves and Holmes, a name and transaction invented by Mr Waldheim to disguise his ethnicity. 'Surely you're not still worried about internment?'

'That danger is past, yes, but if the Germans come....' He left the threat undefined. 'I'm going to change my name to "Woodhouse",' he confided.

William nodded, signalling his approval. 'It's a good name,' he said. Like "Groves and Holmes", it was a cryptic variation on Waldheim, and typical of Waldheim's circuitous way of thinking.

'Enough about problems,' declared Waldheim, picking up the menu. 'We came here to eat.' He scanned it eagerly and said, 'I don't know about you, but I never bother with *entrées*. They take up space better left for dessert.' Mr Waldheim's rotund figure was evidence of his weakness for desserts. 'As far as the main course is concerned, the steak *tartare* is always good.'

'It sounds most inviting.' William had never eaten steak *tartare*, but he was keeping an eye on the time, and he wanted Waldheim to give the waiter his order. There was a limit to the time William could take for lunch.

'Very well.' Waldheim signalled the waiter to come, and ordered for them both. 'Oh, and a bottle of the house claret.'

'Certainly, Mr Waldheim.' The waiter departed with his order.

'You know, William, things are far from easy. That's why I was so pleased when you telephoned me.' He added hurriedly, 'Naturally, it was good to hear from you, anyway, but to hear, also, that you're available for work is good news.'

'I can handle *some* work,' said William, 'in my spare time.'

'Yes, it's good news indeed. I just can't find the talent these days.' Waldheim seemed not to have heard William's caveat, but he was happy, and that was a rare luxury.

◈┅≬◈┼⊱┼⊱◈

That evening, William celebrated his good fortune at the Cross Keys, where he found the public bar only half-full.

'After last night, they don't want to be far from the shelter,' Esme, the barmaid, told him. She was about forty, of formidable build, and never too shy to offer an opinion or sit in judgement.

'I was there,' said William, hoping that the knowledge might deter her from holding forth on the subject.

'Whatever were you doing there?'

'Some of us were clearing the rubble so that the rescue team could get into one of the houses.'

'Well, I never.' She disappeared briefly to serve someone else, but William's story had whetted her appetite.

'The same again, please, Esme.' William placed his empty glass on the bar.

'Was there many trapped inside, then?' Esme hauled on the pump handle with casual forcefulness, making William more than ever resolved never to incur her displeasure.

'A woman and two children,' he told her. 'They were sheltering in the stair cupboard.'

'Well, I never.' It seemed to be her all-purpose observation. 'It's a blessing they got them out.'

William signalled his agreement.

'I'll tell you what, though.'

'What?'

'It must have been a new experience for you, getting your hands dirty.'

102

'Why do you say that?' He knew he was inviting one of Esme's judgemental slights, but he was feeling generous.

'Well, you bein' an officer an' all.'

'Don't you believe it. I was an archaeologist before the war. Now, that really is a way of getting your hands and knees dirty.'

Her face was a picture of incomprehension. She asked, 'What's an archae-whatsit when he's at 'ome, then?'

'Someone who digs up the remains of early civilisations.'

'Well, I never.' Someone was calling for a drink, so she went to serve him. When she returned, she said, 'It sounds clever, that archae-whatsit carry-on.'

'Well, you have to be able to recognise a Roman umbrella stand or a Saxon shaving bowl when you unearth one.'

'Too bleedin' right.' She gave the matter some thought and asked, 'Do they 'ave lady archae-whatsits as well as fellas?'

'I'll say they do. I wouldn't have gone in for it if there hadn't been any pulchritude around.'

'Even so,' she chided him, 'there's no need for that sort of language.' She went to the far end of the bar to serve someone. On her return, she asked, 'Did you enjoy the work, then?'

'I did for a while.'

'Why did you give it up, then?'

'I was tired of having to clean the soil out of my fingernails every night. You've no idea how many nailbrushes I used to go through in the course of a dig.'

'I can imagine.' She seemed to ponder that problem and others, because she said suddenly, 'Of course, I could never do that job. Not with the arthritis in my knees.'

# 15

## NOVEMBER

Commander Challock's tone was unusually severe, at least in William's experience.

'You were seen in a restaurant on the twenty-ninth of October in the company of a man of German-Jewish descent.'

'That's right, sir. He was my employer before the war.' William was inwardly incredulous that the matter had been seen and reported, and that Mr Waldheim had been identified as German-Jewish. The whole business seemed too petty for words.

'Why did you meet him?'

'I had offered to do occasional jobs for him, sir, absolutely in my own time. I also wanted to see him for old time's sake.'

'Challock rolled his eyes upward and asked, 'Don't you think it was bloody silly of you, considering the sensitive nature of your work, to contact a German national?'

'He's actually British by birth, sir, and I'm not normally conscious of his ancestry. As far as I'm concerned, he's always been simply the boss, and he's been damned good to me.'

'Well, you certainly gave MI Five something to think about.'

William could scarcely believe that the secret service was involved. 'In that case, sir, if they take a break from playing hide-and-seek and peep-bo through restaurant windows, and investigate Mr Waldheim in a sensible and grown-up manner, they'll be astonished to learn that his family came to London during the last century, that he served in Flanders in the last war, and that he's now living in fear that the Germans will invade Britain and treat him the same way as they're treating the Jews in Europe.'

'We know all that, Stamford. You, your family and your associates were all soundly vetted before we made the decision to contact you.'

'In that case, sir, I can't see what the problem is. I would never discuss my work with anyone outside this department, and that includes my family and associates.'

'I know, Stamford.' Challock's tone was more conciliatory. 'I'm just saying that you went into this meeting without considering how it might look to the security services. If they'd taken you away for interrogation, we would have been without you at a time when your services are greatly needed.'

'I didn't expect them to follow me, sir.'

'Well, you need to start expecting it. Basically, you need to be very careful. The very fact that you're working with sensitive material means that you're under scrutiny.'

William was beginning to get the Alice in Wonderland feeling he'd experienced when Naval Intelligence first made contact with him. 'Does that mean, sir, that if I call at the offices of Groves and Holmes, I'm likely to be arrested by Special Branch and turned into a double agent, or can I simply expect to be shot?'

'There's no need for sarcasm, Stamford. Now that Groves and Holmes, as well as Waldheim, have been cleared, there shouldn't be a problem, but remember to think twice before you make contact with foreign nationals.' He hesitated and corrected himself. 'Or even British nationals with foreign connections.'

'Aye-aye, sir.' There was little else he could say.

Challock leaned back in his chair, visibly more relaxed. 'We have to be particularly careful, Stamford. As I reminded you earlier, yours is a highly sensitive job, and it's about to become even more sensitive.'

William swallowed his resentment and paid attention.

'We've been given a huge job to do. When I say that, I'm not just talking about the effort involved, although that will probably be considerable. I'm referring to the far-reaching effect we're hoping to achieve.'

'What is the job, sir?' It sometimes seemed to William that Challock might have been highly successful as an author of suspense novels.

'I can't tell you that, Stamford, but I'll be taking you this afternoon to meet someone who can. All I can say for now is that it concerns not just Naval Intelligence or military intelligence as a whole, but that it could alter the future course of the war.'

❧❀❧

William and Challock walked through a long, corridor-like tunnel until they came to what appeared to William to be a cluster, or network, of rooms, the smallest of which Challock pointed out to him.

'It may look like the heads,' he warned, 'but don't use it as such. It's the room where Mr Churchill communicates by telephone with President Roosevelt of the United States.'

'Does the President know we're at war, sir?'

'I think someone must have told him by this time, Stamford. At all events, he's just leased fifty old destroyers to us in exchange for leases on bases in various parts of the Empire. It wasn't the greatest deal that's ever been struck, but we were desperate for the destroyers after Dunkirk, and you know what they say.'

'What do they say, sir?'

'They usually say that beggars can't be choosers, although where I come from, they prefer, "Beggars can't be buggers".'

'Quite, sir.'

Presently, Vice-Admiral Davies, Colonel Loxton and the rest of the Deception committee joined them. William was the most junior of the officers present. It was like being a small boy again in the company of grown-ups.

A civilian in short-jacket morning dress with a wing collar emerged from one of the private offices. 'Good afternoon, gentlemen,' he said. 'Please come this way.'

If William had guessed the identity of the mysterious person he was to meet, confirmation came when the civilian, presumably a private secretary, led the way to a door marked 'Prime Minister'.

The senior officers arranged themselves almost automatically in order of seniority, and William walked in the rear, behind Commander Challock.

106

As the party entered the Prime Minister's office, there was a flurry of salutes followed by the familiar, growling voice.

'Good afternoon, gentlemen. Find yourselves a seat. There should be enough to go round.'

William waited until the senior officers were seated, before sliding discreetly into a chair at the back of the room, where he could hide behind the tall air vice-marshal he'd encountered earlier.

'Ah,' said the Prime Minister, who clearly had X-ray vision, 'I see you've brought the new boy. What is his name?' He consulted a document and said, 'Stamford, stand up and let me see you.'

Obediently, William rose to his feet.

'Interesting name, Stamford. Tell me, it's "Stamford" with an "m", isn't it? Not "Stanford" with an "n"?'

'Yes, sir, with an "m", as in Stamford Bridge, Yorkshire, scene of the battle.' He knew that nerves were making him talk compulsively, but Mr Churchill seemed unconcerned.

'Good, good. A man who knows his history. You come to us with a reputation, Lieutenant, a sound reputation.' He gave a wave of dismissal. 'All right, sit down.'

Still mortified, William took his seat.

'Now, gentlemen, the situation is this. Hitler has postponed his invasion until next spring. After the hiding the Royal Air Force has just given him, not to mention the bloody nose the Royal Navy administered during the Norway campaign, I can't say that I blame him.' He waited for the sporadic laughter to subside, and went on. 'We must not be complacent. My aim, as you know, is victory, but without the participation of the United States, that is impossible. I am happy to report that I enjoy particularly convivial relations with President Roosevelt. Our destruction of the French fleet in July was distressing, I'm sure you will agree, but it proved to him beyond any doubt that we mean business; in fact, he has intimated as much to me. I am, as some of you know, in constant dialogue with the President, but I fear persuasion will be a lengthy task.'

He paused to light a cigar and, confident that it was properly alight, he continued. 'Meanwhile, we must hold the beast Hitler at bay, using all the means at our disposal.' He gestured to the gathering, as if he were expecting some contribution, but continued. 'I hear you ask, "What are those means?" I can only tell you that our means are indeed limited. Our only trump card, gentlemen, is Russia.'

At this stage, Vice-Admiral Davies lifted his hand. 'Sir,' he said, Russia and Germany are allies.'

'They are, indeed, Vice-Admiral, but only for as long as the arrangement is convenient to Hitler. All the signs are, gentlemen, that he has resurrected the Schlieffen Plan, which, if you recall the events of nineteen-fourteen, involved defeating Britain and France before Tsar Nicholas was able to mobilise his troops. So far, Hitler has only defeated France. Before he attempts to invade Britain, we must persuade him to launch an assault on Russia.'

Colonel Loxton was next to raise his hand. 'Sir,' he asked, 'why would Hitler wish to invade Russia?'

'You may well ask, Colonel Loxton. Hitler and Stalin have little in common beyond their obvious partiality for slaughter and butchery, yet such an operation is necessary for Hitler to avoid encirclement and to avail himself of the riches of the Soviet Union.'

'Riches, sir?'

'Oil and wheat, Loxton. Wheat from the Ukraine's vast arable lands and oil from Russia's mineral-rich plains. He will be unable to resist the lure of both. Only one question remains. We know the invasion will take place, but when will it happen? Our task, gentlemen, is to persuade Hitler to mount that invasion as soon as possible.' Then, with his usual, abrupt wave of dismissal, he said, 'I await your propositions.' He rose to his feet and said, 'Vice-Admiral Davies and Lieutenant Stamford, be good enough to remain behind for a moment.'

As the other officers left the room, the admiral and William came forward.

'Yours, Lieutenant Stamford, is a fertile mind. I am relying upon you to furnish me with the schemes and ploys I urgently need. Give the task your most urgent attention.'

'Aye-aye, sir.'

'Vice-Admiral Davies, I want you to have this officer promoted to lieutenant commander. If he's working for me, I don't want him seen as an office boy or also-ran.'

'Aye-aye, sir.'

William shifted uneasily, knowing that he was being dismissed, but compelled to speak. 'Sir?'

'Yes, Lieutenant Commander? Speak up. Time is short.'

'I'm grateful for the promotion, sir, and I thank you for it, but I have a question.'

'Well?'

'Am I at liberty to share this problem with my assistant? I should add that she has Ultra Clearance.'

'Your assistant, Stamford?' The Prime Minister looked puzzled.

'Miss Pendleton, sir. I believe you and she are acquainted.'

Realisation became apparent in the Prime Minister's features. 'Dear Lucinda? Yes, of course you may.' He resumed his stern manner. 'Now, unless you have any further trifling questions, carry on, both of you. In fact, carry on whether or not. I have a war to wage.'

'Aye-aye, sir.'

'Aye-aye, sir.' Both officers saluted and left the office.

When they were clear of the war rooms, the admiral said, 'The Prime Minister can be very rude, Stamford. He sees it as the prerogative of a man of destiny.'

'Who are we to argue, sir?'

'Who indeed?'

They soon caught up with Commander Challock.

'We meet again, Challock,' said the admiral, 'and I have news from the Prime Minister. Lieutenant Stamford is to be promoted to lieutenant commander.'

'Really, sir? I must say, there never were such times. I was a lieutenant for eight years.'

'Those were lean years, Challock.'

'They were indeed, sir. Nevertheless, I am happy to offer you my congratulations, Stamford.'

'Thank you, sir.'

They walked a little further, and the admiral said, 'You'll be a senior officer shortly, Stamford. You'll be expected to behave responsibly.'

'I'll do my best, sir.'

'Hm. I don't recall seeing you on Trafalgar Night.'

'I didn't attend the dinner, sir. I don't possess mess undress.'

'Neither do most of your RNVR colleagues, but many of them nevertheless show respect for our traditions.'

'I intended no lack of respect, sir. My absence was due simply to my reluctance to offend protocol.'

They stopped outside the admiral's office.

'As you're now a senior officer, Stamford, you will be expected to attend wardroom dinners.'

'Aye-aye, sir.'

'Good day, gentlemen.'

The two officers responded.

As they walked further, Challock said, 'You and I are of similar height and build, I believe, Stamford.'

Glancing discreetly at his superior officer, William said, 'I believe so, sir.'

'I have a mess undress uniform I no longer wear. It's perfectly good, but I had one of rather better quality made when I was promoted to commander.' He favoured William with a look bordering on friendliness and said, 'You're welcome to my old one. You'll have to get Gieves to make the necessary alterations. Oh, and you'll need to find a dress shirt and a set of studs as well.'

'That's very kind of you, sir. Thank you.'

'Yes, you've no excuse for not attending dinners, now.' They came to Challock's office, and he beckoned William inside, inviting him to take a seat. 'You mentioned Stamford Bridge to the Prime Minister, Stamford. Any particular reason?'

'I was nervous, sir.'

'But why Stamford Bridge, Yorkshire, rather than London?'

'My grandfather came from Pocklington, near York, sir.'

'Did he, by Jove?' The commander's eyes showed new interest. 'I'm from Stamford Bridge, which is why I was interested.'

'It's not obvious, sir.'

'That I'm a Yorkshireman? We don't all wear it like a pennant number, you know.'

'Of course not, sir.' William couldn't help smiling. 'My grandfather did. He also kindled my enthusiasm for cricket.'

'Oh, you're keen on cricket, then?'

'I'm still a member of Yorkshire, even though I was born in London, such was the strength of my grandfather's influence.' He gave a fatalistic shrug. 'I'm afraid my membership's not much use in wartime,' he said.

The commander allowed himself a rare smile. 'It won't last for ever, Stamford. We may yet see each other at an "away" match or even at Headingley.' The thought evidently pleased him. 'You know,' he said, 'you and I have more than one thing in common.' He left his seat to open the door for William's exit. 'Before we do anything else, though, we have to address the task the Prime Minister has charged us with, and I don't think you'll have much time in your life to write advertisements.'

# 16

Lucy regarded him with dismay. 'Where on earth are we going to start?'

'Let's start with what we know.' William went to the blackboard, hastily borrowed from Anti-Submarine Warfare under the auspices of DMZW. 'The Prime Minister expects Hitler to invade Russia for three reasons.' He took a piece of chalk and wrote:

*To avoid encirclement*
*To capture oil*
*To capture wheat*

'What does he mean by "encirclement"?'

'It's probably not the most appropriate word, but he was referring to Britain in the north-west and Russia to the north-east. France dropped out of the reckoning, as you know, in June. Basically, Hitler has to eliminate Britain or Russia to ensure that he's not fighting on more than one front.' He came to the second item and said, 'The war is already going on for longer than he anticipated, the signs are that he can't rely on the Italians in North Africa, and he needs more oil than ever. It goes without saying, also, that he needs Ukrainian wheat.' He became thoughtful. 'What else is there?' Something had occurred to him during the meeting with the Prime Minister. He wrote on the blackboard: *Hitler needs a quick victory*.

'After a series of relatively easy conquests, his surface fleet has been mauled and his *Luftwaffe* have been given an almighty kick in the pants. So as not to lose face, he needs a quick success, and Russia could provide it, being unready for war.'

'You make him sound like a spoilt child.'

'I'm pretty sure that's what he is. The extremes of politics are essentially childlike because, by definition, they are simplistic.'

'Speaking of Nazi philosophy,' she said, 'if we can dignify it with that label, what about *Lebensraum*, the expansion of the *Reich* to accommodate future generations of the Master Race?'

'Good thinking, Lucy.' He added *Lebensraum* to the list.

'There's no need to sound so surprised. I read *Mein Kampf* when I was at finishing school.' She wrinkled her nose. 'It was good practice at reading in German, but it was very boring.'

'Surely it wasn't part of the curriculum?'

'No, we were never required to read anything. Some of the girls couldn't read the name "Chanel" without moving their lips. I just read Mein Kampf out of curiosity.'

'And you read it in the original German as well.' Suddenly he was back in Wonderland.

'It was the only copy they had in the shop and, after all, we were in Switzerland.'

'Lucy, you're full of surprises.'

'I'll try to find you a few more. Actually, I've been thinking about what you said about Hitler not wanting to fight on more than one front.'

'Go on.' He was prepared for anything.

'It seems to me that U-boats are prowling the Atlantic, attacking anything they find, and if Hitler's not careful, Mr Churchill's dream might come true.'

'And the United States will come into the war on our side, so he must deal with Russia before that happens. You're right, Lucy.'

She gave him a vexed look. 'I wish you wouldn't keep sounding so surprised,' she said.

'I'm not really surprised.'

'Aren't you?'

'No, just impressed.' He gave her a look that showed he was serious, and then glanced at his wristwatch and said, 'Shall we carry on with this in the morning?' He had to make a visit in Camden Town.

He reached the offices of Groves and Holmes a little more than fifteen minutes before closing time. Daisy, the receptionist, gave a little squeal of delight as she left her desk and wrapped her arms round him.

'Just look at you,' she said, running her fingers over the rings on his epaulettes. 'What are you? A captain or something?'

'Or something, Daisy. I'm a lieutenant commander, or I shall be when I can get an extra half ring sewn on.'

'And you've got a scar.'

'Actually, I'm very sensitive about my scar.' He tried to look hurt. 'I don't think any girl will ever want to kiss me again.'

'Oh, don't you, now? In that case, you'll have to come back in a few weeks' time and stand under the mistletoe. Then we'll see.'

'What a prospect. In the meantime, though, I have to see Mr Waldheim.'

'One moment.' Daisy returned to her seat and flicked up a switch on the intercom. 'Mr Waldheim,' she said, 'William Stamford's here to see you.'

William heard Waldheim say, 'Good. Send him in.'

'I'll see you later, Daisy.'

'I'll be here,' she said, looking up at the wall clock, 'Until six, anyway.'

William knocked on Waldheim's door. On hearing the invitation, he opened it and walked in.

'William, my boy, come and take a seat.' The air was heavy with cigar smoke and, as usual, Waldheim was holding a lighted half-corona. William wondered how he would cope when shortages began to bite.

They shook hands and exchanged pleasantries.

'We have a new account,' Waldheim announced. 'It's Sagar and Moreton, and the product is Oralgleam toothpaste.' He picked up a manila portfolio and handed it to William as if he were offering him a lifetime opportunity. 'It's all in there,' he said, tapping the portfolio, 'details of the campaign, the market they have in mind, and the budget.' He smiled and winked. 'There's even a sample tube of the toothpaste. You're welcome to try it. It could give you a few ideas.'

'I doubt it, Mr Waldheim, but I'll certainly try it.' Toothpaste wasn't exactly plentiful, so the sample tube was welcome.

'Have you everything you need, William?'

'I think so. I'll give you a ring if there's anything else I need to know.'

'That's right, my boy.' Waldheim got up to open the door.

'There's just one thing, Mr Waldheim. Do you think we could do this by telephone another time? Working at the Admiralty, I find it difficult to get here inside office hours.' There was no need to mention the brow beating Challock had given him about their meeting at the restaurant.

'Of course we can. Leave your new address and telephone number at reception.'

'I shall.' He took his leave of Waldheim and joined Daisy, who was preparing to leave.

'I thought you'd taken root in there,' she said, checking her make up in a small handbag mirror. She had light-brown hair, which she wore in a fair imitation of Veronica Lake, but pinned up during office hours.

'Are you going straight home, Daisy?'

'Now, where else would I be going?'

'I thought we might go for a drink, just for old times' sake, that is.'

She looked thoughtful for all of five seconds and said, 'All right. Let's do that. I want to know what you've been up to since you ran away to sea.'

'That'll take a while, Daisy. We'd better get started.' He offered her his arm and they left the office together.

As they walked along Kentish Town Road, William returned the salutes of two airmen, and Daisy squeezed his arm.

'Isn't it exciting?'

'What's exciting?'

'Being saluted like that. You're the only officer I've ever been seen with in public.'

He smiled to himself. 'Okay, Daisy, enjoy it.'

They came to the King's Head, a pub William had frequented before the war, and he stopped. 'Shall we?'

'Why not?'

William removed his hat before entering the pub, and Daisy asked, 'Why did you do that?'

'It's so that sailors, soldiers and airmen don't have to salute me.'

'Why shouldn't they?'

'Because they're out to let their hair down and enjoy themselves as well, without being inhibited by officers.'

'Oh, well, if you insist.' Clearly, she disagreed.

'There's also the time-honoured convention that a chap doffs his bonnet when coming indoors,' he reminded her. 'Now, what will you have?'

'Don't naval officers drink pink gin?'

'It's something of a *cliché*, but yes, some do. Would you like a pink gin?' She seemed to be heading on that course.

'Yes, I've never tried it.'

'They say we should try everything once.' He attracted the barmaid's attention. 'Two pink gins, please.'

A woman further along the bar said to her companion, 'Who does 'e fink 'e is? Lord-bleedin'-Nelson?'

William smiled and paid for the drinks, handing one to Daisy.

'Down the hatch,' he said, hoping she would find the salutation acceptably nautical.

'Down the hatch,' she responded. Then, with barely-contained eagerness, she said, 'You were in all the papers, how you got wounded and they gave you a medal.'

'Oh, dear.'

Innocently, she asked, 'What's the matter?'

'A great many were killed and injured, Daisy. It was exciting all right, but for the wrong reason.'

'Oh well, we were excited because we knew you. We didn't know about the others.'

'No, you wouldn't.' It was impossible for civilians to get a clear picture of anything. It wasn't their fault.

'Still, it's good to know you're safe. What are you doing now?'

'Oh, running errands, counting envelopes.... That sort of thing.'

'I don't believe you. What are you doing really?'

He shook his head. 'I mustn't say. I have to keep "mum" about my work, on pain of death.'

'All right.' Having reached a dead end, she tried another avenue. 'Are you going to be around for long?'

'For the foreseeable future,' he assured her. 'As a matter of fact, I've been wondering if you and I could meet again.'

'Do you mean for a proper date?'

'I wouldn't dream of suggesting an *im*proper date. What kind of thing do you like to do?'

She lost no time in thought. 'I love dancing,' she said.

'Then we'll dance the night away. How does Saturday suit you?'

---

Lucy had continued to ponder the current problem, and she was keen to air an idea that had occurred to her. She put it to William the next morning.

'A girl I met in Winterthur,' she said, 'told me her parents were involved in helping Russian fugitives. Her father was something at the Foreign Office. She told me some amazing stories of their escapes from the Bolsheviks, but she told me some awful things as well, about men, some of them high up in the army and air force, being arrested and taken away, never to be seen again.'

'Yes, I remember hearing about those trials. It was a shocking business.'

'But they didn't all get a trial, fair or otherwise, William.' She continued impatiently. 'I don't know who the individual victims were, there were so many of them, but just suppose Stalin unwittingly had some of his best generals imprisoned or even executed....' She let him consider the possibility.

'You're right, Lucy. We don't know that, but neither does Hitler.' He was instantly enthused. 'The knowledge might just give him the nudge he needs.' He made a note on the blackboard and asked, 'What else can we think of?'

Lucy had a question. 'Do you think Hitler might be concerned that another power could come to Russia's aid, or is that a silly idea? I suppose it is, really.'

'Not a bit of it.' It disturbed him, and he felt like hugging her when she lapsed into self-doubt. 'I think you've hit another nail on the head.'

'Oh, goody. What have I said?'

'I think Hitler needs to be assured that Britain will never form an alliance with Russia.'

Lucy grinned at the idea. 'I couldn't see Mr Churchill and Stalin side by side. Could you?'

'Not for one moment. The Bolshevik and the arch imperialist?' He chuckled. 'What a thought.'

'You know,' she said, 'it's all very well having these ideas. I mean, they really are the cat's pyjamas, but how is anyone going to convince Hitler that the dope about Russia, the generals and so on, is the genuine article?'

He thought for only a moment and said, 'Those immigrants, the fugitives you told me about, could be the source of intelligence. Assumed names, of course.'

'Of course.'

They pondered the problem further, until William said, 'Speaking of generals has given me an idea.'

'Trot out your idea, William.'

'Right.' He sat for a minute, formulating his thoughts, and Lucy waited patiently, knowing better than to nag him while he was thinking. Eventually, he said, 'Generals plan land battles, don't they?'

'Yes, even I understand that.'

'Hitler's not a general; he never got further than corporal, but he's still a product of the army, which means he thinks like a soldier.'

'Presumably.' Lucy waited for him to continue.

'He's literally out of his element planning a seaborne invasion, and the battering the RAF have given his *Luftwaffe* will have taught him one lesson. That much we know.'

'What lesson was that?'

'That he can't use his *Luftwaffe* as airborne artillery ahead of his ground troops, as he did in Poland, Belgium, France and the rest.'

'How do you know?'

'Because Göring had to stop sending *Stuka* dive-bombers over here after they turned out to be sitting ducks for the RAF. On the other hand, Russia's air force, with its primitive aircraft, is unlikely to provide the same resistance.'

'So, invading Russia would be much more his kind of party piece. I see what you mean, now.'

William made a few notes.

'I can't think of anything else,' said Lucy.

'I think I've scraped the bottom of the barrel. Right, Lucy. I'll collate all this stuff and type a report. After that, it's up to the top brass.'

'And Mr Churchill,' she reminded him.

'Mr Churchill most of all.'

# 17

News that Jack White and his Collegians were soon to end their contract led William and Daisy to The Astoria Ballroom in Charing Cross Road to hear the band and dance to it for possibly the last time.

The evening began well, and they danced to some of their favourite numbers. Daisy wasn't a natural dancer, but she was capable, and compensated with genuine enthusiasm for any lack of flair. William was naturally careful to appear unaware of any shortcomings. In any case, he was happy to be in the company of an attractive young woman, dressed as she was in a mid-blue shirt dress that complimented her slim figure.

At shortly after eight, however, the air raid sirens sounded, and dancers were advised to take cover. The nearest place of safety was Leicester Square Tube Station, so William duly bought two tickets, and they found a place where they could see out the raid. Daisy was unimpressed, particularly as the bedrolls were all taken.

'I suppose we're going to be here all night,' she sniffed.

'It wasn't part of the planned entertainment,' he told her, 'but it's on the cards.'

'I don't know how you can joke about it, I really don't.'

'I try not to, honestly.' He unfastened the last of his buttons.

She watched him remove his greatcoat and asked, 'What are you doing that for?'

'So that we can lie on it. It'll keep your clothes clean.'

'Your coat will get dirty.'

'I know,' he said, trying to look like Leslie Howard at the end of *The Scarlet Pimpernel*, 'but history is being re-enacted tonight.'

She stared at him, nonplussed. 'What are you talking about?'

'I'm talking about a man laying down his outer garment to preserve a lady's dignity. It's been a while since the last time it happened.'

She joined him on the greatcoat, laying her head on his shoulder. 'Do you mean you've done this before?'

'Not I, my dear. No, the last man to behave in such a chivalrous manner was a well-known tobacco and potato importer.' He squinted sideways at her, but failed to detect a reaction. 'He also gave his name to a bicycle factory.'

'He keeps his fingers in a few pies, then.'

'Yes, it's enough to make a man lose his head.' He placed his cap over his eyes to shade them from the light.

'William?'

'Hm?'

'You were at Groves and Holmes when I started there, weren't you?'

He removed his cap to speak to her. 'That's right.'

'Have you always been in advertising?'

'No, I used to be a make-up artist.' The words were out almost before he was aware he'd uttered them.

'Where did you work?'

'At the Windmill Theatre.' He was conscious of a mother nearby, who was telling her children a bedtime story. They seemed fascinated. It must be a good story, he decided, but he had to concentrate on his own.

She whispered, 'Isn't that where the girls go on stage in the altogether?'

'Yes, but I hardly noticed them after a while. You can get used to anything, you know.'

'But, I mean, they do it without a stitch on, don't they? Which part of them did you have to make up?'

'Their faces, mainly.'

'Mainly?' She sat upright, eager to hear more.

'Yes, I occasionally had to apply a spot of rouge here and there.' He corrected himself. 'Well, *there* and there, actually.'

'Surely not,' she breathed, involuntarily covering her chest with both hands.

'And every now and again, I was obliged to wield the razor.'

'What?' Her eyes and mouth widened to their fullest extent.

'Yes, the underarms, you know. Girls are hopeless at shaving. They cut themselves quicker than you can say "Sweeney Todd".'

'Well, I've never had a problem with it.'

'Relax, Daisy. I'm not offering my services. I've retired from the dressing room.'

Now that the discomfiture was past, she had to ask, 'What made you give it up? Was it the embarrassment at working with nude women?'

'No, it wasn't that.' He adopted an earnest expression and said, 'It had been my custom to call at the fish and chip shop on the way home. Have you ever tried eating fish and chips with the smell of greasepaint lingering in your nostrils?'

'I can't say I have.'

'Either one or the other had to go, and I've always been keen on fish and chips.'

❦

After seeing Daisy safely home the next morning, and indulging in a few hours' sleep, William addressed the matter of Oralgleam toothpaste.

According to the marketing brief, Oralgleam was to have universal appeal. That was a challenge in itself, and William set about the forbidding task of reaching out to the factory worker, the bus conductress, the shop worker, the accounts clerk, the schoolteacher, the bank manager, the business executive and the debutante. The last one was easy; the closest example William could find to a debutante was Lucy, and her teeth were perfectly shaped and spotlessly white. Glamour was clearly the key to her world.

After some reflection, he resolved not to spend too much time thinking about Lucy. He found it difficult enough to close his eyes to her obvious charms when they were at the Admiralty, where he had, at least, the distraction of work; at home, it was a matter of self-preservation.

He sparred with the problem of universal appeal until it became evident that it called for a dose of Mozart. There were times when William had no other course than to call on the spoilt little bugger. Childhood tantrums apart, though, Mozart was widely held to be one of the greatest musical geniuses of all time, so it wasn't surprising that his music stimulated creative thought.

The score on the piano was of the Piano Concerto in F Major K. 459. Apparently, the 'K' stood for Köchel, the scholar who catalogued Mozart's music, a boring occupation if ever there was one. The music, however, was superb, and one of William's secret pleasures was to play the piano part whilst hearing the orchestra in his head. Short of playing music of his own composition, it was musical masturbation on a grand scale, which was why he kept quiet about it.

After a while, an idea began to form, and he forsook the piano for a pencil and notepad. The cover of the latter bore the familiar official anchor and was marked *Admiralty Property*. It was another of William's secrets, albeit a very minor one.

At one end of the spectrum was the debutante, who simply wanted white teeth and fresh breath. At the other, the factory worker had other priorities. Anything more than routine dental care was beyond the means of the lowest-paid workers, so a toothpaste that protected the teeth, thus reducing the need for dental intervention, would be a welcome prospect. He juggled a few ideas until he had one that appealed to him. It was in the form of a strip cartoon but, instead of telling a story, it depicted people from a range of backgrounds, each stating a reason for using Oralgleam toothpaste. He selected four from his original list, beginning with a girl behind a lathe or similar contraption.

GIRL WITH LATHE: I brush with Oralgleam to keep my teeth healthy and avoid fillings.

TEACHER: I brush with Oralgleam to keep my teeth healthy and to set the best example to my children.

BUSINESSMAN: I brush with Oralgleam because a man in my position must look smart and groomed.

PRETTY GIRL: I brush with Oralgleam to keep my teeth beautifully white and my breath as fresh as peppermint.

As a final caption, he wrote, *Oralgleam gives you fresh breath and healthy, white teeth. Remember, when you brush with Oralgleam, a brushing per day keeps the fillings at bay!*

Although Mozart could never have known it, he might just have made a significant contribution to the dental health of the British nation.

⊕⊣3⊹⊱⊢⊱⊣⊕

On the following Tuesday, Commander Challock sent for William.

'The Committee have approved your scheme, Stamford,' he said. 'Well done.'

'Thank you, sir.'

'No, really, credit where it's due. It's a splendid piece of work.'

'Thank you, sir.' William was embarrassed. 'I can't, in all honesty, take all the credit. Much of the kudos must go to Miss Pendleton, who played a full part in the planning.'

'Really? Very well, Stamford. That's noted.' Challock consulted his diary and said, 'Make yourself available at six bells.' He looked at his watch. 'In exactly two hours' time, Stamford, we have a meeting with the Prime Minister.'

'Aye-aye, sir. Do you think Miss Pendleton might be allowed to attend the meeting?'

After a moment's consideration, Challock said, 'I applaud your loyalty to your assistant, Stamford, but no, I think we're better treating this matter as official service business, which it most certainly is.'

William spent the next two hours with a piece of charcoal and a large pad of white paper, which Lucy had found for him in the stationery store.

⊕⊣3⊹⊱⊢⊱⊣⊕

He, Commander Challock and Vice-Admiral Davies met for the second time outside the Prime Minister's office and waited to be received. Eventually, his secretary opened the doors and invited them in.

124

'Come in, gentlemen, come in,' called the Prime Minister. 'Take a seat, all of you. I've just received most welcome news from Admiral Cunningham, regarding *Operation Judgement*.' Mr Churchill's eyes twinkled with satisfaction as he delivered the news. 'Last night,' he said, '*HMS Illustrious* launched a force of Swordfish strike aircraft, which attacked the Italian battle fleet in Taranto Harbour.' With a broad smile, he went on. 'I have to tell you that the Italian battle fleet is now reduced by fifty percent. Our aircraft sank or crippled no fewer than three battleships.'

Protocol demanded that the admiral was first to speak. 'Absolutely magnificent, sir,' he said.

'Amazingly well done,' said Commander Challock.

In his capacity as the most junior officer present, William said nothing, but nodded his agreement.

The Prime Minister turned to him and looked over his spectacles. 'Ah, Lieutenant Commander Stamford,' he said, 'I see you have something to show me.'

'Yes, sir, but before I do, I should like to make it clear that I can accept no more than half the credit for this initiative. The other half must go to Miss Lucinda Pendleton because it is rightfully hers.'

'In that case, why is she not here?'

'It was my decision, sir,' said Commander Challock. 'Lieutenant Commander Stamford asked me if Miss Pendleton might be included in the meeting, but I felt that the proceedings should remain an official service matter.'

'I see.' For a moment, it looked as if Mr Churchill were about to administer a reprimand, but his current good humour prevailed. 'In future, if Miss Pendleton makes a significant contribution to an initiative of such import, I shall expect her to be here to receive my thanks and, if applicable, my approval, Commander Challock.'

'Aye-aye, sir.'

'You did what you thought was right, and I cannot expect more from you than that, Commander.'

'Thank you, sir.'

The Prime Minister looked over his spectacles at the wall clock and said, 'Now, Lieutenant Commander Stamford, as time is pressing, perhaps you would be good enough to enlighten me.'

'Aye-aye, sir.' William opened his display at the first page and proceeded with his presentation.

Mr Churchill listened intently, interrupting occasionally with a question or observation, until William reached the end of the presentation.

'I must congratulate you on a meticulous piece of work, Lieutenant Commander Stamford. You will, of course, convey to Miss Pendleton, also, my gratitude and appreciation?'

'Of course, sir.'

'I fully intend writing to my good friend Edgar Pendleton. Without my giving anything away, I should make him aware that his granddaughter is making a vital contribution to the conduct of the war.'

As the party made its way back to the Admiralty, William at last had an opportunity to speak to Commander Challock.

'I'm grateful to you, sir, for what you said. I mean about Miss Pendleton.'

'I told the truth, Stamford. I owed you that at least.'

'Even so, sir, I'm grateful.'

The admiral, who had been listening to the conversation, made his contribution. 'It's an important principle of leadership, Stamford, that loyalty operates in both directions, and I was pleased to hear you express your loyalty to Miss Pendleton. I think the Prime Minister was also impressed.'

They reached the admiral's office and, before leaving the two officers, he said, 'Would you both be good enough to escort Miss Pendleton to my office? I should like to speak to her.'

'Aye-aye, sir,'

'Aye-aye, sir.'

<hr />

A few days later, Commander Challock had news for William.

'There's going to be a formal dinner on Saturday, Stamford, this time to celebrate the success of *Operation Judgement*. Perhaps there is a lady of your acquaintance whom you might wish to invite?'

'There is, sir.'

'Very good. I look forward to meeting her.'

William had to think about that. He and Daisy had been out together twice, including the night spent in the tube station, and she was game for more, but he couldn't take her to a wardroom dinner. He hated himself for thinking it, but she would be an Easter egg in a Christmas stocking. He was no snob, but he had to be realistic. Consequently, when Lucy came into the office, he surprised her by inviting her to the dinner.

'But I thought you were seeing someone,' she said. Her attitude surprised him, as she'd reacted somewhat coldly when she first learned about Daisy.

'It's nothing serious. Daisy's just someone I used to work with.' He wondered how to assuage her misgivings without sounding completely heartless. He felt guilty enough already. In the end, he said lamely, 'It's a very casual arrangement.'

'I don't know, William. It's lovely of you to invite me, and I do appreciate it, but I can't help feeling awkward.'

'I wish you wouldn't. There's no future for Daisy and me, and there's something else.' He searched his mind again for a tactful way of saying something that, despite his reluctance to say it, was essentially snobbish. 'You see, it would be the most awful experience for her. She would feel out of place, excluded and the object of disapproval. It just wouldn't work.'

'Whereas I'm the social equal of the naval officers' wives?' It was clear that she disapproved of the argument.

'I'm not a snob, Lucy, but, essentially, yes, and there are other reasons why I'd like you to come.'

'I'm listening.'

'You're part of this establishment, an important part now, and it's right that you should be asked to take part in its social life.'

She viewed him through half-closed eyes, seemingly unconvinced.

'I'd like you to come also because I enjoy your company, and I think we'd both enjoy the evening.'

She looked down at her hands, whether making her decision or wondering how to say, he had no idea. Eventually, she said, 'I appreciate the situation you're in, William, and I understand your argument. Normally, I wouldn't dream of doing something like this, I mean behind another girl's back, but you've been more than good to me, and for that reason I will go to the dinner with you.'

'Thank you, Lucy. There's no suggestion of your doing anything underhand. It's just an isolated arrangement, as I said, but thank you again.'

# 18

William and Lucy arrived at the wardroom at seven for seven-thirty. William introduced Lucy to the most senior officer present, a full admiral, and to Commander Loveday, the Mess President.

Lucy looked around her, saying, 'I wonder if we're going to get an *aperitif*?' She wore a plum-coloured evening gown with a diamond brooch, a present on her twenty-first birthday, the previous January.

Her question was answered when a steward appeared with a tray of drinks from which they each took a glass of dry sherry.

'Hello, you two.'

Hearing the Welsh accent, William turned to see Dai, whose luck with women had evidently changed, because he was accompanied by Beatrice Dean, looking demure in her mess gown.

The two couples greeted and complimented each other, and Dai asked, 'Have they rung the bell yet?'

Bea asked, 'What bell?'

'The bell for "Ease Springs".'

It was Lucy's turn to ask, 'Ease what?'

' "Ease Springs", Dai told her. 'When a ship is tied up alongside, as well as the mooring lines there are usually two ropes called "springs" that prevent movement for'ard and astern, and they have to be adjusted; that is, taken in or eased, as the tide ebbs and flows. In this context, however, it's an opportunity to powder your nose before dinner, because it's your last chance until after the Loyal Toast.'

'I still think it's a revolting expression,' said Lucy.

'The Navy's full of them,' remarked Bea, whose mind appeared to be elsewhere. 'I've brought a change of clothes,' she said, 'in case we're caught in an air raid. Have you, Lucy?'

'Oh yes.'

'I think we all have,' said Dai.

William looked at the time. 'Ten minutes to the bell,' he remarked. 'If you ladies want to powder your noses, now's the time before the heads become too crowded.'

'You sound like my mother,' said Bea, 'although....' She looked thoughtful for a moment.

'Maybe we should,' said Lucy.

William watched them disappear towards the heads and said, 'I thought they'd never go.'

'Neither did I, mun.'

'Okay, how are things proceeding with the fair Beatrice?'

'Nicely, mun. How about you and Lucy?'

'They're not. I've been seeing someone else lately. Nothing serious, though, and I couldn't bring her here tonight.' He explained the situation.

'You probably did the right thing, William. Still, it's a shame, because Lucy's still keen on you.'

'How do you know?'

'I hear it all second-hand from Bea. They talk, you know.'

William wasn't convinced, and it really didn't matter. Even so, he couldn't resist saying, 'You wouldn't have thought so if you'd heard her laying the law down because I didn't want to bring Daisy.'

'Daisy being the one you're currently seeing?'

'The same.'

'And Lucy thought you were wrong not to bring her?'

William nodded. 'You guessed correctly.'

'Laid it on the line, did she?'

'Well and truly.'

'Women can be funny buggers, can't they?'

William peered over his shoulder. 'Hush, they're coming back.'

Lucy and Bea returned just as the bell sounded.

William looked at Dai and said, 'Ease springs?'

'Yes, mun, we'd better ease springs while we can.'

During the course of the meal, William was heartily relieved that he hadn't subjected Daisy to the experience. The snobbery and bitchiness of some of the more senior officers' wives had surprised even him. Happily, however, Lucy was holding her own.

'Ladies and Gentlemen,' called the President, 'The King.'

Port glasses were raised in the toast. 'The King.'

'Ladies and Gentlemen, in honour of those who took part in *Operation Judgement*, I give you "The Fleet Air Arm".'

The toast was repeated, and permission was given for those who wished to leave the table, the President having evidently decided that 'Ease Springs' was a term unfit for mixed company.

When the partakers had returned, cigars were placed on the table.

'Gentlemen,' said the President, 'you may smoke.'

The lady seated opposite Lucy said to anyone within earshot, 'I believe it used to be the practice for a lady to choose a cigar for her escort, although I've absolutely no idea how it was done.' She ended with a nervous laugh.

'As far as I'm aware,' said Lucy, 'it remains the practice to this day.'

'Oh?'

'I'll show you if you wish.'

'Go on, Lucy,' said Bea, 'give us a demonstration.'

'Very well.' Lucy took a Corona from the box and held it for everyone to see. 'A good cigar should be perfectly packed,' she said. 'If you roll it between your thumb and forefinger, you can feel its texture, which should be even throughout its length. You can also hear its texture.' She demonstrated by rolling it beside her ear. 'Like a polo field, it should be free from divots and recesses. The ash from a well-packed cigar retains its shape until it is disturbed.'

The woman opposite her stared, open-mouthed until eventually collecting herself.

'The aroma of the tobacco is, of course, a matter of personal taste,' she said, passing it beneath her nose and scenting its bouquet, 'but a lady is usually aware of the gentleman's preference. Now, will one of you gentlemen please oblige me with a cigar cutter?'

Several hands dived into as many pockets, and Lucy was confronted with an array of cutters.

'Thank you.' She took the nearest. 'The ends of the cigar are distinct from each other, the head,' she said, indicating the domed end, 'and the foot.' Here, she pointed out the end to be lighted. 'The head is cut, preferably with a cigar cutter. Should you use a knife, you must take care not to unravel the outer leaves.' She cut the cigar expertly and offered it to William amid enthusiastic applause from the officers and most of the ladies.

'As I recall from a dinner party at home,' she told the woman who had brought up the subject, 'Mr Churchill prefers to choose for himself. He is, of course, a connoisseur.'

With immaculate timing, the air raid siren wailed. The Mess President announced, 'Ladies and gentlemen, I think it would be safest for us to repair below.'

An officer's wife picked up her place card and slipped it into her evening bag. 'I always take mine home,' she said, 'as a souvenir.'

William picked up Lucy's and his. In the absence of a pocket in his mess jacket, he resolved to put it into his greatcoat pocket at the first opportunity. It was an evening he, too, wanted to remember.

Later, amid the noise of bombs, fire engines and ambulances, William said privately, 'Thank you for the best entertainment I've had in a long time, Lucy. Your cigar tutorial was magnificent.'

'Oh, the ridiculous woman was asking for it.'

'Can you see now why I couldn't bring Daisy this evening?'

'Yes, I can now.'

'Actually, I have it in mind to let her down gently. It's a relationship that's going nowhere.'

'Don't prolong it for her, William.' Lucy regarded him seriously. 'Make it a quick and clean break for her sake.'

❖⊱⊰❖

It was good advice, and William would have acted on it had fate not stolen a march on him. It happened the following weekend, when they returned to Daisy's bedsitter after a tea dance at the Regent Palace Hotel in Soho.

Daisy took his greatcoat to hang it up. As she did so, a glove fell from one pocket. William saw her pick it up and said, 'Thank you, Daisy. Just shove back into the pocket.'

'No, they're good gloves. I'll fold them properly.' She felt inside the pocket for the other glove and frowned.

'What's the matter?'

'There's something else in here, getting in the way.'

'Don't worry about it. I have to go soon, anyway.'

She pulled out the offending articles, which turned out to be the place cards from the wardroom dinner. 'What on earth are these? She read, "Lieutenant Commander W J Stamford DSC, RNVR" and "Miss Lucinda Pendleton".' Holding the second card up so that he could see it, she asked, 'Just who the hell is Miss Lucinda Pendleton?'

'She's my assistant at the Admiralty.'

'And what are these doing in your pocket?'

It seemed an odd question. 'I must have forgotten to take them out.'

'Don't get clever with me, William. What are they about?'

'They were place cards at a wardroom dinner to celebrate the attack on the Italian battle fleet, that's all.'

'That's all? You took someone else to dinner and you say, "That's all"?'

'It was an official dinner, Daisy. Miss Pendleton works at the Admiralty and was invited along with everyone else. There was nothing underhand about it.'

'All right, then, why did you put these things in your pocket? It must have been a very special occasion for you to do that.'

'It was. Three modern battleships had been either sunk or crippled. It was a battle worth celebrating.' He was becoming impatient and more than ever resolved to end the relationship.

'I wonder how many other functions you've attended with this Miss Pendleton.' She almost spat the name.

'There was only one other occasion,' he told her coldly, 'and that was simply a way of thanking her for speaking to higher authority on my behalf. She rescued me from a difficult situation.'

'And I could never compete with that. I suppose she's on nodding terms with the Prime-sodding-Minister.'

William let that observation go without comment, but it was time he took the initiative. 'Daisy,' he said, 'this situation is too unpleasant for words, and I can't see it being resolved, so I think the best course will be for us to stop seeing each other.'

'I couldn't agree more,' she snapped, handing him his coat and cap.

⊕∺⅏⅏⅋∺⅏⅏

'It was most unpleasant,' he told Lucy after he'd described the incident to her, 'but I have the place cards here if you want them.'

'Thank you. It's nice to have a memento.' She took the cards and said, 'I can't help feeling sorry for the poor girl, although I've never been in that situation, so I don't really know what it's like.'

'Have you never been given the heave?'

'Never,' she confirmed. 'Have you?'

'More times than I care to relate.'

'And if you ever did, I've no doubt each would be a work of fiction.'

He ignored the jibe, saying, 'I'm fascinated, though. If you've never been rejected, you must have known men of the worthiest kind.'

'Not exactly.' She went on to explain. 'As you can imagine, being at a boarding school and finishing school offered no opportunities for liaisons with the opposite... you know. I was engaged to be married, however, when I was eighteen.'

'A baptism of fire, you might say.'

'In more senses than one. My *fiancée* was a fiery man.'

'Quick-tempered?'

She nodded. 'I'd heard of black eyes, but I'd no idea what they looked like until I saw mine in a mirror.'

'Oh, Lucy.' On an impulse, he reached for her hand and held it between his. Then, realising what he'd done, released it quickly. 'I'm sorry,' he said.

'There's no need to apologise.'

More to cover his embarrassment than out of curiosity, he asked, 'Did you break off the engagement immediately?'

134

'No, I told myself that it was an isolated incident. It was wishful thinking, I suppose.' She forestalled his next question by saying, 'I concealed the evidence from my family, that time, by staying with a friend, and things seemed fine at first. Then he did it again, and my mother saw what he'd done. She told me the truth about violent men.'

'Thank goodness.'

'How she knew, I don't know, because she never had that problem.'

The picture she'd painted was so awful, he could say nothing at first. She broke the silence by saying, 'You're very protective, aren't you?'

'You have that effect on me,' he admitted.

'I know.'

Again, he could think of nothing to say, and he was relieved when the telephone rang.

'Room Thirty-Three. Lieutenant Commander Stamford speaking.'

It was Commander Challock. 'Stamford, come to my office, will you? I've something to tell you, and I can't do it over the telephone.'

'Aye-aye, sir.'

He took his cap from its peg and gave Lucy a puzzled look before taking the short walk to Challock's office.

He arrived to find his superior in an affable mood. He returned William's salute and welcomed him inside.

'Come in, Stamford. Take a seat. It was good to see you and Miss Pendleton at the wardroom dinner.'

'Thank you, sir.'

'Now, I'll come straight to the point and tell you that the *Abwehr* and the *Marinenachrichtendienst*, the *MND*, have given the go-ahead for research to be carried out into the behaviour of marine mammals. In other words, your story about porpoises has got them thinking. Well done, Stamford.'

'Thank you, sir. That's good news.'

'Good news indeed, and we need all the good news we can get. I'll be in touch again.'

# 19

## DECEMBER

William was surprised and disappointed to find that for the first three weeks of the month he was required only to read reports of how his and Lucy's arguments were being leaked to the Nazis through two trusted double agents. To maintain credibility, it was important that the intelligence was leaked gradually, and in spite of his frustration, he found the process fascinating.

As Christmas drew nearer, however, thoughts turned naturally to leave, and he learned that he would have from Christmas Eve until the following Saturday, five days in all. Lucy was granted the same and was looking forward to being with her family again. That was until the morning of the 23rd, when she received a message requesting her to telephone her parents without delay.

To respect her privacy, William left the office and hung around the corridor for the two minutes she was allowed for the call. He was about to re-join her, when he heard her pick up the receiver again and request another number, so he absented himself for a further two minutes.

He returned to find her quiet and despondent.

'What is it, Lucy?'

'I'm not going home for Christmas,' she said quietly. 'Manchester was bombed last night. I'm told it was quite awful, and because of the likelihood of it happening again, my parents have told me to stay in London.' She said bleakly, 'They don't seem to realise that London is being bombed as well.'

Again, he felt desperately sorry for her. The sensation was becoming familiar to him. 'Come to us, Lucy.' He said. 'It won't be the same as home, obviously, but you'll be made to feel welcome.'

She gave him a watery smile. 'Thank you, but the people where I'm staying have invited me. I phoned them after I'd spoken with my parents.'

'All right. By all means spend Christmas with them, but come down to Ashford afterwards. My family would love to have you. You could get a train on Boxing Day and we could travel back together on Friday.'

She said nothing for several seconds. When she did speak, she forced a smile and said, 'I'll let you know, William.'

'Okay. I need to have a word with Dai, so I'll leave you for a while.' It was an excuse to give her some time to herself, as she no doubt realised.

A short while later, when they met for a drink, Dai said, 'It's that boarding school thing, mun. You and I never had the problem, but they had to endure cold showers, rugby in freezing weather—'

'Girls don't play rugby, Dai.'

'Well, whatever they play. I was speaking generally, mainly from what chaps have told me about boarding schools. I was really trying to say that holidays were a beacon, something that made everything else bearable. That's what Bea told me, anyway.'

'Did she play rugby?'

'Don't be silly, mun. Can you see Bea in shorts, covered in... mud and grappling with... the... other... girls?' His eyes took on a distant look. 'I don't know, though. It's an appealing picture, isn't it?'

'I couldn't possibly say, Dai. It's your picture.'

'Yes.' Dai recovered his composure. 'I'm only saying that home for the hols is special for them, so it's no surprise that Lucy is less than joyful this festive season.'

'She's going to the people she lodges with, but I've suggested she comes down to us on Boxing Day. My mum's happy to have her stay.'

'Oh, well, there's lovely, then. She'll feel wanted, at least.' He put his glass on the bar and asked, 'Another one?'

'Go on, Dai, you've persuaded me.' It would give Lucy a little longer as well.

⊕⊷∃⊷⊹⊱∈⊷⊜

When he returned to Room 33, he found that Lucy had a visitor. Bea was in his chair, and the two appeared to be ardently in conversation. It was a fleeting impression, however, as they both stopped talking when he entered the room.

'I'll leave you both for a little longer,' he offered.

'No, sir, I wouldn't hear of it.' As Bea stood up to go, an image of her in rugby kit sprang immediately to mind, but he banished it and forced himself to concentrate.

'Don't feel that you have to go because of me, Bea.'

'Thank you, sir, but I've been absent long enough.' She paused at the door to say, 'I hope you have a lovely Christmas in spite of everything, Lucy. You as well, sir. Have a happy Christmas.'

'Thank you, Bea. You too.'

As her footsteps down the corridor faded, he said, 'I really didn't mean to chase her away.'

'It's all right, William. We were only indulging in girl talk. It was nothing important.' She picked up a handwritten note and said, 'Commander Challock telephoned half-an-hour ago. He said he'd try again later.'

'I'll try him now.' He lifted the receiver and asked to be connected with Commander Challock. A few moments later, his voice came on the line.

'Commander Challock speaking.'

'Good afternoon, sir. Stamford here. I believe you wish to speak to me.'

'Yes, Stamford. Can you and Miss Pendleton come to the wardroom in half an hour's time? I've already spoken to Hughes, so he'll be there.'

'Of course, sir.'

'Good. I can't let my team secure for Christmas without buying you each a drink.'

'That's very kind of you, sir. We'll be there.'

138

'Good. Carry on, Stamford.'

'Aye-aye, sir.' William replaced the receiver. 'Commander Challock has invited us and the rest of his team to a drink in the wardroom in half an hour, Lucy.'

'Lovely.'

'Also, I've spoken to my mum, and she would like you to come on Boxing Day and spend the rest of your leave with us.'

She gave him her first proper smile of the day. 'Thank you,' she said. 'It's very kind of you both. I'd love to come.'

'I'm glad we've sorted that one out.'

She looked at his desk inquiringly and asked, 'What's next on your list, William?'

'I have a question for you. It's got nothing to do with Christmas. Actually, I've been wondering what outdoor winter game you played at school.'

'Hockey. Why do you ask?'

'I was just curious. Tell me, did you have cold showers?'

Her eyes registered surprise. 'Good heavens, no. We had lovely, hot showers, a whole row of them. We had baths as well. We needed them when we came in from the hockey field and the weather was below freezing.' She blinked and asked him, 'What on earth made you think we had cold showers?'

'A salacious Welshman. Let's go to the wardroom and have that drink.' He needed something to dispel the image of Lucy and the others luxuriating in a steamy ablution block.

<hr />

It was a special Christmas for the Stamford family. When William arrived home after a slow and interrupted journey, his sister Jane and her children Harry and Pamela were already there. Jane's husband George was due to arrive later, although it would be a short leave for him, as he had to return on the 27th.

'I hope he won't come when Father Christmas is here,' said Pamela, mindful that any interruption of the magical event might have disastrous consequences.

'Don't worry,' Jane told her. 'Father Christmas doesn't mind

daddies coming home at funny times. He knows there's a war on.'
Jane shared William's colouring and gentle features. She was also
adept at improvising answers to her daughter's incessant questions.
Pamela was six and she had an enquiring mind.

'Is there a war where he lives?'

'No, darling. The North Pole is a happy place.'

'Tanks can't run on ice,' said Harry, 'and you can't have a war
without tanks.'

'Quite right, Harry,' said his mother.

'It wouldn't be a proper war.' Harry was eight-and-a-half, and
conscious of his standing as the elder sibling.

'No, darling.'

'And as well as that, they couldn't land an aeroplane on ice. It
wouldn't—'

'All right, Harry. You've made your point.'

It was time for a diversion, and it came when Mrs Stamford said,
'Hush, everybody. We have company.'

The voices that came from the front doorstep were young and
naïve, qualities that made them as welcome as the carol they sang.
'Once in Royal David's City' would always raise the curtain on
Christmas, so it was the perfect choice, and the family listened to
the whole of it before sending William to the door.

He was about to congratulate the children, when they decided to
favour him with an encore, so he stood in the doorway and listened
to 'Away in a Manger'.

'That was very good,' he told them. 'Now, let me see. There's
one, two, three, four.... Good heavens, there are five of you.' He felt
in his pocket and took out a coin. 'So,' he said, 'if I give you half-a-
crown, that works out at sixpence each, doesn't it?'

'Thank you.' One of the children remembered her manners.

'You're welcome, but let me tell you something before you go.
When you sing 'Away in a Manger', it's "... until morning is *nigh*, not
*night*".'

He handed the coin to the girl who had thanked him. 'A happy
Christmas to you all.'

There was a chorus of 'Merry Christmas' before they processed to the next house to sing again, hopefully with the correct words, if only because the occasion deserved it.

As he turned to go inside again, a taxi drew up and a passenger in RAF uniform got out. He paid the driver, picked up his luggage, and then noticed William in the doorway.

'William,' he called, 'how are you?'

'Fit to drop, George. How about you?'

'Oh, I'll survive,' he said as they shook hands. 'I had a foul journey from Lincoln, but I'm here now.' He was taller, darker and five years older than William.

'It's good to see you again, George.' He let him in and closed the outer door to avoid breaching the blackout. Opening the inner door, he announced, 'George is here.'

Jane and the two excited children came out of the sitting room to greet him. William tactfully left them and re-joined his mother.

'Those kiddies will take some settling tonight,' she said. 'They were excited enough about Christmas, and that was before their daddy came home.'

'Kids will be the same all over the country, Mum, at least those whose dads are free to come home. Not everyone will have Christmas leave.'

She smiled at him sadly. 'I know,' she said. 'I went through all that with your dad.'

'Of course you did, Mum. I'm sorry, I spoke without thinking.'

'Well, let's not mention it again over Christmas.'

'No,' he agreed, 'we'll keep things light-hearted.'

In fact, the proceedings remained light-hearted for the next two hours, when the time came for Jane and George to take the children home to bed. They would be back in the morning. Meanwhile, William and his mother could look forward to the midnight Celebration of Holy Communion at Christ Church. It was a family custom.

---

Christmas morning was the usual bustle of activity, with over-excited children, Jane and her mother in the kitchen, and the two men dragooned into laying the table amid copious comments about the hopelessness of the male where domestic duties were concerned.

At Mrs Stamford's suggestion, William and George took the children for a walk. Jane had gone to much trouble to find a clockwork train set for Harry, so they took the children to see some real locomotives, as they were the enthusiasm of the moment. On their way, they counted babies in prams for Pamela's benefit. Her main present was a doll that said, 'Mamma' in a strangled voice whenever it was thrust into an upright position, an occurrence that became wearing after a while, but which the adults accepted as part of the diverse ensemble that was Christmas.

Harry was delighted to see his father and uncle saluted by passing sailors, soldiers and airmen, and complained strongly when the two adults removed their caps so that saluting was no longer necessary.

Pamela had another preoccupation. 'I haven't fed Spencer yet. He'll be hungry.'

'He'll enjoy it all the more when we get home,' said her father.

William was puzzled. He asked, 'Why do you call him that, Pamela?'

'Because that's his name,' she said matter-of-factly.

'She thought "Winston" wasn't a suitable name for a baby,' explained George.

'Some names are not,' agreed William. 'Herbert Morrison was given an old man's name.'

'Maybe so, but it's still no excuse for behaving like an old woman.'

'No, it's not. What about Clement Attlee?'

'I wouldn't call a baby "Clement",' said George.

'Neither would I.' William mused for a while about names and said, 'You could have called Spencer "Leonard", Pamela. That's another of Mr Churchill's names.'

George expressed his surprise. 'Is it really?'

'Yes, on Sundays, he's Winston Leonard Spencer Churchill.'

'No,' said Pamela firmly. 'He's called "Spencer", and that's that.'

'Listen to her,' said George. 'She sounds just like her mum. Suddenly I'm afraid of my daughter.'

The two men walked on, smiling at the thought. The children simply looked around them, commenting or asking questions. Most of the questions came from Pamela. In fact, Pamela had a seemingly endless list of questions that she posed throughout lunch and until it was time to go home. William was worn out, but not as exhausted as his mother, who could only look forward to a spell at the First Aid Post.

'I'll make a cup of tea, Mum,' said William. 'Then you can get your head down for an hour or so before you go to the Post.'

'Thank you, William. You're a good boy.'

Her words made him feel like a child again, but he was conscious of the affection that came with them.

⊛⊷⋈⊷⋈⊷⋈⊷⊛

For Lucy, Christmas Day had been the strangest she'd ever known. The Cohens had tried hard to make it festive in some way but, being Jewish, they had only the vaguest idea of what Christians, or gentiles generally, got up to at Christmas. They'd been terribly kind, but she was relieved to be on the train to Ashford. She didn't know William's family, but spending time with them could be no more eccentric than the kosher Christmas she'd left behind.

Eventually, the train crept into the station. An arch voice announced, 'Eshfoord, This is Eshfoord. The twelve-fifty to Westenhanger, Sandling, Folkestone West—' The rest of the announcement was drowned out as the engine released a blast of steam, leaving onward passengers to hope that their destination had not been removed from the schedule, as sometimes it happened.

Lucy joined the crush of passengers leaving the train and eventually found herself on the platform, looking for the exit. As she waited for a cloud of smoke to clear, she heard a familiar voice.

'Happy Christmas, Lucy.'

'Happy Christmas, William,' she said, offering her cheek.

'Let me take your bags.'

'Thank you. Be careful with this one,' she said, holding up the smaller of the two. 'There's food in it.'

'Food? How did you manage that?' He took the bags and led her to the exit.

'There's bacon for six people. The family I'm staying with are Jewish, so bacon's no use to them.'

'Not that I'm complaining, but can't they get something instead of bacon?'

'They're allowed cheese in lieu, but for some reason, they can't get kosher cheese.' She handed her ticket to the collector, who tore it in two, handing her the return half.

'That's no good, is it?'

'It's very unfair,' she agreed. 'Speaking of cheese, by the way, I've brought a selection of cheeses. Thank goodness it's not rationed.' She added, 'Yet.'

'This way, Lucy. We're going to the car park.'

'I've brought some pusser's tea as well.'

'Naughty old you. Still it'll be welcome.'

'I didn't pinch it. Bea did, and she gave me half.'

'Here we are.' He unlocked the car and opened the door for her.

'What a surprise.'

'It's my mum's car. She lent it to me so that I could meet you.'

'That was kind of her.'

He left the station and joined the main road for the short journey to his mother's house. 'She has it to ensure the supply of medicines,' he explained. 'She has to deliver them, sometimes, to people who can't leave their homes.'

'You know, that never occurred to me, I mean, that it might be necessary. It makes perfect sense, though.'

'Here we are.' He turned right across the road and parked on his mother's drive. 'Fortunately, the kids aren't here today, so we can hear ourselves think. It was bedlam yesterday.'

'Don't be like that, William.'

'You haven't met them yet. Come in and meet my mum.' She was standing in the doorway. 'Mum, this is Lucy.'

'Happy Christmas, Mrs Stamford. It's terribly kind of you to have me stay.'

'Happy Christmas, Lucy, and don't give it another thought. We're pleased to have you. How was your journey?'

William took Lucy's coat and hat, and then took her case up to the guest room while they chatted.

'I've brought a few things to help out,' said Lucy, opening her bag.

'Oh, there was no need to, but thank you.'

'It's just bacon, cheese and tea. I explained to William how I came by the bacon. It's absolutely above board, I assure you.'

'I would never have doubted it, and it was lovely of you to bring these things. Now, the sitting room is through here. Take a seat and I'll make some tea. Is tea all right for you?'

'Lovely. Yes, please.' Lucy sat in one of the armchairs, pleased to see the Christmas tree with all its ornaments, and the decorations around the room were equally reassuring. She wondered what her family were doing, and then dismissed the thought. For the time being, her Christmas was with William and his lovely 'mum', as he called her.

When William came downstairs, he'd changed out of his uniform and was now wearing a flannel shirt, a jumper and grey flannel trousers.

'Oh,' said Lucy, 'what happened to Lieutenant Commander Stamford?'

'He's on leave. Anyway, I don't need to go out again, so I can wear civvies and relax.'

Mrs Stamford came in with the tea things on a tray. 'You'll have to take us as you find us, Lucy,' she said. 'I have to go on duty at the First Aid Post tonight, but William will be here, and tomorrow I'll be in the shop.'

'You've made me feel very welcome, Mrs Stamford. I just don't want to be in the way at all.'

'If you get in the way, Lucy,' said William, 'I'll just pick you up and move you.'

'William,' said his mother, 'that's no way to speak to a lady.'

'Lucy knows me well enough, Mum.'

'It's just as well.'

The relaxed atmosphere was just what Lucy needed, and she slept soundly that night, grateful as ever for the hospitality she was receiving.

The next day, she met Jane, George and the children, who turned out to be nothing like the hooligans William had described; in fact, she found them quite engaging. She was already "Auntie Lucy", a title she'd never previously been awarded, and that made her feel included all the more. It was as well that the children had a distraction, although Lucy had no idea how much of a distraction she might be, as George had to leave them in order to catch his train at ten o'clock.

It appeared that Göring was bored with Christmas, because the siren sounded at 6:30, just as Jane was preparing to take the children home.

Mrs Stamford poured boiling water into a vacuum flask so that those in the shelter could brew tea. She said, 'You know where the shelter is, don't you, Jane?'

'Yes. Come along, you two.' She picked up Pamela, who was already sleepy, and beckoned to Harry to follow her.

William took down Lucy's coat and hat as well as his own. 'Have you got everything, Lucy?'

'I've got everything I need, thank you.'

'I have to go now,' said Mrs Stamford. 'I'm due at the First Aid Post in five minutes.' She handed the bag with the flask, tea and mugs to William. 'Good luck, everybody.'

They returned her good wishes and followed Jane to the public shelter.

Lucy asked, 'Do you think we'll all be welcome?'

'The shelter's never full,' Jane told her. 'There'll be room for us.'

They made their way into a building designed to house eighty people, with a narrow aisle down the middle and chairs and bunk beds along the sides. As Jane had prophesied, the shelter was far from full.

'Some people prefer the shelter of their stairs and kitchen

tables,' she said, undressing the children and placing them head to toe in a single bunk.

To the south, the coastal anti-aircraft batteries were easily audible.

Someone said, 'A merry Christmas that was while it lasted.'

A man said, 'That's Adolf and Hermann off my Christmas card list, the miserable buggers.'

The woman next to him said, ''Ere, watch your language. There's kiddies in here.'

'Sorry, kiddies.'

Pamela and Harry listened to the guns, their faces white and drawn. Jane sat beside Pamela, while Lucy, taking her cue from Jane, went to Harry's end of the bunk.

'It's all right,' said Jane, trying to sound convincing, 'no one can hurt us in here.' It was patently untrue, as Jane knew, but it was one of those things that had to be said.

Soon, they heard the droning beat of approaching aircraft and the whistle of falling bombs followed by the deafening sounds of detonation.

'I know,' said Lucy, 'let's see how many Christmas carols we can think of. Do you know one, Pamela?'

Terror gave way to concentration and finally to inspiration. ' "Away in a Manger",' she said.

'Good girl. Let's sing it.' She led them into the carol in a gentle soprano that seemed, in some way, to beckon others to join in, so William and Jane added their weight to the singing and, by the time they'd reached the third verse, other children were joining in, seemingly oblivious to the carnage outside.

The woman who'd admonished her husband for swearing, said, 'It beats "Roll Out the Barrel" and "The Siegfried Line." I've heard them two so many times in this place, I'm sick of 'em.'

A stick of bombs fell, shaking the shelter like the hand of a petulant giant.

'Harry,' said Lucy, 'it's your turn to think of one.'

Harry made a conscious effort and said, ' "While Shepherds Watched Their Flocks by Night".'

'Good boy. Let's sing it.'

They sang despite the horrors taking place on the outside of the shelter, even though, if only from William's point of view, it had to be one of the most boring carols in existence.

When they were finished, Lucy said, 'I know a better tune than that. I'll teach it to you.' To William's surprise, she sang a version of 'While Shepherds' to the tune of 'On Ilkley Moor Baht 'At', explaining afterwards that it originated on the other side of the Pennines from hers, but that she didn't see why Yorkshire people should have the exclusive right to it.

She proceeded to teach it, line by line, to the children, who now included several further along the shelter, and they picked it up quickly and eagerly. It seemed to William the maddest situation of all, that bombs were falling outside, and here were children having a rip-roaring time. Even their parents were joining in, although it was 'While Shepherds' as they'd never heard it sung.

Suddenly, the whistling outside became unusually loud and shrill.

'Here it comes,' said the man whose wife had forbidden him to swear.

The whistling stopped short, and there was a thunderous crash that shook the shelter with a new violence, so that pieces of cork from the anti-condensation layer on the ceiling showered down, covering the bunks and everyone around them.

'It's just like snow,' remarked the irrepressible Lucy, urging the children to sing again. 'Let's sing "Good King Wenceslas".'

Now everyone in the shelter was singing so enthusiastically that William imagined that the airmen overhead might be tempted to join in.

They reached the end of 'Unto Us a Boy is Born', and parents were putting tired children to sleep. Bombs were now falling some distance away, but the 'All Clear' had not yet sounded.

The woman who had welcomed carol singing as a change from the popular songs of the day, said, 'It's bizarre. That's what it is.'

Lucy asked, 'Why do you say that?'

'Well, us hiding down here, them up there trying to kill us, and us singing carols. Don't get me wrong. It's been lovely, but you have to admit it's a funny way to spend Christmas.'

'I don't think so.'

'What?' The woman gave her a strange look.

'I'm reminded of a baby boy and his parents, forced to go into hiding, much as we are now, but in his case because a jealous king wanted to murder him. It seems Christmassy enough to me.'

Eventually, with Jane on one side and Lucy on the other, their heads resting on his shoulders, William drifted into sleep thinking about this exceptional young woman and the circumstances that kept them regrettably apart.

# 20

## JANUARY 1941

'What did Commander Challock want, William?'

'He wanted to tell me about a hitch. It's to do with the changes to the Wrens' uniforms.' He wondered how to phrase the problem. 'It's actually to do with the bell-bottomed trousers. I reminded him that it was your triumph, but he asked me to explain it to you.'

'Why didn't he just send for me?'

'He's shy, Lucy, and I think I can sympathise with him on this occasion.'

'What's the problem?'

He squared his shoulders, eased his collar away from his throat and took a deep breath. 'The trousers come in three lengths: Long, Average and Short,' he began. 'A tailor was engaged to measure Wrens chosen to represent each size.'

'Well, what's wrong with that?'

'Only that the trousers turned out to be either too long or too short. Of course, if they're too long, they can be shortened, but....'

'If they're too short, they're useless,' she agreed. 'But how did it happen?'

'Well, you see, the tailor had to take two measurements: waist and....' He was floundering. 'If you imagine a Wren standing with her feet apart, the other measurement is from the instep up to the... the apex, as it were, of the triangle.'

She gave him a straight look. 'The inside leg measurement,' she prompted.

'Well, yes.' It was probably going to be easier than he'd thought.

'And what went wrong?'

'Ah, well, out of respect for the girls' sensibilities, the tailor didn't actually take the measurement. Instead, he estimated it.'

'And got it wrong?'

'Exactly, and now the replacements have been inevitably delayed.'

Lucy groaned.

'There's just so much serge cloth available, and it goes without saying that sailors at sea have to come first. There was an unfortunately-worded signal about it, that will almost certainly be used in signals instruction for years to come.'

She looked at him patiently and asked, 'What did it say?'

' "Wrens' skirts will be held up until the requirements of the fleet have been satisfied." '

She allowed herself a shallow smile. 'All this,' she said, 'could have been avoided in the first place if they'd got a woman to take the measurements.'

William shrugged. 'Or a less-scrupulous tailor.'

'I'll make some coffee. You've suffered long enough.'

He had to agree. The matter of Wrens' clothing continued to be an embarrassment. He wished it would all disappear. Not the clothing, of course, just the embarrassment.

He forced himself to think about the other matter Commander Challock had raised, about Airborne Interception Radar, and was agonising about it when Lucy returned with the coffee.

'I'm going home soon, just for a weekend,' she said. 'Christmas was lovely, and your mum was a real sport to have me stay, but I want to see my family.'

'Of course you do. What's the bombing been like in Manchester?'

'That's just it. There were two massive raids just before Christmas, but there's been nothing more since the early hours of Christmas Eve.'

'Thank you.' He took the coffee she'd poured for him. 'That's good news, at least, because there's been no let-up over London.'

'You can say that again.'

'Night fighters have had some success,' he told her. 'One pilot, a chap called John Cunningham, is particularly successful, so much so that they've already dubbed him "Cats' Eyes" Cunningham.'

She blinked and asked, 'Are his eyes green?'

'No, but he behaves as if he can see in the dark. He can't, obviously. It's all because of Airborne Interception Radar.' He corrected himself. 'I shouldn't say "all". Much of it is down to his ability as a night fighter pilot, but AI Radar is an invaluable tool, and the enemy mustn't get wind of it.'

She nodded. 'It's like the HF/DF thing, then?'

'Exactly. We have to think of a convincing reason for the RAF's success that'll hoodwink Hitler so that he doesn't give radar a second thought.'

Lucy frowned. 'Surely it's the Air Ministry's job to deal with this kind of thing.'

'In the ordinary way of things, it would be, but word's got around the corridors of power that the Admiralty have two people working for them, who can crack any problem at sea, on land or in the air. We're famous, Lucy, you and I.'

She picked up the coffee pot. 'More coffee?'

'Please.'

She refilled his cup and asked, 'Have you had any ideas yet?'

'I've wondered about a special training course involving total immersion in darkness for thirty days,' he said.

'That would drive me potty.'

'I think it would have that effect on most people,' he conceded, 'so what next? We can't use porpoises, and birds don't fly at night.'

'Owls do.'

He considered that and rejected the idea. 'We can't use owls. It would be too much like the porpoise idea.'

They both sat, lost in contemplation, until Lucy gave a start. ' "Dr Carrot, the Children's Friend". That would kill two birds with one stone.'

'Yes, tell the population that carrots help them see in the blackout and people will eat more carrots. That would please Lord Woolton, at least—'

'And let it be known that night fighter crews enjoy a carrot-rich diet that helps them see in the dark, and we have the perfect cover for Airborne what'sit'sname.'

Pulling the typewriter towards him, he said, 'You've done it again, Lucy. You've whacked the nail right on the bonce. They're going to sack me and give the job to you.'

'Not before I've been home, I hope.'

That stirred his memory. 'I've been thinking about that, Lucy. When you come back, why don't you bring your violin, and we can do something together?'

She looked at him in surprise. 'Good thinking, William. It's time I got back into practice.'

⊷⊷⊰⊹⊱⊷⊷

During the weekend that Lucy was in Cheshire, the Luftwaffe intensified its attacks on London. On Friday, Saturday and Sunday nights, William lay awake, listening to the din outside until weariness finally overtook him and granted him sleep.

On Monday morning, he went to Room 33 at the Admiralty as usual, and waited to hear about Lucy's weekend. By nine-thirty, it was evident that she'd been delayed. It was no surprise after the past three nights; the railways would be in chaos and the roads would be no better. He concentrated on his work, concerned for her comfort and safety, but expecting her to arrive at any time.

She arrived shortly after five in the afternoon, dazed, exhausted and clearly troubled. She carried a suitcase and a wooden violin case, which she placed carefully on the floor before sinking wretchedly into her chair.

# 21

William could only wonder as he stood in the galley, spooning tea into a pot. Experience had taught him not to press for information, but to wait until Lucy was ready to talk.

He scalded the tea and carried the tray back to Room 33, where he found her still hunched in her chair.

'I pinched a couple of biscuits for you,' he said, putting the plate with her cup and saucer on his desk. Rather than wait for the tea to brew, he gave it a vigorous stir and poured it for her. As he did so, he stroked her shoulder, quite absent-mindedly until he realised what he was doing, and then stopped abruptly.

'I see you brought your luggage,' he remarked. 'You evidently haven't been home yet.'

'There's no house to go to,' she told him quietly. 'The street was bombed last night.' She shook her head slowly, incredulous. 'Everything's gone.'

He crouched by her chair to speak to her. 'What about the family?'

'They were in the shelter. None of them was hurt.' She had been staring down at her hands, which were in her lap, but now she turned to speak to him. 'They've gone to stay with friends in Burnt Oak,' she said. 'They left a message for me at the wardens' post. They couldn't get through to Stalybridge or Manchester.' She lowered her eyes again. 'Too many lines down.' After a while, she said in the same dazed voice, 'I've nowhere to stay. I suppose Bea might put me up on her sofa.'

'I've got a spare room, Lucy. Come back with me.'

'It's a lot to ask.'

'You're not asking. I'm offering, and you'll be perfectly safe.'
She attempted a smile. 'I know I shall. Thank you, William.'

⊕◅⌁⊰⌁⊱⌁▻⊕

With the open fire going nicely, he was able to air the sheets for the spare bed.

'There,' he said, 'I'll make up the bed in a minute. More tea?'

Receiving no response, he refilled her cup. 'Are you ready to think about eating yet?'

She shook her head hopelessly. 'It was horrible,' she said. 'People were killed.' She seemed to dwell on that before moving on. 'Things were sticking out of the bricks and tiles, things that had belonged to people. There was a dolls' house and pram next door, and the Cohens' beautiful velvet curtains, torn and filthy....' Her voice tailed off as if the list had become too awful to be put into words.

'When did you last eat, Lucy?'

She looked at him blankly. 'I can't remember.'

His mind travelled back to his childhood and the celebrated panacea for shock, disappointment and distress. He thought it was worth a try. 'Lucy,' he said, 'could you eat a boiled egg and toast sailors?'

She reacted slowly. 'Sailors?'

'Like soldiers, but not as stiff and straight.' He'd never been very good at cutting straight soldiers, so it was as well to warn her, although, in her present state, she was unlikely to be too critical.

She surprised him by saying, 'Yes, please. That would be nice.'

He set to in the kitchen and soon emerged with a soft-boiled egg and a plate of toast cut into sailors.

'Dinner is served,' he announced.

'Oh, lovely.' She took her place at the table and then put her hand to her mouth. 'William,' she said, 'When you offered me this, I wasn't thinking. This must be your fresh egg ration for the week.'

'And you're more than welcome to it. As a matter of fact, I'm trying to give them up.'

'I don't believe you.'

'Don't let it get cold.'

'Why would anyone want to give up eggs?' She nevertheless broke the top of hers and removed the broken shell.

'For humanitarian reasons,' said William, as though the answer were obvious. 'I've been torn with guilt, many a time, about the inconvenience, not to mention the discomfort, a chicken must suffer in laying an egg. I mean, it's not as if there's any satisfaction in it either, when, as soon as it's laid, someone comes into the henhouse and makes off with it. Anyway, I've decided to act. It's a matter of principle.'

'But they do it every day. They're used to it.'

'Oh, Lucy,' he said, favouring her with his most pious and earnest gaze, 'people used to say that about the slaves in the sugar plantations and cotton fields.' Relaxing his expression, he said, 'But don't let that thought put you off your egg.'

She made no reply, but continued to eat her yolk-laden sailors with evident enjoyment. Finally, she said, 'That was lovely, thank you. I couldn't have eaten anything more.'

'Good.' He would make himself a sandwich later. Meanwhile, other matters competed for his attention. He asked, 'Do you know how to make up a bed?'

'Of course I do. We had to do it at school.'

'In that case you can give me a hand with the spare bed.' Taking the aired sheets and pillowcases off the clothes horse, he led her to the spare room, where they made up the bed. Her assistance was completely unnecessary, but it served as a distraction.

'If you fancy an early night,' he said, 'don't feel that you have to be sociable. I have some copy to write, anyway.'

'If you really don't mind, I will.'

'The fire's been going long enough for a bath,' he said. 'I'll find you some towels.'

'Do you keep spare towels?' She sounded surprised.

'You wouldn't believe some of the things the owner left behind.'

'It's a nice flat,' she said, looking around her for possibly the first time. Her eye fell on the telephone, and she said, 'I really must tell my family what's happened.'

'You're welcome to call them from here, but I really think you should wait until tomorrow, when you've had a sleep and you're feeling more in charge of yourself.'

She nodded. 'I'll have a bath now and call my folks tomorrow,' she decided, going to the spare room to undress.

William took the opportunity to read a letter from David Waldheim offering him a new account. The client was H J Marston and Co. Ltd, manufacturers of ointments and associated remedies, and the product was Cremoloid, an unguent that, its manufacturers claimed, afforded instant relief from the itching and discomfort caused by haemorrhoids, by going to the seat of the problem. This revolutionary preparation, they maintained, dealt with the fundamental cause of the condition.

William made a note to the effect that the client should be advised to avoid using the words 'seat' and 'fundamental' or, for that matter, any word associated with the product's ultimate destination. It seemed to him also that explicit reference to the condition should be avoided as it could easily embarrass a great many sufferers. It would be better, he felt, to concentrate on the sufferer's state of mind, on how he/she felt at having to endure the symptoms day in, day out, and how the prospect of relief beckoned. It occurred to him, as well, that the ointment might also be sold as a soothing emollient for general use. Then, purchasers would have no need to disclose the fact that they had a more intimate problem. He resolved to work on his idea after he'd made a sandwich and a cup of tea. Lucy's emotional state had ruled out the meal he'd had in mind.

He made a cheese sandwich and ate it while he waited for the kettle to boil. It tasted of very little without pickle or condiment but after twelve months of food rationing he was used to that.

He carried the tea things through to the fireside table and sat down to think about Cremoloid ointment and how he was going to present it.

After a while, he heard the bathroom door being opened. He turned his head to see Lucy in dark-red pyjamas and a matching silk dressing gown.

He asked, 'Do you feel better for that?'

'Yes, thank you. It was lovely.'

'Would you like a cup of tea? I've just made it.'

'Yes, please.' She perched on the end of the sofa nearer the fire while he poured the tea. 'It's very kind of you to put me up like this,' she said. 'I'll find somewhere to live as soon as I can.'

'You're welcome to stay for as long as you like, and you're pretty safe here as it's a basement flat.'

'Are you sure?' She still sounded distant, but hopeful.

'Nothing's completely safe, not even an air-raid shelter. If the bombing comes close, we'll just get under the table and play "house".'

'That would be a new experience for me.'

He was about to say something about childhood experiences, but checked himself when the warning siren sounded. From its first rising note, Lucy had taken on a look of dismay. He left his seat to sit beside her. Taking her hands in his, he said, 'We'll be all right down here.' Her obvious anxiety led him to put his arm round her shoulders. She huddled closer to him.

After a while, she said, 'William?'

'That's me.'

'Have you always been called "William", I mean even when you were a tiny tot?'

At such a time, the question surprised him until he realised that she was possibly trying to distract herself, maybe to banish the worst of the memory of the afternoon's experience.

'My memory of tiny-tothood is a trifle hazy, but I've always insisted on being called William,' he told her. 'I've always found the diminutives, "Bill", "Will" and "Willy" unsatisfactory. I mean to say, a bill is usually bad news, a will is associated with the dear departed as well as being an old-fashioned name, and it goes without saying that no man wants to be called a willy.'

Her eyes opened wide at that last disclosure, but suddenly, the anti-aircraft batteries to the south opened fire, making her blink nervously.

'We're okay here,' he told her again.

'Don't go anywhere,' she pleaded.

'I shan't. I'll stay with you until the "All Clear" sounds.' He wrapped both arms round her, which was what she seemed to want, and she clung to him as if he had some mystical power to shield her from the bombing.

Before long, the familiar giant footsteps approached, followed by the whistling of the falling bombs and the detonation as they landed. It seemed to William, going by experience and aural direction, that the main targets were to the east as well as north of the Thames.

'I think they're giving us a miss tonight,' he said with no real confidence, but in the hope that the news might calm her, at least until events proved otherwise.

With her cheek pressed hard against his, she repeated urgently, 'Don't go.'

'I'm going nowhere,' he assured her.

They sat like that until tiredness overtook William, and, in spite of the bombing, his eyes closed, and he fell asleep.

***

When he'd blinked the sleep from his eyes, he saw from the clock that he'd slept for almost two hours. He looked at his companion and saw that she was asleep. He was conscious of the heat emanating from her body. Also, his hands were perspiring against the silk of her dressing gown. Otherwise, he was mercifully unaffected by her proximity. Several thousand tons of high explosive falling from the skies imposed celibacy more surely than a papal decree.

She opened her eyes and seemed disoriented for a few seconds. Then, she remembered where she was, and why. As the bombs continued to fall, she clung to him again.

After a while, he thought of a distraction. Reaching for the pad and pencil he'd used when he was working on the advertisement, he said, 'Let's make a list of the things you need to do tomorrow.'

'There's lots to do,' she said, her attention divided between him and the horrors outside. 'I hardly know where to start.'

'That's why I suggested making a list. Your first job, of course, is to tell your family what's happened.' On the pad, he wrote, *Telephone home.*

'What about a ration book?' She was making herself concentrate.

'Okay, but before that, you need to inform the authorities of your change of address. Your National Registration details need to be altered.' He wrote, *Town Hall, to report change of address.*

'Ration book,' she prompted.

'Good.' The distraction seemed to be working. He added to the list, *Food Office. Ration book.*

'What about work?'

'Don't worry about that. I'll send a memo to the Civil Service in triplicate, signed, countersigned, checked, double-checked, triple-checked, rubber-stamped twice in various colours and approved.'

'By whom?'

'By me. They have to remember that signatures are hard to come by in wartime. They have to accept whatever comes.'

She managed a half-smile. 'Everyone's rude about the Civil Service,' she said, 'including you.'

'Isn't that their function, to entertain the fun-loving masses? I've always thought so.'

'I don't really think you mean that.'

'Don't be so sure.'

'What else?' She was looking at his notepad.

'As soon as I can, I'll take you to the shops I use so that you can register with them as a customer.'

'But what are we going to do until my registration is confirmed?'

'We'll buy breakfast at the Admiralty and dine out.'

'Won't that be expensive?' The receding noise of the detonations appeared to be having little effect on her now.

'When I say we'll dine out, I don't mean at the Savoy.'

'Even so....'

'Don't worry,' he said, patting his notebook. 'My little side-line will keep the wolf from the door.'

'I insist on going Dutch,' she said.

'If you insist,' he agreed.

Listening carefully, she said, 'They seem to have gone.' There was more life in her voice. 'Twenty-two years old,' she reflected, 'and I behaved like a little girl.'

'Twenty-two? When did that happen?'

'At the weekend. That's why I went home.'

'I didn't know it was your birthday. I'd have....' He wasn't all that sure, but he'd have done something.

'William,' she said, stroking his tie with the tips of her fingers, 'you did something for me tonight that's more precious than anything tied up in a ribbon.'

'It was no trouble.' Looking at the clock, he asked, 'Are you ready to go off to bed now? You'll know where to find me if there's another raid.'

'All right.' She stood up and adjusted her gown. 'Thanks again.'

'It was no trouble. Is there anything you need? Ovaltine, a bedtime story?'

'Another time perhaps. Good night.' She offered her cheek and he kissed her goodnight.

'I'll bring you a cup of tea in the morning, but you've no need to get up early. Just sleep well.'

⊕⊷⨝⊶⟨⊱⨝⊷⊕

He'd considered leaving her to sleep on, but he decided to tap on her door. A drowsy voice answered, 'Come in.'

He pushed open the door and found her snuggled up to a worn and seemingly well-loved teddy bear.

'Tea.' He put it on her bedside table. 'Did you sleep well?'

'Like a top.'

'Good. There was another raid,' he told her, 'further north, between two and four o'clock.'

'I'd no idea.'

'Good. In any case, you'll get used to it.' He inclined his head towards her companion and said, 'It was a good thing you had him with you at the weekend.'

'Ted goes everywhere with me.'

'That could be a surprise for your future husband, but I'm sure you'll work things out. There are some wheat flakes in the larder, or you could have toast if you prefer it. I'm off to work now. Take care.'

# 22

William had been wondering how Lucy was coping with her various tasks, when she surprised him by walking into Room 33 after lunch.

'I've done all the jobs on the list,' she announced, 'and I've bought some clothes to replace those I lost. Thank goodness they're not rationed.'

'Yet.' William was inclined to be realistic.

'There's just one problem.'

'Tell all, Lucy. What's happened?'

She took her usual seat on the other side of his desk, and he could see that she was concerned about something.

'I said I'd find somewhere to live as soon as I could, didn't I?'

'Yes, I remember that.'

'Well, my parents are not keen for me to sleep under the same roof as a single man, unchaperoned, that is, and they don't see how they can find alternative accommodation for me. Basically, they don't know anyone else in London.'

William considered the news and was obliged to see their point. 'It's bound to cause them concern,' he agreed. 'After all, they don't know me from Bluebeard.'

'Who?'

'A chap I once knew. He had an accident with a pot of paint one day, leaning forward to inspect his handiwork.'

'Oh. Anyway, my father is coming down by train tomorrow, and he wants me to go back with him to Stalybridge.'

'For good?'

'That's about the size of it.' Her expression was glum. 'You know, there was a time when I would cheerfully have dropped everything and gone home, but it's the last thing I want now.'

It wasn't what William wanted either. He asked, 'Is he open to reason?'

'Not for one moment, I'm afraid. Mother and I are very much alike, and we get on like a house on fire, but my father's not the easiest man to deal with.'

William was thinking. 'Maybe we could find you a service flat,' he suggested.

'What's a service flat?'

'It's one where the cleaning and laundry are done for you, and there's usually a modest restaurant on the ground floor. You order what you want to eat, and they cook it and have it ready for you.'

Suddenly, she perked up. 'That sounds perfect,' she said. 'Are there many around?'

'I don't know. I'll ask the letting agents who look after my flat. They should know.'

<hr>

It seemed a good idea, and the agents reported that they had several on their books, one quite nearby. The solution appealed to William, who had been concerned about having Lucy in close proximity, temptation lurking as it was wont.

Everything pointed, therefore, to a successful outcome. All that remained was to convince Lucy's father that his fears were now groundless.

<hr>

Arthur Pendleton was at the flat when William arrived home. Lucy was serving tea.

'William,' she said, 'this is my father.'

William greeted him formally and shook his hand. He was tall and dark-haired, with a blue chin and a mournful look that might have graced a Victorian undertaker's countenance.

Mr Pendleton came immediately to the point. 'I've inspected my daughter's sleeping quarters,' he said, 'and they're far from satisfactory.'

'Oh, really?'

Lucy interrupted urgently. 'Dad, I've already told you that I'm perfectly safe with William. In any case—'

'Far from satisfactory,' he repeated. 'I have business in London tomorrow, but we'll leave for home on Friday morning. Meanwhile, Lucinda, I shall reserve a room for you at my hotel.'

'Mr Pendleton,' said William, 'Lucy and I have gone to some trouble to locate a service flat that would be ideal for her. She would be in easy reach of Clapham Common tube station and about twenty minutes from the Admiralty.'

'Lucinda is coming home with me on Friday, and that is an end to it.'

'Have you forgotten that Lucy's work at the Admiralty is vital to the conduct of the war?'

'Nonsense. How could her work be so important? What could she possibly do that would make any difference to the outcome of the war?'

'Dad—'

'Be quiet, Lucinda.'

William bit his lip before answering. 'I'm not at liberty to tell you that. Both Lucy and I have signed the Official Secrets Act, and we must honour that undertaking.'

'Dad, will you—?'

'Be quiet, Lucinda, and if you must use that common form of address, at least use it when we're alone, although, frankly, I'd rather you didn't use it at all.' He turned to William and said, 'As for you, young man, I don't take kindly to gross exaggeration, especially when it concerns my daughter.' He seemed about to elaborate, but William's patience had found its limit.

'Mr Pendleton—'

'Now, you listen to me.'

'No, I advise you to listen to me. Lucy is a civil servant engaged in essential war work, and to take her away would be in breach of the National Service Act. Also, when I tell you that her contribution is vital, I don't expect to be called a liar.' He was aware that his voice had risen, but he was angry. 'The fact that you inspected my flat without my permission, that you've spoken to me in the curtest possible terms and that you see nothing wrong in such behaviour is water off a duck's back as far as I'm concerned. I've been insulted by experts and, believe me, you have much to learn from them. However, I will not have my integrity or my professional judgement called into question.'

Clearly outraged, Mr Pendleton picked up his hat and coat. 'Come along, Lucinda. We're leaving. We'll be back to pick up your things tomorrow evening.' He made for the door and stood, waiting, in the porch. Meanwhile, William helped Lucy on with her coat and handed her hat to her. 'I'm sorry I had to say that, Lucy,' he said.

'You were right to stand up to him. I only wish I could.' She was embarrassed and close to tears.

'Lucinda, come along now.' Her angry parent had his hand on the doorknob.

'Don't worry, Lucy,' said William. 'I'll speak to Commander Challock in the morning.'

'You may speak with the devil for all I care, Mr Stamford. My daughter is coming home with me on Friday morning.'

⊕⊢∃⊰⊱⊱⊣⊕

William had to wait to speak with Commander Challock, who was involved during most of the morning in conference with the Deception Committee. When he was finally allowed to put his case, Challock's response was disappointing.

'I'm sorry, Stamford, there's nothing we can do. I suppose the Civil Service could object, but I doubt if they will. The most likely outcome is that Miss Pendleton will be conscripted into one of the women's services, the Land Army or factory work.'

'What a horrible prospect, sir,' said William. 'I mean working in a factory. Until she came here, the poor girl had only ever known a girls' boarding school and a finishing school in Switzerland. I don't know how she'd survive.'

'Finishing school?' Commander Challock considered the concept. 'They're a trifle old-fashioned now, aren't they? Rather like debutantes.'

'Her father is an old-fashioned tyrant, sir.' William told him about the previous evening's conversation. 'He sent his daughter to finishing school because he saw no future for her other than as a wife and hostess. That was in spite of distinctions at School Certificate in Latin, Greek, German, English Language and Literature, and a credit in French, as I recall.'

'Your memory for detail does you credit, Stamford; in fact, I wonder if your interest in Miss Pendleton is entirely professional.'

William shook his head minutely. 'I've never considered anything other than a professional relationship, sir. There's too much at stake in our line of work to risk any distraction.'

Challock smiled at his argument. 'Speaking as a long-serving naval officer who's spent more years at sea than you can imagine, I have to say I find that a little "distraction" oils the wheels.' He put on his serious face again and said, 'Still, the subject is an academic one for you now, Stamford. Thinking more practically, we'll have to see if we can find you another assistant, although I haven't a clue where to begin looking.'

Neither had William, but he had little interest in finding a successor. He wanted Lucy, although he'd run out of ideas for the moment.

During the afternoon, he was distracted from his deliberations when the telephone rang. It was Lucy, and she sounded angry.

'He's out on business,' she said, 'and he's left me cloistered in this hotel like… Rapunzel in her… *rotten* tower.'

'I presume you're talking about your father.'

'Who else?' Her tone changed and she said, 'I must say, you gave him what-for last evening. He's not used to it, you know. He was quiet all the way to the hotel.'

'I'm sorry I had to do it, but I was pretty angry, as you know.'

'Oh, well, I don't know whether it did any good or not. I tried telephoning Grandpa, but he wasn't available. I left a message.'

The changing forms of address in Lucy's family amused him enough to ask, 'Does he let you call him "Grandpa" nowadays?'

'Yes, he likes it. He's not at all like my father. You'd be surprised if you met him.'

'Would I?'

'I think so. My father and brothers, you see, are products of their school. They all went to the same one, as boys do. If it comes to that, I suppose I'm a product of mine, too.'

It was an alien world as far as William was concerned. Even so, he said, 'I think your school was kinder to you than your father's was to him.'

'Oh yes, boys have an awful time, you know, with cold showers, sadistic and humiliating traditions, beastly punishments and that sort of thing.'

The picture of Lucy in her hot shower at school returned to him, and he put it to flight immediately.

'Anyway, I shan't keep you, William. I'll see you this evening. *Vale.*'

''Bye.'

He wondered how he could possibly manage without her.

⚬⊷⊱⊰⊷⚬

William was at home in good time to receive Lucy and her father.

As Lucy was packing her purchases and her overnight bag, he made a final entreaty.

'Mr Pendleton,' he said, 'won't you reconsider your decision? This is the first job at which Lucy has been successful, and it gives her tremendous satisfaction.'

'I've made my decision, and that's—' The telephone bell drowned the end of his sentence.

William picked up the receiver. 'Stamford.'

'Oh, is that Lieutenant Commander Stamford?'

'Speaking.'

'Edgar Pendleton here.'

William tensed himself. If another member of the Pendleton family wanted a fight, he was more than ready. When he spoke again, however, the caller sounded conciliatory, even friendly, and William remembered that Lucy had left a message for her grandfather.

'I'd like to thank you for looking after our Lucy, as she calls herself these days. Do you mind if I call you "William"?'

'Please do, sir.'

'Don't call me "sir". I'm not in the Navy.' His accent reminded

William of someone he'd heard on the wireless. A great many entertainers seemed to hail from the north-west.

'Very well, Mr Pendleton, but I've only done for Lucy what most men would have done.'

'Well, she's told me all about you, how you put her together again when she were so unhappy, and she left a message telling me how you took her in and cared for her after the house got bombed.'

'Oh, it was a pleasure, Mr Pendleton.' He noticed with some satisfaction Lucy's father's surprised expression at hearing his surname.

'Lucy said you were a gradely chap, and I know what she meant. Now, is that son of mine with you? I tried calling his hotel, but he'd left. Honestly, he prances about like a curate at a christening.'

'He's here, Mr Pendleton. Would you like to speak to him?'

'Yes, please. It's been nice talking with you, William.'

'And with you, Mr Pendleton. Goodbye.' He handed the receiver to Lucy's father. 'Mr Edgar Pendleton for you,' he said.

The younger Mr Pendleton put the receiver to his ear. 'Father?'

To afford him some privacy, William went in search of Lucy. He tapped on her bedroom door.

'Come in.' She was closing the lid of her case on a squashed teddy bear.

'Your grandfather called,' he told her. 'He's speaking to your father now.'

'Hush.' Lucy put a finger to her lips, unashamedly going to the door to eavesdrop on the conversation, of which only one side was audible.

Her father was saying, 'Yes, Father... But how was I to know? Yes, Father, she's here. If you say so, Father.' He called, 'Lucinda?'

'Yes?'

'Grandpapa wishes to speak with you.'

'Oh, goody.' She took the receiver from him, and this time William headed for the kitchen, wondering if perhaps a change of heart might be on the way.

After a moment, Lucy's father found him. 'Lieutenant Commander Stamford,' he said soberly, 'it seems I owe you an apology. My father tells me he has it on good authority that Lucinda's work is, as you said, of vital importance, although I don't know how he could possibly know that.'

'I imagine Mr Churchill will have told him,' said William. 'The Prime Minister said he would write to him.'

'This is beyond my comprehension.' He looked completely bewildered.

'Mr Pendleton, Lucy has found a job that she does remarkably well, and I find her assistance invaluable. I know, also, that Mr Churchill is equally impressed with her work. Let me ask you again to reconsider your decision to take her home.'

'Lieutenant Commander—'

' "William".'

'Very well, William, my father has already made his feelings known and given me my instructions. If you'll help Lucinda, or Lucy, as you insist on calling her, find a service flat, I'll let her remain in London. I said some very harsh things to you, William, as well as doubting your word, and I take it all back.'

'Thank you, Mr Pendleton. I accept your apology.' They shook hands.

'No hard feelings?'

'None that I'm aware of.'

'I must say, William, you're not afraid to stand your ground, and I respect that.'

William smiled at the compliment. 'My first experience of this war was a David and Goliath match,' he said, 'with the battleship *Admiral Graf Spee*, and that rather puts anything else into perspective.'

'I imagine it does.' He consulted his watch and said, 'I should go now. I don't want to miss my train.' He turned and called, 'Lucinda, are you coming to the station, or will you stay here?'

'I'm expected at the Admiralty, Dad; in fact, you might almost say, "England expects".'

'Very well, darling. Here's something to help with the new wardrobe and accommodation.' He pushed a bundle of banknotes into her hand and kissed her. 'Take care.'

'I will, Dad. I'll write soon.'

Finally, he turned to William. 'Goodbye, William, and thank you for what you've done for Lucinda.'

'It was my pleasure.'

When he was gone, Lucy opened her arms to William and hugged him. 'Thank goodness that's settled,' she said.

'Yes,' said William. 'Maybe now we can get on with the war.'

# 23

## MARCH

'I never really saw the appeal of daily practice.' It was Sunday afternoon, and William was looking through the sheaf of music for violin and piano that Lucy had brought over to try.

'It does help when you're learning something new,' she told him tactfully. 'Anyway, how did you manage to satisfy your teacher if you didn't practise regularly?'

'I took the short-cut.' He sat on the duet stool to explain. 'I once played something for her, and she, not being the most tactful and encouraging of her calling, told me that it sounded like gifted sight-reading. She meant it to hurt, but it gave me an idea. I tackled every piece of music I could find until eventually I became a fairly proficient sight reader, and that solved my problem: I didn't need to practise ever again.' He considered his claim and added, 'Well, not very often.'

It was clear from Lucy's admonishing look that she wasn't impressed. 'There's more to it than simply playing the notes,' she told him, 'and some things only come with practice.' She picked up a score from the pile and took out the violin part. 'Let's try something from the second eleven,' she suggested.

'What do you mean?'

'Well, you play a lot of music by Mozart, Beethoven and Debussy, and they're all in the first team and they're wonderful, but there's also a lot of fun to be had with some of the lesser composers.' She put the piano part on his music desk. 'There's Cesar Franck, for example.'

'*Sonata in A*,' he read. 'Okay.' He was game for a challenge, and the Cesar Franck looked challenging enough. He waited until Lucy was ready, and then began the introduction.

After a while, she stopped playing.

'What's the matter, Lucy?' It seemed to be going fine.

'It's what I was talking about,' she said. 'Some things are not obvious when you just play the music through. You have to listen to the cadence and phrasing, and think about expression to get the most out of it. Listen to this.' She played the sixteen bars up to where they'd stopped, and William had to admit that her playing had something extra. The way she leaned into the strong beats and shaped the phrases gave the music a yearning quality that drew the listener in.

'Franck wore his heart on his sleeve,' she said when she'd finished playing, 'and, as long as it's not overdone, it's wonderful. Let's go back to the beginning and put some passion into it.'

As William took his lead from her, shaping the phrases and making the most of the cadences, it seemed to him that the aching, driving quality of the music was highly suggestive of the one activity he tried to exclude from his thoughts when he was with her. Temptation was a relentless adversary.

⚬⊰⊱⚬

Dai Hughes was also a victim of carnal longing, as he told William when they met for a drink at the Old Shades.

'I don't know how long it's been since I last raised my periscope,' he complained. 'I make the mistake of spending my time with virtuous women, mun. That's the reason for it.'

'And you lack subtlety, Dai. It has to be said.'

'There is that to it as well,' he admitted. 'There are times when the urge gets the better of me, and somehow, women don't seem to find my ardour all that flattering. I don't know why.'

William had been considering his friend's plight. 'What you need,' he advised, 'is a change of approach.'

'Go on, mun, I'm listening.'

'You need to adopt the mantle of the Celtic poet rather than the Welsh battering ram.' He lifted his glass. 'Another?'

Dai nodded, more interested, for the moment, in William's advice. 'Tell me more,' he urged.

'Soft lights, sweet music and beguiling words.' He stood up. 'Let me get these in.'

When he returned to the table, Dai was still waiting for enlightenment. 'These beguiling words, mun, what are they?'

'I'm not going to give you a script, because it has to sound authentic, as if it's from you, but I would advise you to abandon the direct approach. "*O fy duw*, Bea, you don't half make me feel randy" is never going to make her throw caution to the four winds and melt into your arms.'

Dai looked uneasy. 'That was a terrible Welsh accent, William, and who said we were taking about Bea?'

'How many other women are you seeing?'

'Oh, well, I'm found out, I suppose. Anyway, how did you know about "*O fy duw*"?'

'I knew a Welsh girl before the war. She was always saying it.' He corrected himself. 'At least, when we were, you know, *cael rhyw*.'

'When you were having sex?' Dai whispered the sentence as if it were a dark and dangerous secret.

'Yes, she used to say it repeatedly. "*O fy duw*! Ie! Ie! Oh, my god! Yes! Yes!" '

'She must have been an excitable girl, mun.'

'Only when we were—'

'Having sex.' Dai's attention was locked into place.

'That's right. She wanted me to go back to Wales with her and become apprenticed to her father. He was a baker, you know.'

'And did you?'

'For a while. I was quite celebrated in the local area, although not exclusively for my baking.'

'What made you come back, mun?' He spoke as if it were the most ridiculous thing to do.

'Have you ever made six dozen Welsh cakes and then tried to get the flour out of your trouser turn-ups?'

'I can't honestly say I have, mun, but I have to say it sounds like a job-and-a-half.'

Commander Challock picked up the message form for the fourth time, and put it down again. He'd done the same with the request about Wren recruitment, and William realised that the task was not to his liking.

'The Ministry of Information have asked for our help, Stamford, and I'm becoming rather tired of being at the beck and call of every government department under the sun, although I have to admit this is partly a naval matter.' He smoothed out the form with a deliberate gesture and said, 'It's basically about wasting food and commodities. They want a message for the population that will make them think twice before behaving recklessly with imported goods.'

William had no need to think about it. The answer was plainly obvious. 'We have to appeal to the public conscience, sir. I think the image of a merchant ship sinking and men in the water should start people thinking, especially with a caption that says something along the lines of "They're risking their lives to feed you. Don't waste food and make their sacrifice in vain!" '

'All right, Stamford, let me have a proposal in writing and I'll get it off to them. Maybe then, they'll leave us in peace.'

'To get on with the war, sir?'

'Yes.' Challock smiled at his clumsiness. 'That's what desk work does to us after a while, Stamford. It dulls our senses and makes us say bloody silly things.' He was clearly in a resentful mood, because he said, 'Believe it or not, I joined *HMS Audacious* in nineteen-thirty-five, as Commander. I went from second-in-command of an aircraft carrier to farming out silly tasks to officers who would be better employed doing other things.'

'I'm sorry, sir, I mean, that you had to forfeit a sea-going appointment.'

'It's the same for all of us here. I expect you sometimes feel frustrated.'

William thought back to the previous May, and his feelings at the time. 'Not now, sir. When I was appointed, I felt that I should have been at sea again as a gunnery officer, but I enjoy the challenges of this job, and I'm quite reconciled now to intelligence work.' He added sympathetically, 'I suppose it's different for you, sir, being a professional naval officer.'

'Maybe it is, Stamford, but I think you've just put me in my place.'

'Sir?'

'Don't worry about it. Just let me have that proposal when you can.'

❂┄❬┄❂┄❬┄❂

William's proposal went to the Ministry of Information, where it was considered with uncharacteristic promptness – and rejected.

Commander Challock read the message before him and said, 'They feel that your suggested image of a sinking ship and drowning seamen would be too powerful for the general public's appetite, and that it might even be seen in some quarters as defeatist.'

'Incredible.'

'They're civil servants, Stamford. They don't enjoy the same human thought processes as we do. In any case, bugger them.' He screwed up the message and shied it into the Non-Classified Waste bin. 'That's as far as it's going.'

'Amen to that, sir. We have more important things to attend to than smacking the wrists of....' He searched his mind for an appropriate epithet, and found one. 'Squander bugs.'

Commander Challock nodded appreciatively, making a note on his blotter. 'I like that name. I'll suggest it when they come pestering me again.'

❂┄❬┄❂┄❬┄❂

'You know, Bea, you remind me of a statue in the Public Library at home. I used to notice it every time I went delivering the newspapers.' They were at Bea's bedsit, and she had just brewed tea.

She was suspicious but curious. 'What did it represent?'

'It was Diana, the Huntress. She had magnificently-proportioned legs, slender arms and a long, smooth neck.'

175

Bea handed him his tea and sat, for the moment, on the bed, quite taken aback by his description. 'You were impressed,' she said. 'I can tell.'

'Oh yes, she was lovely.'

'And I remind you of her?'

'Very strongly,' he confirmed.

'I'm flattered, Dai. Tell me more.'

He closed his eyes to aid recollection. 'Her hands and feet were delicately sculpted so as to be almost perfect.' He reopened his eyes. 'And, of course, she had magnificent breasts.'

'You would notice them,' she commented.

'I was a boy at the time, but I could recognise quality even in those days.'

'You were doing ever so well, Dai,' she told him whilst trying to maintain a straight face. 'I was very impressed by your aesthetic appreciation right up to the moment you referred to her breasts, and then you reverted to the Dai I know so well.'

'They were very special,' he insisted.

'And you called them "breasts", which is in itself a step forward.'

He stirred uncomfortably and asked, 'You don't mind me talking about them, do you?'

'As long as it's only occasionally. I'd worry if I thought it was becoming an obsession.'

'Somehow, I always seem to say the wrong thing.' He left his chair and joined her on the side of the bed. 'I make an effort to get it right, but just when I want to be intimate, I put my foot in it.'

She eyed his size eleven shoes and winced. 'Maybe you try too hard,' she said.

'But you see what I mean, don't you?'

'I do,' she said, taking his hands and stroking them, 'but you know, there's no substitute for just being yourself.'

He kissed her tentatively. 'I've never met anyone quite like you, Bea,' he said.

'That same thought has crossed my mind,' she said cryptically, nevertheless allowing him to kiss her again, more comprehensively.

The air raid siren began to wail, but they ignored it; Bea's bedsit was fairly safe, in the basement of the building, and their attention was diverted along pleasanter lines.

He ran his hand beneath her skirt and encountered the welt of one black, artificial-silk stocking and the enticing sensation of exposed thigh beyond it.

'Just a minute, Dai. Stockings are precious.' She unfastened them and peeled them off, placing them on an arm of the chair he'd occupied earlier. 'In fact,' she said, 'I'll be back in two shakes.' She disappeared into the bathroom, emerging after a minute or so. 'Right,' she said, unhooking her skirt so that it fell to her feet, 'your turn. Come on, join in.' She proceeded to unbutton her shirt, while he, stunned by the sudden turn of events, fumbled with his trousers.

Clad only in her underclothes, Bea hopped into bed, smiling as she saw him reach inside a pocket of his tunic. 'There's no need for one of those things,' she told him. 'I have a cap.'

For a second, he stared uncomprehendingly.

'Not a uniform cap, silly, a *Dutch* cap.'

Bemused, he asked, 'Have you done this before?'

'Once or twice,' she admitted. 'Now, do come and join me before you walk into something and hurt yourself.'

'Okay,' he said, glancing down self-consciously at his eager manhood. 'We Hughes have always enjoyed more than our fair share.' He eased himself into the narrow, divan bed and took her in his arms, kissing her eagerly. To the south, the anti-aircraft batteries were firing, but they went unheeded.

After a few seconds, he released the fastening of her brassiere and removed it, throwing it towards the armchair, where it hung obligingly next to her stockings. 'Oh, Bea,' he breathed, 'the Public Library is welcome to Diana. She's not a patch on the real thing.'

'That's a relief.' She reached down and, after a momentary struggle, retrieved her French knickers. 'You do it,' she said, handing them to him, 'you're a better shot than I am.'

He obliged, and completed the set of underwear on the chair arm just as the first bombs fell.

They kissed and teased until neither of them could delay matters any longer, and then they merged as one in their own rapturous domain, unhurried and oblivious to the violence of the other world around them.

⚜

'You'll never believe this, Stamford.' Several days had passed, and Commander Challock had received a proof of the Ministry of Information poster. It depicted a pot-bellied insect with pointed ears tempting someone to waste left-over food, and the caption read: *Beware the Squander Bug*.

'Pathetic,' said William.

'But it's a good name. What was the aphorism you left loafing, the one Commander Bonnington found?'

' "There is no limit to what man can achieve as long as he doesn't mind who takes the credit", sir.' He added, 'I've been trying to forget that episode.'

'I shan't mention it again, Stamford.'

'That's very decent of you, sir.'

# 24

## APRIL

'We're about to become involved in more Ministry of Information propaganda, Stamford.' Commander Challock referred to another of their unwelcome messages. 'This time, it's about security. It's all your fault, of course.'

'Why is it my fault, sir?' William had become used to his superior's flippancy, but he was interested to know what lay behind the assertion.

'You're too bloody good at giving them what they want.'

'Thank you, sir.'

'It was more by way of a complaint than a compliment.'

'In that case, I'm sorry, sir, but I suppose security affects us all. I had a reminder of it last evening, on my way home.'

Challock was suddenly interested. 'Oh?'

'It was on the tube, sir. I had to remind a junior officer from the War Office about the fact that "Walls Have Ears". He was talking with a colleague about the Sten gun, a new automatic weapon the army are adopting. I thought it sounded like a good idea, and it's possible that the other passengers agreed with me, because they all heard what he was saying.'

'Good for you, Stamford. Mind you, I'd have roasted the bugger if I'd been there.' He looked again at the message on his desk and said, 'They want a poster warning against careless talk. I said I'd ask you to come up with something.' He added with a knowing smile, 'Even if it's only a catchy name for a chatterbox.'

'I have an idea, sir, maybe two.'

'Already?'

'Yes, sir, I wonder about a sort of strip cartoon.'

The commander looked surprised. 'Like *Jane*?'

'Not that kind, sir. I'm thinking of a series of window pictures with speech balloons, rather like those in a children's comic. In the first window, a sailor, soldier or airman is sharing a secret with his girlfriend. The speech balloon would read, *You mustn't tell anyone, but....* In the second, she's talking to a friend, and the speech balloon says, *You'll never guess what he told me....* In the third, the friend is speaking to a man. Her balloon reads, *Don't tell anyone else, but I have it on good authority that....* The fourth is of the same man sending a message via a portable wireless transmitter. The whole thing is headed, *She Meant No Harm....*'

Commander Challock was impressed. 'I like that, Stamford. Not even the dimmest matelot, soldier or whatever could fail to understand that.'

'I'm glad you like it, sir. I have another, which may well suffer the same fate as my suggestion for avoiding waste, but it's probably worth a try. Again, the picture would be of a sinking ship with or without men in the water, and the caption would read, *A Careless Word Could Result in This.*'

'Yes.' the commander was hesitant.

'I know they don't like sinking ships, sir,' he said, 'but they'll have to face reality sooner or later.'

'I'm afraid so. I've been looking at last month's losses and I've found them dispiriting, to say the least. Unfortunately, it's difficult to see how the situation in the Atlantic can be reversed, and the threat doesn't end there.'

William was intrigued. 'What do you mean, sir, when you say that the threat doesn't end there?'

'We know that the battleship *Bismarck* has been undergoing sea trials in the Baltic. It's only a matter of time before she breaks out into the Atlantic.' His tone was as bleak as his message.

'What have we got that can measure up to her, sir?'

'That's a good question, Stamford. *King George the Fifth* and *Prince of Wales* can probably match her firepower, *Nelson and Rodney* could with their sixteen-inch guns, the *Queen Elizabeth Class* possibly, but our older battleships would be outclassed, and the battle-cruisers *Hood*, *Renown* and *Repulse* are too lightly armoured to be pitted against a ship as powerful as the Bismarck. We can only hope that she doesn't do too much damage before we can sink her.'

Lucy put down her violin and bow to ask, 'What are you doing for Easter, William?'

'Assuming that I get leave?'

'A weekend's stand-down shouldn't be difficult.'

It was true. 'No, it shouldn't. I suppose I'll go to my mum's place, as usual. Are you going home?'

'Yes, the reason I asked was because my folks are inviting you to spend the Easter weekend with us.'

He closed Franck's *Sonata in A* and gave her his full attention. 'That's kind of them,' he said, 'and completely unexpected.' His thoughts returned to the running battle with her father, even though they'd parted on friendly terms.

'I think my father wants to make amends for the earlier business,' she explained, as if reading his mind. 'Otherwise, they just want to thank you for everything you've done for me, and "they" includes my grandpa, whom you're bound to like when you meet him.'

'In that case, I'm grateful for the invitation, and I'm looking forward to meeting your family.' Easter was only a week away. He had to get organised. He asked, 'Do I need anything special? I mean, do you dress for dinner and that kind of thing?' He'd seen it happen in films, and he'd wondered.

'Good heavens, no. There's nothing grand about us.' She pulled up a chair and sat facing him. 'You think I'm posh, don't you? Well, if I am, I'm second-generation posh, and that's meaningless. You'll see what I mean when you meet grandpa.'

'You had a nanny, though, didn't you?' That, alone, was a being from another world.

'Yes, we all did, but that was just my father being pretentious and my mother being disorganised.' She looked thoughtful for a moment and said, 'Actually, I wasn't terribly keen on Nanny, and she wasn't carried away with me either. She preferred my brothers.'

'Tell me about your brothers.'

'All right. Eric and Francis are twins, but they're not identical, so there's no problem telling them apart. They're twenty-three and they're both in RAF Coastal Command, based in Connel. It's in Argyllshire. They may be home for Easter, but I'm not sure.'

'I see.' He wondered if they were at all like their father. It was as well to know. 'What kind of people are they?'

'They're all right, quite easy-going and relaxed. They're clever; when we're not at war, they work in the family business, but for now, Francis is a pilot and Eric's a navigator. The RAF won't let them fly in the same aircraft, though, in case something goes wrong and they're both killed.' She shuddered at the thought. 'I suppose they learned that lesson in the last war.'

'Maybe they did. My father and his brother were both killed at Passchendaele.'

'I'm sorry.'

'I never knew them, but it was a tragedy, all the same.'

Suddenly, she brightened and asked, 'Who else do you want to hear about? My mother?'

'Yes, let's not leave her out.'

'She's sweet. I think that's the best way to describe her. The two family members who mean most to me are my mother and Grandpa. I think it's because they've always taken my side, and there have been times when I've needed support.'

It seemed to William that wealth was a poor substitute for emotional security. Almost unconsciously, he reached for her hand and held it. She moved to his side, so he shifted along the duet stool to make room for her.

'You shouldn't think of me as coming from a different world,' she said. 'I'm flesh and blood, like anyone else.'

He already knew that. He could feel the warmth of her body through the dark-green worsted dress, and it disturbed him in the most confused way. Common sense told him that personal involvement was a distraction in the workplace but, at the same time, he was acutely conscious of her physical appeal, and he was fonder of her than he would ever admit. Most appealing of all, though, and therefore disquieting for him, was her childlike vulnerability.

'I know we'd both like things between us to be more than this,' he said, 'but it's really not a good idea.'

'Do you still believe we come from different worlds?'

He slid his arm round her waist to soften his words. 'Yes, but I was thinking more of how it would affect our working relationship.'

'How would it affect it?'

Her face was temptingly close to his; he was very much aware of her Chanel perfume, and he tried not to think about it. 'It would create a kind of tension,' he explained, 'pleasant enough in itself, but a distraction from what we're trying to achieve. Don't you see that?'

'The tension is already there. Surely you've noticed it.'

In truth, he had, but he'd been so quick to ignore it that until that moment he'd truly believed it to have dispersed, like a trifling disagreement.

'I feel it all the time,' she admitted. 'I thought you did.'

'You're very astute.'

'It's a female thing,' she assured him.

'There's also the fact that you've been hurt in the past, and I really don't want you to be hurt again.'

'I know. Let's just keep our fingers crossed that it won't happen.'

As she spoke, he felt her breath touch his cheek, and with it, his remaining resistance ebbed. He kissed her cheek, and then she turned her head until her lips brushed his.

'I'm surprised,' he said, delaying the moment, 'that, after your experiences, you want anything to do with men.'

'But men are not all the same, are they?'

He made no reply, but framed her trusting face gently with his hands, and kissed her properly for the first time.

# 25

After a journey made interminable by detours because of bomb damage, William and Lucy arrived in Manchester only half-an-hour before sunset.

William picked up their cases, having reminded Lucy a second time that he had no need of a porter, and followed her to the exit, where he was surprised to see Lucy heading straight for a shiny black-and-maroon Rover. Their lift was waiting for them.

The driver stepped out and waited to greet them. She was quite tall, dark-haired and slim, and her features identified her unmistakably as Lucy's mother.

'Mum.' Lucy embraced her.

'Hello, darling.' Her mother kissed her and turned immediately to William. 'So you're William.' She shook his hand with surprising firmness. 'I've heard so much about you and I'm keen to hear more.' She unlocked the boot so that he could stow the luggage.

'I was going to introduce you,' said Lucy, 'but you didn't give me time. William, this is Mother.'

'I'm "Mum" now,' explained her mother, 'now that Lucy's renamed us. My husband is still adjusting to it, but I really don't mind what she calls us as long as it's polite.'

'How do you do, Mrs Pendleton?' William opened the boot lid and placed the cases inside.

'Mum, are you going to let me drive?' Lucy was already holding out her hand for the key.

'Lucy doesn't care for my driving,' her mother confided. 'She finds it too exciting, don't you, darling?'

Grimacing, Lucy took the key and climbed into the driving seat.

'Sit in the back with me, William,' said her mother, 'and we can become better acquainted.'

William waited for her to take her seat, and then closed the door and went round to the other side.

Once inside the car, he looked through the window for the first time at the bomb damage. 'I never realised how bad it must have been,' he said.

'The bombing? It was terrifying, and it was more than kind of you and your mother to have Lucy stay over Christmas when she couldn't come home.'

'Not at all. We enjoyed having her.' His mother had told him about the letter of thanks from Lucy's mother, and the letter that followed it from Lucy herself.

'Mum,' asked Lucy, 'are Eric and Francis coming home?'

'I'm afraid not, darling, not until next week. They say someone has to hold the fort, and the job's fallen to them this time.' For William's benefit, she explained, 'Both my sons are in the RAF. They're stationed in Argyllshire.'

'Yes,' said William, 'Lucy told me. It's a shame they can't be here this weekend.' He thought of Dai, stuck in London, but he did have Bea to keep him company, and they'd both been looking very pleased with life recently.

He looked out of the window and watched Manchester recede into the distance. Another of Lucy's talents was that she was a safe and confident driver. He was impressed.

'Lucy's grandfather, I should say "grandpa", is looking forward to meeting you,' Mrs Pendleton told him. He'll be home soon, and then everyone will be home for the weekend.' As another thought occurred to her, she said, 'Grandpa says that Yorkshire people work on Good Friday. Isn't that odd?'

'But they have a holiday on Tuesday as well as Monday,' Lucy reminded her. 'William's grandpa was a Yorkshireman.' William wondered if she'd supplied that information to forestall any gaffe that might otherwise have been forthcoming.

'But you're a Londoner, I believe, William.'

'That's right, Mrs Pendleton, although I'll admit now that I'm a member of Yorkshire County Cricket Club.'

'Really? How did that happen?'

'My grandpa introduced me to cricket. He took me to see them play Surrey, Middlesex and Kent, so it became the most natural thing for me to become an honorary Yorkshireman with a funny accent.'

'I'm sure Lucy's grandpa won't take it amiss.'

'Carrbrook,' announced Lucy as they passed a group of houses. 'Much has happened since I left home, I mean the first time.'

'When you were very unhappy in London, and you never said a word,' her mother reminded her.

'I didn't want to admit to yet another failure.'

'That's all in the past,' William put in quickly. 'Lucy is easily worth twice her weight in gold now.'

'It's very kind of you to say so,' said her mother.

'I'm only speaking the truth.'

'How wonderful. Well done, darling, and thank you for taking her under your wing, William.'

'I'm just grateful that I have the ideal assistant, Mrs Pendleton.'

'Here we are,' said Lucy, driving past a pair of gates and turning into a circular drive. '*Chez* Pendleton,' she announced.

The house, which was possibly two centuries old, appeared to have three storeys and an attic. William imagined the attic would be the servants' quarters. In films he'd seen, they usually were.

Mrs Pendleton opened the boot for William to take out the bags. 'It's help yourself time,' she said, taking William's coat and cap. 'The only servant we have now is a cook-general. The others went to do war work, so we closed some of the rooms for the duration, and a woman comes in three times a week to clean for us.' She must have thought William was looking bemused, because she said reassuringly, 'We've opened up one of the bedrooms for you, William. I hope you'll be comfortable.' She looked around for Lucy and saw her locking the car. 'Lucy,' she said, 'take William up to Eric's room.'

Lucy led William up to the first floor, where she opened the first door in the passage and said, 'This is your room, William.' She switched on the light to reveal a large, well-appointed bedroom. 'The bathroom,' she said, indicating an internal door, 'is through there.'

'Is it for the whole floor?' He visualised a procession of family members crossing his room as they made for the bathroom.

'No, it's all yours. I'm at the other end of the passage and I've got my own too.' She watched his expression. 'It all seems terribly grand, doesn't it? I suppose it was at one time, but chances are, after the war, we'll have to move to a smaller house that doesn't need staff.' She could evidently see he was only half-convinced, because she said, 'I think servants will be an outmoded concept by that time.'

'I imagine so,' he agreed.

'Good. Well, I'll leave you to unpack and freshen up, and I'll see you downstairs in the morning room for tea, first left as you came into the house. We use it as a sitting room nowadays.'

He unpacked his clothes for the weekend, placing them in the wardrobe and chest of drawers, and then took his spongebag to the bathroom, which was another surprise. The suite had probably been installed during the early part of the century rather than earlier, because it was old-fashioned without being primitive. Even so, it created an impression of opulence, of a world separate from his by a long way.

When he'd freshened up, he went downstairs to join Lucy and her mother in the morning room for a welcome cup of tea. Lucy was making excited and affectionate noises, and the reason became apparent when he entered the room and found her fussing with a blue roan cocker spaniel.

'Her name's Dora,' She told him. 'That's short for "Pandora", not the Defence of the Realm Act.'

' "Pandora" is a good name, though.'

'Lucy chose it,' said her mother, 'but we persuaded her that any other member of the family would be embarrassed at having to call her with a name like that.'

'Pandora,' said Lucy with mock archness, was the first woman in Greek mythology.' She added in a darker tone, 'She led men to their doom.'

Mrs Pendleton picked up the teapot and asked, 'How do you like your tea, William?'

'With milk, but no sugar, please, Mrs Pendleton,' he said

gratefully. The story of Pandora interested him, but he had gone too long without tea.

Before long, Lucy's father and grandfather arrived. First to greet him was Lucy's father.

'William,' he said, shaking his hand, 'I don't know what you must have thought when we met in London. I was worried about Lucinda….' He corrected himself. 'About Lucy, but that's no excuse at all for the way I behaved.'

'Don't give it another thought, Mr Pendleton. 'As far as I'm concerned, the matter is closed.'

'You will have something to apologise for, Arthur,' said the old man, 'if you don't introduce this young man to me.'

'I'm sorry, father. This is William Stamford. William, my father.'

The two greeted each other and shook hands. Edgar Pendleton was shorter than his son, but still very erect, and his grey hair and whiskers were immaculately groomed. Most striking of all, however, even though William had heard his voice on the telephone, was his local accent, which contrasted starkly with his son's refined vowels.

'Has Lucy shown you round yet, William?'

'Only to my room, sir.'

'No, I mean the local area, and don't call me "sir". I told you that on the telephone, if you recall.'

'Very well, Mr Pendleton.'

'I'm going to take Dora for a walk,' announced Lucy. Would you like to come, William?'

'Yes, and then you can show me around the neighbourhood.'

'Take him round the golf club,' suggested her grandpa. 'It's a good walk, and he'll see they have something in common.'

'Dinner's at seven,' said her mother.

'We shan't be as long as that.' She disappeared towards the rear of the house and returned wearing a battered pair of flat shoes and with a dog lead in her hand. 'Right, Dora, heel.' Dora sat obediently at Lucy's feet. 'You'll need your coat, William,' she said, clipping the lead to Dora's collar. 'I'll get it for you if you'll hold the lead.'

It was William's turn to be obedient, and he held on to the lead, although Dora showed no sign of straying.

Lucy helped him on with his coat and then handed his cap to

him. Her mother asked, 'Are you insisting that the poor man wears his full uniform just to take a dog for a walk?'

'Yes, you never know who's likely to see us, and I want to be on his left arm when he returns a salute.'

'Suddenly my daughter is a naval socialite. She never fails to surprise me.'

William could only smile and shake his head at Lucy's nonsense. On their way out, he heard her grandfather say fondly, 'It's just like having her home from school again.'

'What was that about the golf club?' William had never played golf and couldn't imagine what the old man was talking about.

'Oh, that's just his sense of humour,' said Lucy, closing the gate. 'It's called Stamford Golf Club.'

'Ah.'

'Never mind. I forgot to ask if you were used to dogs, but you seem to be happy to have Dora around.'

'She's lovely.' He looked down and saw her trotting happily by Lucy's side. It was a clear, starry night, and the blackout posed no problem. 'My grandparents had a spaniel.'

'What colour?'

'Liver.'

'Lovely.'

'We could never have one, you see, because there was never anyone at home to look after one.'

'Which grandparents were they?' It seemed important for her to know.

'My mother's parents,' he explained.

She took his arm as they crossed the road and asked, 'What about your other grandparents? I don't think you've mentioned them.'

'I never knew them. They both died in the 'flu epidemic at the end of the last war.'

'How awful. That's your father, your uncle and both pairs of grandparents you've lost.'

'Well, as I said, I never knew most of them.' He stopped and touched her arm. 'Are you ready for this?'

'What?'

'Your ambition is about to be realised. There are two... airmen, I believe, coming towards us.'

'Oh, my beating heart.'

The two airmen approached and saluted William. He returned their salutes, wishing them a good evening.

'Good evening, sir.'

'Enjoy your leave.'

'Thank you, sir,' said one of them.

The other said hurriedly, 'You too, sir.'

Lucy said, 'I know one of those boys. He lives not far from here.' She corrected herself by saying, 'When I say I know him, I mean that I know him by sight.'

'I didn't think you meant it in the biblical sense.'

'Of course not.' She squeezed his arm. 'Why do sailors salute differently from everyone else?'

'Tradition. In bygone times, sailors had to handle ropes and cordage covered in tar, and they could never get their hands properly clean, so they saluted with the wrist cocked, so that the palm faced downward and slightly inward, so that the officer they were saluting couldn't see their dirty hands.'

They stopped to let Dora relieve herself on a patch of grass. Lucy was still curious. 'Why don't marines salute that way?'

'They salute with the palm forward because they're so used to cocking an ear.' He demonstrated, pushing his right ear forward with his fingers. 'You must have heard the expression "Tell it to the Marines".'

'Yes.'

'Well, they have to keep cocking an ear so that they don't miss anything.'

'But they don't salute behind their ears.'

'That's because they don't know their ears from their eyebrows.' He stopped and considered that. 'At least,' he said, 'I think that's the expression that's used.'

'I give up. I really do.'

⸻◈⸻

On Saturday morning, the elder Mr Pendleton suggested that he and William might take a stroll together. William naturally agreed, having realised earlier who was the power behind the Pendleton family.

They had only walked a hundred yards or so, when the old man asked, 'Where did you go to school, William.'

'It was a grammar school in London, Mr Pendleton, but I left at sixteen to help with the family finances.'

'There's no shame in that, lad, and my name's Edgar. If you go on calling me "Mr Pendleton", I'll think you're talking to my son.' He was silent for a short spell, and then said, 'When you have children, don't send 'em to boarding school, whatever you do. I sent Arthur to his, thinking I was giving him the best start I could, and all it did was give him airs and graces.'

William hardly knew what to say. Wisely, he said nothing.

'He sent his children away to school,' Edgar went on. 'It seemed to suit Eric and Francis, and they've turned out all right, but what he did to Lucy was wrong.'

'I don't understand, Edgar. What did he do to Lucy?'

'I'm talking about sending her away to school an' then off to Switzerland like that. The trouble was, the way he saw it, she was a lass in a man's world. Do you know what I mean?'

William was reluctant to discuss such a sensitive matter, but he felt he had to respond. 'Do you mean in the world of gears and differentials?'

'Not only that. She couldn't get on with accounts either.'

'The Sports and Social Club? I heard about that. She felt she'd let you down.'

'I know, an' it wasn't her fault. Some folk are equipped to deal in numbers, and others....'

'I was never very good at maths either, Edgar.'

'Maybe not, but I'll tell you what you are good at.'

'Go on.'

'Maybe you know this already, but you're good at people.' He waved his stick in the direction of a public house along the road, and it was clear that it was to be their first stop. 'I'll make no bones about it, William. Lucy had me scratching my head. I knew she could do something, but I was buggered if I knew what, and you found it just like that.'

'I had to work at it, Edgar. I got her to talk about her experiences and what she liked to do, and it all came together. Suddenly, I had the assistant I needed. I can't tell you what we do, or what Lucy does that's so important, but rest assured, she's found her niche.'

'I know.' Edgar took his arm and guided him to one of the tables outside the pub. A barmaid collecting empty glasses saw him and said, 'Good morning, Edgar. What can I get you?'

'I'll have a pint of bitter, love. What about you, William? The bitter's passable, even in wartime.'

'I'll join you with that, then.'

'Good. Two pints of bitter then, Edna. Put it on my slate.'

'Right you are, Edgar.'

He gave William his full attention. 'Winston wrote to me, you know.'

'He said he would.'

'You don't know what that meant to me, hearing that Lucy was doing so well. I gather you've got your name up in neon letters an' all.'

'I'm glad it worked, Edgar. I felt desperately sorry for her when she told me how she'd been treated. She'd written herself off as a failure, but she hadn't done it all by herself.'

Edgar patted his arm. 'I know, lad, an' I were the one that got her the job.' He seemed to find a knot in the wooden table fascinating, and William realised he was feeling quite emotional. Eventually, he said, 'They sent her to that finishing school because they reckoned she'd never be anything more than a wife and hostess. Catherine has a good heart, you know, an' she's an affectionate mother, but she usually does Arthur's bidding.'

William realised that 'Catherine' must be Lucy's mother. For the present, though, he was more interested in Lucy. 'As I told you, Edgar, I can't divulge anything of what we do, but I have to say there have been times when Lucy's education has been invaluable.' He stopped when the barmaid arrived with two pints of bitter. When she was gone, he went on. 'There is something I can tell you about her schooling in Switzerland, because it had nothing to do with our work.' He described the wardroom dinner, the overbearing wife of the senior officer, and Lucy's impromptu demonstration with the cigar. When he repeated her reference to Mr Churchill choosing his own cigars, Edgar began to shake with laughter.

'Bless her,' he said. 'I never thought she had it in her to do that.' When his laughter had subsided, he said, 'I'll let you into a secret, William. The last time Winston came to dinner, he sat in the same place at the table where you've been sitting, but Lucy wasn't there. She'd be in the nursery. You see, she was only three or four at the time.'

William had to laugh too, but Edgar's thoughts were evidently still at the dinner party eighteen-or-so years earlier, because he said, 'We had a nursery then, an' that were a daft idea, that and the nanny. I tell you, William, when you have children, give 'em the home life they need and bring 'em up so that you've only yourself to blame if they don't turn out as you'd like.'

'I can't see myself ever having the income to do otherwise,' said William, 'but I take your point.'

Clearly, Edgar had done a great deal of thinking. 'We should keep in touch, you and me, William. You never know. We might be able to do each other some good when this war's over.' He took a long pull at his beer and asked, 'How do you think it's going?'

'The war? If we can hold Hitler off until the Americans decide to join us, we have a chance.' He deliberately made no mention of Russia.

'Aye, I can see that.' He looked thoughtful again, and surprised William by saying, 'You probably think the way we live is rather grand,' he said.

'Grander than I'm used to,' agreed William.

'Listen, lad. I went to the local elementary school until I was fourteen, an' then I left to go into t' "snuffy". Do you know what that is?'

William shook his head.

'It was the cotton mill. It was a horrible place, and as soon as an opportunity came up, my parents took me out of the mill and apprenticed me to a blacksmith. I served my indentures and became a master blacksmith myself, and that's where it all started.' He caught Edna's attention and ordered two more pints.

Ray Hobbs

'Let me get these, Edgar.'

'Take your hand out of your pocket, lad. You're my guest.' He went on with his story. 'I saw the first motor car driven through the valley where I lived, an' that told me something. I realised that the internal combustion engine was the coming thing. I knew manufacturers would be fighting each other to make parts for cars, so I decided to concentrate on gearboxes, prop shafts, differentials and back axles for buses and wagons.'

'And tanks, I believe.'

'Eventually,' he agreed, 'but what I'm trying to say is that I'm no better than you are. We're both blessed with special ability. The only difference is that I saw an opportunity and I was lucky, that's all.'

'You've been very successful.' It was as if Edgar had forgotten that, although William doubted it.

'I started a long time ago.' He made a dismissive gesture, saying simply, 'Keep in touch, William.'

# 26

## MAY

Lucy closed her violin part and said, 'I think the Cesar Franck's coming along nicely. We should try something new next time.'

'You're a hard taskmistress.'

'Nonsense. You're just lazy.'

'All right.' He closed the fall and stood up. 'What do you have in mind?'

'We could go for one of the greats, maybe Beethoven.' She considered that briefly and said, 'We could have a bash at one of the shorter sonatas, not the *Kreutzer Sonata* just yet, but you never know.'

'I thought that was the German word for "cruiser".'

'Different spelling, I think. He dedicated it to the ungrateful violinist Rodolphe Kreutzer, hence its name.' She left the music on her stand and sat on the sofa.

'Why do you call him ungrateful?'

'He criticised it and he refused to play it.'

'They're a strange lot,' he said, joining her on the sofa.

'Who? Violinists or Germans?'

'Oh, violinists. Germans are all right when they're not listening to a megalomaniac with a chip on his shoulder.'

'Have you known many violinists?'

He put his arm round her and drew her closer. 'Only one, really.'

'You do talk nonsense.' Nevertheless, she snuggled up to him. 'Tell me,' she said, 'have you noticed the quality of your work falling off since we became better acquainted?'

'Not measurably, but I'm keeping a close eye on it.'

'You served in a cruiser, didn't you?'

'What has that got to do with you distracting me from my work?'

'Nothing.' She snuggled closer. 'I was changing the subject. I'm allowed to, you know, and you mentioned cruisers earlier, so I was only referring to an earlier conversation.'

'All right. *HMS Exeter* is a *York Class* heavy cruiser.'

'How heavy?'

'About eight-and-a-half thousand tons, but the description "heavy" refers to her armament.'

She raised her head to say, 'William?'

'Yes?'

'Are you going to kiss me?'

He bent and kissed her, conscious as ever of her perfume and the warm softness of her body. The moist feel of her lips against his added to the temptation.

As they broke apart, she said, 'You remember that ship with something akin to affection, don't you?'

'Yes, but I never kissed her like that.'

'I know. I'm only saying that you remember her with such fondness in spite of the horrible injuries you suffered.'

'It wasn't *Exeter*'s fault, Lucy. You have to blame the *Graf Spee* for that; in fact, it wasn't even her fault. It was all down to Hitler.'

'I curl up inside whenever I see your scar and think about what happened.'

'Don't think about it.'

'I'll try not to.' As something else occurred to her, she asked, 'What were you laughing at when you came from Commander Challock's room?'

'You asked me that yesterday.'

'And you wouldn't tell me.'

'It's classified information.'

'Rot. Anyway, I have Ultra Clearance.'

His eyes teased her for a moment longer, and then he relented. 'There's a new submachine gun, a brilliant idea, because it can be made almost anywhere, and it can fire captured enemy ammunition.'

'I don't see what's funny about that.'

'All right. The Sten gun, as it's called, has a weakness, namely that it's vulnerable to water and dirt, which is bad news, as it will most likely be used in North Africa, where, admittedly, there's very little water, but there's a hell of a lot of sand.'

'I still haven't heard anything funny.'

'Be patient.' He patted her knee. 'It's been decided that, to protect it when it's not in use, its muzzle must be covered by a condom sheath. That's a sort of....' He wondered quite how to explain it without being too graphic.

'I know what a condom sheath is. Is that the funny bit?'

He gave her a stern look and asked, 'How do you know what a—'

'Never you mind. Is that the whole story?'

'No, it's not. When Commander Challock told me that, I had an idea. Chances are, you see, that at least one gun and its... accessory will, at some time, fall into enemy hands, so I suggested that each man should be equipped with a box of large condoms, but that the box should be labelled "Size: Normal".'

'Sort of boasting?'

'Sort of,' he agreed. 'Anyway, the plan was put to the Prime Minister, who endorsed it. Apparently he said, "Let's give the Master Race an inferiority complex. Hitler as well. With any luck, it will have the bugger peering down his trousers with acute dismay." '

Lucy regarded him seriously. 'It's boys' humour, isn't it?'

'I'm afraid so, but you're remarkably unfazed by it.'

'Maybe I'm not as posh as you think.'

'Maybe not,' he agreed, 'if you know what a condom is.'

'Did Grandpa convince you that we don't come from another planet?'

'Yes, he did, but I'm still surprised that you're as knowledgeable as you are. Did you learn about condoms at finishing school?'

Lucy looked at her watch. 'The siren hasn't sounded yet,' she said, 'but I should go, anyway.'

'You could stay here. You'll be all right if there is a raid, and tomorrow's Sunday, so we don't have to go to work.'

She considered his offer, and then asked, 'Have you enough food?'

'There's a Woolton pie with Bovril gravy and a hint of sausage meat.'

'Anything to follow?'

'Only the pleasure of my company.'

'I'll stay.'

Her presence overnight would present him with further temptation, but he felt equal to it.

⊷⊶⊷⊶⊷⊶

'The siren hasn't sounded yet,' said Bea.

'Don't worry, you can stay here.' Dai sounded absent but reassuring.

'I think I will.' She watched as his forefinger slid through the water, representing a torpedo that finally made contact with the floating loofah.

'Pow!'

'Do you ever use this bathtub for bathing, Dai, or is it just for playing boats?' They were at Dai's flat, which had the advantages of a double bed and its own bathroom with a six-foot bathtub. Because there were two of them, they were taking advantage of more than the approved five inches of water.

'Deep down, I'm still a submariner, Bea. I have to have my moments.'

'I thought you had your moment earlier, when you grabbed the bedrail and shouted, "It's a try!" I felt like a pair of rugby goalposts, and it came as quite a shock.' She fanned herself with a facecloth.

'I was just overcome with emotion. You know how it is.'

'And I thought you'd turned over a new leaf. Was the poetry no more than a flash in the pan?'

'What poetry was that, Bea?'

'Your description of the statue of Diana at the Public Library, and the particularly extravagant compliment you paid me.'

'That was no flash in the pan, Bea. No, I was only thinking, looking at you just now, you remind me of what we're fighting for.'

She laughed. 'A woman in a bathtub?'

'Not just any woman, Bea, but a Diana-like embodiment of British womanhood at its finest and most desirable.' He took a bar of 'Lifebuoy' and began soaping her legs, starting below the knees and

198

continuing upward, leaning forward to afford the same attention, albeit more gently, to her torso and her delightful breasts.

'I thought Diana was a Roman goddess.'

'I believe she was, when everyone had their own. She's just a close parallel in this case.'

'You say the sweetest things in your rugged, Celtic way.'

'I try to be poetic, Bea, honestly I do.' His eyes went up to the bathroom clock. 'Now you're staying the night,' he said, 'we can play the second half of the match. That's if you're game.'

❧❦❧

Sunlight was streaming in through the only window. William poured a cup of tea and took it to the spare room. A sleepy invitation answered his knock, so he pushed open the door.

She sat up in bed and, remembering her nudity, covered herself again.

'Oh, bloody hell, Lucy, I'm sorry.'

'No, it was my fault. I should have worn the pyjamas you left out.'

'No, I should have....'

'Let's both stop apologising,' she suggested. 'The tea will go cold.'

'All right.' He started for the door.

'No, be sociable and sit on the bed for a minute.' She tucked the sheet under her arms and across her chest.

'Do you think I should?'

'I think decency will be preserved.'

He sat at the bottom of the bed. 'You're very relaxed,' he observed.

'I was brought up with two brothers. I used to wander about the house completely starkers.'

'How old were you when you stopped doing that?'

'Seventeen.'

'What?'

'Gotcha! You're not the only one who can tell whoppers.' She took pity on him and said, 'I was about five, actually.'

Changing the subject for the sake of his own composure, he said, 'I never heard a single bomb all night, but I'm a heavy sleeper. How about you?'

'I heard nothing. What do you think it means?'

'Maybe Göring's found a new hobby: collecting man traps or pulling the wings off insects.'

She nodded slowly. Perhaps we'll never know.' She stirred, and said, 'I need to use the bathroom.'

'Feel free.' He left the room.

❦❦❦

On Monday morning, Commander Challock was similarly intrigued. 'The evidence is pointing to an offensive in the east,' he said. 'It's too early to say, yet, but it could be the end of the Blitz.'

'Oh, from your lips to God's ears, sir.'

'What?'

'It's something my civilian employer says. If you remember, he's Jewish.'

Challock looked at him sharply. 'Are you still working for him, Stamford?'

'Occasionally, sir.'

'You amaze me.'

'I'm keeping my options open for the end of the war, sir, but the agency job is a bird in the hand.'

Challock raised both eyebrows. 'One night without an air raid, and you're making post-war plans. It'll be a long time, yet, Stamford. Meanwhile, we have yet more bloody silly requests from the Ministry of Information.'

'Isn't it time I did something for the Admiralty, sir?'

'My sentiments entirely, but there's nothing doing for the time being. Everyone's looking nervously towards Danish waters, where the Bismarck is believed to be hiding.'

William decided to concentrate on the job in hand. 'What do the Ministry want, sir?'

'Jokes about Hitler, would you believe? Make it as original as you can, Stamford. No need to go down the monorchid route. In any

200

case, it's been done already. I believe the pongos sing a song about it to the tune of "Colonel Bogie".'

William nodded. He had heard soldiers in a pub singing, 'Hitler has only got one ball!' It was quite amusing, but he took Challock's point.

# 27

Commander Challock shuffled William's collected offerings, chuckling to himself. Eventually, he said, 'I'm afraid we can't use these, Stamford. Too near the knuckle.' He put them down with apparent reluctance and said, 'When I told you to avoid reference to Hitler's singular appendage, I didn't mean that you could make jokes about the size of his equipment or, for that matter, his choice of sexual accomplice. As a matter of fact, I have it on good authority that he favours the all-male scenario, but we can't use that either.' He gave the document a good-natured but dismissive pat and said, These would go down well in a four-ale bar, a messdeck, a barrack room or even a wardroom, but they're not suitable for the general public.'

'With respect, sir, you never mentioned the identity of the audience when you gave me the job. You simply asked for jokes about Hitler.'

'In that case, Stamford, I apologise, but you'll have to try again, hopefully with your mind somewhere above your middle.'

'Aye-aye, sir.'

'I'm sorry I can't give you a more rewarding task, but the powers have their attention firmly on the Bismarck, and now Crete.'

'What's the situation on Crete, sir?' William had heard nothing about it.

'Of course, you don't read the papers, do you? Our people on Crete are helping the Greeks defend the island. So far, they've seen off an airborne invasion and given Jerry a hiding into the bargain, but it's not going to end there. We're expecting the enemy to launch another major assault.' He banged the desktop with his fist in frustration. 'If Hitler would only stop dithering, take your advice and invade Russia, we'd know where we stood. The trouble is, he's such a capricious bugger, he could make the decision and then change his mind at the drop of a hat. We shan't know for certain until his tanks cross the Ukrainian border.'

⸎⸎⸎

When William went to Challock's office the next day, he found his superior in an even blacker mood.

'The Germans have taken Maleme airfield, Stamford. They have an airstrip now, where they can land troops and supplies.' It was clear to William that Crete wasn't Challock's worst preoccupation, because he went on to say, 'The *Bismarck* has been sighted off Norway. Just when we didn't need any more bad news, she's bloody-well put to sea.'

'Are they able to shadow her, sir?'

'No, they've lost her. Apparently, it's a guessing game, now, which route she'll take into the Atlantic. She's got most of the Home Fleet tied up, trying to cover every eventuality. It's a bloody shambles.'

'If she gets among one of our convoys—'

'We'll have no convoy left, Stamford.'

William returned to the purpose of his visit. 'It's probably the worst possible time, sir, but I've written some more of those jokes.'

Challock forced himself to concentrate. 'All right,' he said, 'let me see them.'

William handed over three sheets of foolscap, which Challock took and read. At first, he appeared unmoved, and William prepared himself for another rejection. It was the worst time to sell an idea. He was beginning to regret bringing up the subject, when Challock began to chuckle. It was possibly the first laugh he'd had in twenty-four hours, and it was good to see him enjoying it.

'Damned good, Stamford,' he said eventually. 'I especially like the one about Hitler's hunting trophies.' He read it again with unabated enjoyment and said, 'I'll pass these to the Ministry. Let's hope it satisfies them.'

'Thank you, sir. I'd like to go back to what I'm supposed to be doing, working for the Admiralty.'

'Your *magnum opus*, Stamford, if it ever comes off, will be persuading Hitler to invade Russia. If anything, it's a damned sight more important than finding the bloody *Bismarck*, and that's important enough.'

⊕⊦⊣⊰⊢⊱⊦⊰⊣⊢⊕

That weekend, William forsook his habit of ignoring printed news, and bought a copy of *The Evening Standard*. It told him no more than he'd heard from Challock, which only reinforced his ideas about newspapers, but on the following day, he was compelled to buy another. The reason was the alarming news written on the vendor's 'A' board. It read: *Hood Sunk. All Feared Lost.*

He stood in a daze, scarcely able to read beyond the stark headline, and unable to believe that 'The Mighty Hood', forty-seven-thousand tons of battlecruiser, and pride of the Royal Navy, now lay on the ocean bed.

He hurried home to read the report in full.

It seemed that *Hood* and *Prince of Wales* had intercepted the *Bismarck* in the Denmark Strait, and that, in the ensuing battle, *Hood* had been blown apart by a colossal explosion and sunk. *Bismarck* and her consort, the cruiser *Prinz Eugen*, had then turned their guns on *Prince of Wales*, the unfortunate battleship having lost almost half her firepower due to a manufacturing defect. She had been badly damaged and had withdrawn behind a smokescreen.

William's eyes were drawn repeatedly, however, to the report of the *Hood*'s sinking, simply because his mind was unable to accept it.

⊕⊦⊣⊰⊢⊱⊦⊰⊣⊢⊕

When Lucy arrived at his flat the next day, he was more in charge of himself, but manifestly less than vibrant, because, having accepted a half-hearted kiss, she asked, 'Why so soulful?'

'Have you read the news about *HMS Hood*?'

'Yes, I think everyone has. It sounds terrible. What kind of ship was she?'

'A battlecruiser.'

'Like *Exeter*?'

'No.' He motioned to her to sit down. '*Exeter* is a cruiser. A battlecruiser is like a battleship, but with less armour plate and a hull designed for speed.' He stood up, remembering his manners. 'Would you like a cup of tea?'

'I'll do it. I know where everything is. Come and talk to me while I do it.'

'All right.' He went with her to the kitchen. It was a strange feeling because it was his kitchen and she was making tea for them both.

'How many men would a ship like *Hood* have on board?'

'There was no ship like her. She was unique, and I believe she had a complement of about fourteen-hundred. I still haven't heard anything about survivors.'

'Horrible.' She put her arms round his waist and rested her head against his chest. 'What happens now? They've got to find a way of sinking the *Bismarck*, haven't they?'

'It's their first priority.'

'Have we got ships capable of doing it?' She released his waist to stand back and look at him directly.

'According to Commander Challock, *King George the Fifth*, *Nelson* and *Rodney* have the firepower, and any of the *Queen Elizabeth Class* might do it at a pinch, although their guns are of quite an elderly design. The first job, though, is to find her.'

'What was the problem with the *Prince of Wales*? The papers said she was defective in some way. Apparently, she still had civilian workers on board.'

'Her after quadruple turret was faulty. It fired one salvo before breaking down again. It's thought that she landed a few shells on the *Bismarck*, though. We can only hope they caused real damage.'

Lucy scalded the tea. 'I can't help thinking about those men in *HMS Hood*.'

'I've been thinking of little else.'

'Let's take the tea into the sitting room.'

He sat with her on the sofa. 'I'm afraid I'm not good company today.'

'You're not,' she agreed. 'You're a misery, but I see it as my role to hold your head above water until you remember how to swim again, and if that doesn't deserve a kiss, I don't know what does.'

'You'll have to overpower me, Lucy.'

'Very well.' Pinioning his hands to the sofa, she leaned over him and kissed him. After a minute, she said, 'You're not struggling.'

'There was no need. I was enjoying it.'

'Ah. Success at last.' She inclined her head towards the piano, asking, 'Are we going to do anything this afternoon, or are you a lost cause?'

'It'll be a distraction, I suppose.' He needed it after being manhandled by Lucy.

Monday at the Admiralty was like the gathering before a funeral. William knew there was no point in going to see Commander Challock, who was said to be in a bitter frame of mind. He had known some of Hood's officers personally, and he'd taken the news very much to heart. A report that three survivors had been picked up did nothing for his mood.

Lucy was missing for most of the morning, saying that she had a medical appointment. William presumed she was going to see the Principal Medical Officer, and respected her privacy by saying nothing about it other than wishing her well.

On her return, he and she worked on some more jokes for the Ministry, and by the end of Monday, they had a collection of harmless merriment for both sexes, a feat William could never have accomplished alone.

On Tuesday, they worked until William looked at his watch and said, 'I'm going for lunch. Are you coming, Lucy?' She rarely ate lunch, but he always asked her, just in case.

At that moment, Dai burst in without his usual polite knock and said, 'Hey, you two, they've sunk the *Bismarck*!'

'Hooray,' shouted William.

'Hoorah,' said Lucy.

'It happened an hour-and-a-half ago, apparently. She was finally sunk with torpedoes from *HMS Dorsetshire*.'

William was impatient for detail. He said, 'Start at the beginning, Dai. *Dorsetshire* can't have done it alone.'

'Nor did she. It's thought that a Swordfish from *Ark Royal* must have torpedoed *Bismarck* in the steering compartment, because she was unable to steer a straight course when *Rodney* and *K G Five* arrived on the scene. Anyway, those two battered her into a blazing hulk, but she still wouldn't go down, so *Dorsetshire* had to do the honours with torpedoes.'

Lucy asked, 'What is *K G Five*?'

'Sorry, Lucy. *King George the Fifth*.'

'Well,' said William, '*Hood* is avenged, and the threat has passed.'

'In that case,' said Lucy, 'I think I'll join you for lunch.'

# 28

## JUNE

Beethoven's *Appassionata* appeared on William's 'Impossible' list, although he still enjoyed hearing it. He and Lucy were in the National Gallery, at one of the lunchtime piano recitals given by Myra Hess, and the sonata was the main and final work in the programme.

The last movement ended with its three thunderous chords, and the audience broke into eager applause. William exhaled more audibly than he'd intended, prompting Lucy to say, 'You were holding your breath through the final section, weren't you?'

He nodded self-consciously.

'I've done that a few times.'

They sidled out quietly. Miss Hess was likely to play at least one encore, but they had to forego that, having ten minutes in which to return to the Admiralty.

As they walked down the steps into Trafalgar Square, Lucy said, 'Isn't she wonderful? I mean, she's a superb musician, of course, but to play throughout the Blitz was something truly remarkable.' There had been no air raid for more than forty nights, so it seemed right to refer to the Blitz historically.

'Saints and sinners.'

'What?'

He returned a rating's salute and said, 'Saints and sinners,' he repeated. That's what war produces.'

'Oh, I think there are lots of ordinary people as well, all doing the best they can to keep the flag flying. Don't forget them.'

'I suppose you're right.' They waited until it was safe to cross.

'I always am.'

As they moved across the road, William tried to pick up the conversation. 'You always are what?'

'Right. Anyway, how do you class yourself? Saint or sinner?'

'Sinner, of course. As a matter of fact, I have something quite sinful in mind.'

'Oh?' They showed their passes at the door, but Lucy naturally waited until they were out of earshot before asking, 'What kind of sin are you planning?'

'I was only thinking that we should have a celebration soon.'

'What are we going to celebrate?'

'Well, we never did anything to mark the sinking of the *Bismarck*, did we? It didn't even prompt a wardroom dinner, because everyone was too busy with other things.'

They mounted the stairs to their floor, and Lucy said, 'There was the evacuation of Crete as well.'

'That was as much an embarrassment as an achievement. Let's stay with the *Bismarck*.'

'Why not celebrate nothing in particular?'

'That's a good idea.'

Once in Room 33, they resumed their seats and continued to plan their celebration.

'We could do it on Saturday,' said William.

'No, Saturdays are too busy. Everyone else is out celebrating or carousing. Sunday would be better.'

'All right. What do you suggest we do? Dinner and then on to somewhere else afterwards?'

Lucy clapped her hands. 'Perfect,' she said. 'The Glass Slipper was lovely.'

'Yes, I took you there once, didn't I?'

'And you gave me a dozen red roses,' she reminded him, recalling the event with apparent fondness.

'They'd be almost impossible to find nowadays, with everyone Digging for Victory.'

'Never mind. It's time to put on our organising hats. Now, so that neither of us has to worry about getting home late at night, why don't you leave some clothes at my flat and stay over?'

He spotted a flaw immediately. 'You have only one bedroom,' he reminded her.

'There's the sofa bed. It extends to six feet.'

'How impressive.'

It seemed that their plans were complete, which was as well, because Commander Challock chose that moment to summon William.

'Stamford.'

'Sir?'

'Come to my room. I have a task for you…. No, damn it, I'll come to Room 33. That assistant of yours makes a first-rate cup of tea. I'll see you in a few minutes.' He put the telephone down.

'Lucy, your tea-making skills are not only famous, but required now. Commander Challock is on his way here.'

'Aye-aye, sir,' she said, attempting a salute.

As she left the room, William visualised her in a blue uniform with black stockings, but decided that it was a daydream to be saved for later. With Challock on his way, he had to concentrate.

By the time Challock arrived, Lucy had made the tea and had it ready in Room 33. She inspected it and declared it ready just as he knocked at the door and entered.

'By Jove, Miss Pendleton,' he said, 'you knew I was coming.'

'Yes, Commander.'

His eyes explored further. 'Biscuits,' he said. 'How did you come by them?'

'I believe they were left over from a meeting, Commander.'

'Do you make a practice of this? Biscuits are reserved for officers of flag rank.'

'Certainly not. I only picked them up because I knew you were coming.'

Addressing William for the first time, he said, 'How very thoughtful, eh, Stamford?'

'Miss Pendleton is the very epitome of hospitality, sir.' Over Challock's shoulder, he saw Lucy's collaborating smile.

She asked, 'Milk and one lump, isn't it, Commander?'

'That's correct, Miss Pendleton. You remembered.'

'Of course, Commander.'

'Now, the reason for this visit is to charge you both with a new task,' said Challock. 'On this occasion, I'm not wasting your time with a lot of nonsense from the Ministry of Information, although, I have to say, they have approved and accepted your work, so well done, both of you.'

'Thank you, sir.'

'Thank you, Commander.'

'Credit where it's due, no more than that. Now, this is purely a naval task concerning mines. In particular, it concerns the acoustic mine.' Seeing a questioning look from Lucy, he explained. 'There are several types of naval mine, Miss Pendleton. There is the contact type that explodes when one of its horns comes into contact with a ship, and that kind is bad enough, but there are two other types, which are more difficult to counter. The magnetic mine explodes when triggered by a ship's magnetic field, and there is the acoustic mine, which is detonated by the sound of a ship's engines.'

'How beastly.'

Challock adopted a soothing, avuncular tone. 'War is a vile and inhuman business, Miss Pendleton.'

'Are you saying that there are no countermeasures, as yet, for the magnetic and acoustic types, sir?'

'No, Stamford, I'm not. Countermeasures are in place, and mines are being detonated safely. The problem is, as you will have guessed, one of information. The way we deal with the magnetic mine was equally obvious to both sides, but the enemy would give their eye teeth to know how we're dealing with the acoustic variety.'

'May I ask, sir, what that method is?'

'You may. Minesweepers are equipped with electric breakers, or hammers, that make enough noise to detonate acoustic mines safely. It's as simple as that, but the enemy don't know that. If they did, they'd refine their acoustic trigger somehow to make it immune to our electric hammers. Our information is that they're looking for something much more technical, and your job, Stamford and Miss Pendleton, is to invent that equipment and make it sound convincing.'

William also had a new project from Groves and Holmes, an advertisement for an ointment that claimed to restore feminine softness to the work-roughened hands of women in munitions factories. He was both unconvinced and unenthusiastic about the project. In any case, he had to put it on one side until he and Lucy were able to solve the acoustic mine problem.

That evening, he tried Mozart, practising his 11th piano sonata for a full two hours, but even the *wunderkind* was powerless to help him on this occasion. He knew why he was failing. The fact was, he needed Lucy. They had worked together for so long that their partnership was more effective than they were as individuals. He remembered how Lucy had once quoted Aristotle: 'The whole is greater than the sum of its parts.' She and Aristotle were right: there was an undeniable wholeness about them, and it applied in other ways unconnected with their work at the Admiralty.

⊕⊢⇃⊰⊱⊢⊕

In the morning, he learned that Lucy, too, had been unable to make headway with the problem, so they set about tackling it together.

'I've been tempted to fall back on Zoological Warfare,' he confided, 'but I'm reluctant to use it again.'

'Why?'

'I don't want to run the risk of them realising the truth about the Department. The cracked pitcher, you know.'

She was making notes on a sheet of paper. Either that, or she was doodling. He wasn't sure, but suddenly, she said, 'Remember what Aristotle said about the suspension of disbelief.'

'You know him better than I do, Lucy. What did he say?'

'He said, "Probable impossibilities are to be preferred to improbable possibilities".'

'He said it in Greek, too, which is particularly clever. What was he driving at?'

'He was talking about the theatre,' she explained patiently. 'The purpose of theatre is to make us believe something that's not true, isn't it?'

'Agreed.'

'Just as an example, everyone knows that coincidence happens in real life.'

'Yes.'

'But if a play relies too heavily on coincidence, the plot becomes incredible, doesn't it? It becomes an "improbable possibility".'

He was beginning to follow her argument. 'Like *The Force of Destiny*,' he suggested.

'All right, but that was the fault of the librettist, rather than Verdi.'

She had him there. 'Right.'

'Let's move away from the theatre and consider weapons of war, which is what we're supposed to be doing. Let's take the tank as an impossibility.'

'But it exists.'

'I know, but it didn't always. There was a time when it was impossible because no engine was capable of propelling a gigantic steel box across muddy wasteland. Trust me, I have it on good authority.'

'The highest authority,' he agreed.

'And then, when they had the engine, there was no gearbox capable of doing the whatsit.'

'To use a technical term, but yes, that overcame the impossibility, but what made it probable?'

'The need to break the stalemate on the Western whatnot.'

'Front,' he prompted.

'All right, I'm just a weak and feeble woman. I don't know all the terminology.'

'But you can launch a telling argument.'

She shrugged. 'That was Aristotle, not me.'

'Give him my thanks when you see him, and ask him how we can crack this problem.'

'That's just what I'm saying, William. Let's use the DMZW, but not that alone. If we don't use it again, the enemy will suspect something, and if we over-use it, they will, but if it makes a small contribution backed up by something concrete, it retains its credibility.' She set about drawing a diagram. 'Let's consider using porpoises to detect metal objects on the seabed. Then, when they're detected, an improved form of radar or something – I'm sure there is such a thing – identifies it as a mine. Then, whether it's magnetic or acoustic, it can be destroyed on the seabed by something-or-other.'

'May I?' He took her diagram and studied it. 'You know, Lucy, you have something here. A mine could be identified by an improved form of ASDIC and destroyed by a delayed-action explosive charge placed remotely by... by compressed air directed down a pipe, like a miniature torpedo tube.'

'You see,' she said, smiling, 'those Greek philosophers still have their uses. I was only thinking, today, about the day we met, when I was feeling so useless, and you bucked me up.'

He was floundering again. He had to ask, 'Where did the Greek philosophers come into it?'

'You realised I had certain qualities and you drew on them. That's how Socrates taught his pupils, by drawing out knowledge they didn't know they had. He began with facts that they knew, and then he got them to realise something connected with those facts.' She smiled wistfully and said, 'If only more teachers could take a leaf out of his book.'

'You should teach classics, Lucy. You'd be brilliant at it.'

'Without maths, I couldn't matriculate, so that was never an option for me. I had to learn, instead, to be a wife, hostess and mother. My duty would be to serve my husband by entertaining his guests at the table and by serving him in the marriage bed.'

Surprised as he was to hear her speak so frankly, he said lamely, 'That's a very unmaidenly thought, Lucy.'

Her expression became serious. 'Maybe,' she said, 'that's because I'm not a maiden.'

'What?' He tried to look less surprised, but it was too late.

'I've been meaning to tell you, and this is as good a time as any. You know I was engaged to be married. I told you about that.'

'To a man who ill-treated you.'

'Yes, he was also impatient. He decided he could wait no longer for his conjugal rights. I was nervous, of course, and not at all keen, but I was afraid of him, so I went along with it.'

'Oh, Lucy. That must have been horrible for you.'

'It was horrible. For a while, I wondered why people did it, and then I decided there must be some inducement, otherwise the human race would have become extinct after the frolic in the Garden of Eden.'

'You must have had a bloody awful experience.'

'You don't think less of me, then?'

'Of course not. I feel…. I don't know what I feel. If anything, I feel bloody angry. I wish I could lay my hands on him.'

She smiled, possibly relieved by his understanding and sympathetic reaction. 'Don't worry, William. It's in the past, but I thought you should know that I'm not pretending to be something I'm not.'

'Well,' he said, taking her hands in his, 'it makes no difference at all to you and me.'

She made no reply, but tears were forming in her eyelids.

'Let me type up this proposal.' He released her hands, kissed her surreptitiously before anyone could call in and see them, and then drew the typewriter towards him.

❦

On Sunday evening, he arrived at Lucy's flat and presented her with a dozen red roses.

'William! Thank you. They're lovely. Where on earth did you find them?'

'The Savoy Hotel. I told them I was a resident, but I wanted to pay in cash because I didn't want the roses to appear on the bill.'

'How clever of you, and what a lovely thing to do.' She wore a dark-red, flared evening dress that clung to her slender figure, and her air of excitement made it all the more glamorous.

'You look wonderful,' he said, and he meant it.

'Thank you.'

'Where shall I leave this?' He held up his overnight grip.

'Leave it in the sitting room, unless you want to lay out a shirt or something.'

'I'd better. I don't want to appear before Commander Challock in a creased shirt.' He took out his shirt, placing it on a hanger that

Lucy brought for him. 'The taxi's waiting,' he said. 'Let me help you on with your coat. That's if you need it. I've left mine at home, it's so warm out there.'

'I'd better take it. I've been caught out before,' she said, letting him help her.

As they walked out to the taxi, she said, 'I have a feeling about tonight. I don't know why, but I think it's going to be special.'

'I hope so.' He opened the door for her and followed her into the taxi, saying to the driver, 'Henri's in the Strand, please.'

'Henri's in the Strand, guv'nor,' the driver confirmed.

William settled back in his seat beside Lucy, luxuriously inhaling her perfume.

'You like it, don't you?'

'It's like a drug. How do you find these things nowadays?'

'Perfume? I'm afraid I was naughty when they told us not to stock up. I bought clothes, perfume, make-up, cold cream, silk stockings and all kinds of things that I thought might be in short supply. It seemed to me that the previous war went on for four years, and it was possible this one would do the same.' She looked at him guiltily from beneath the brim of her hat and asked, 'Do you think that's awful?'

'Stocking up? No, and you weren't the only one.' He gave her an unnecessarily appraising look and said, 'Besides, when you look as sensational as you do tonight, I can't find it in my heart to blame you for anything.'

⊕⊢⪥⪥⊢⊕

The meal at Henri's matched their expectations and, confident that an air raid was now unlikely, they took another taxi to the Glass Slipper, where they were welcomed and taken to an alcove similar to the one they'd occupied a year earlier.

Their host brought them the wine list and lit the candle on their table. 'I'm afraid we've finished serving food, sir, but perhaps you'd like to choose something from the wine list.'

'That's all right. We've already eaten, but I'd like to order a bottle of....' He scanned the list until he came to the champagnes. 'A bottle of the *Dom Pérignon* 'thirty-seven, please.'

'William,' said Lucy when they were alone, 'can you afford champagne?'

'I've been doing a lot of work for Groves and Holmes,' he told her. 'They're paying for it. Anyway, I'm only trying to create the special evening you're anticipating.'

'I should have realised that, although I don't know how you fit the work in.'

'It won't be for much longer.'

'Oh?' Her eyes registered surprise.

'I'm disenchanted with advertising. Since I've become involved in lying for a good cause, I find that lying to innocent and unsuspecting shoppers leaves an unpleasant taste.'

She said nothing, which was as well. Work belonged to another time, whereas the evening was theirs.

William asked, 'Would you like to dance?' The band was playing 'The Last Time I Saw Paris', and the distress that had been associated with it had now faded with the passing of time. It was also an excellent song.

'Let's.'

They took to the floor, which was less than half-full. Lucy's prediction had been right, and they were able to enjoy the space and the music.

When they returned to their table, they found a bottle of the champagne William had ordered, standing in a bucket of ice.

William removed the foil and the cage. 'Here goes,' he said, easing the cork until it left the bottle with a pleasingly discreet 'pop'.

'Well done,' said Lucy, who had clearly heard a few corks drawn during her young life.

'A wardroom steward told me that a champagne cork should never pop loudly,' said William, filling her glass.

'And he was right. I don't know what difference it makes to the champagne, but that is the received snobbery as I understand it.'

William was already thinking of something else. 'Lucy?'

'Yes?'

'Would you send your children away to school?'

'If it were my decision, no.'

'Good.'

She peered at him in the light of the single candle. 'What made you think of that?'

'It was just something your grandpa said that struck me as important.'

'What did he say?'

'It was a piece of advice. He said, "When you have children, don't send 'em to boarding school". That was all, but I'm glad you and I agree with him.'

They danced several times, the last being to 'A Nightingale Sang in Berkeley Square.'

'It seems to follow us around,' said William.

'It's only happened once, and that was a year ago. Let's just enjoy it.'

The floor was crowded by this time, so they shuffled, enjoying the music, the ambience and the nearness of each other. With his cheek against Lucy's, and before he could help himself, William said, 'Lucy?'

'What?'

'I love you.' Realisation had caught up with him only in the last few days, and saying it seemed to eradicate any previous doubts and to underline the truth.

'There,' she said, 'I told you it was going to be a special night.' She kissed him lightly and murmured in his ear, 'Confidentially, I love you too.' They danced on to what seemed to have become, quite by chance, their song. It would always be so, and William wondered, that night, if Aristotle's 'probable impossible' might be at work again. He would check with Lucy, but not immediately. For now, they would simply enjoy the new turn of events and the euphoria that came with it.

The taxi dropped them at the block of flats, leaving them to pick their way through the blackout. Lucy stumbled once on the stone steps, but William caught her.

'I used to field at first slip for my school,' he said.

'I don't believe you.' It had become almost an automatic response.

They reached the flat and closed the door behind them.

'We'll have to draw the blackout curtains before I can switch the light on,' she said.

'Let's not. We can see what we're doing.' Even through the

narrow basement window, the brilliant new moon was enough to illuminate the sitting room.

'All right.' She drew him down to the sofa. 'I love you,' she whispered.

'Why are you whispering?'

'Because what we're doing is very private.'

'In that case,' he whispered, 'I love you too.'

She still wore her coat, but they kissed, oblivious to everything. Eventually, she said, 'Let me take my coat off. I'll be back in a tick.'

While she was gone, he removed his tunic, tie and shoes, wondering how long it took her to hang up her coat. The moon was making its relentless journey towards the western sky and taking its light with it.

'Done,' she said, removing her stockings and draping them over his tunic. 'I'd better take this dress off. It's rather precious. Will you unhook me?'

He stood up to unhook the top of her dress and pull down the zipper, kissing her neck where it curved into her shoulder.

'No one's ever kissed me there,' she said, pulling her dress up and over her head.

'I should hope not. It's part of an advanced technique known only to a few.' He stepped out of his trousers, deftly removing his socks. He always felt foolish, half-clothed and in socks, even when he was alone.

'Men's collars are ridiculous,' she remarked, struggling to remove the front stud.

'Let me do it,' he suggested. 'It's a man's job, after all.'

She busied herself with his shirt buttons while he attended to his collar.

'My turn,' he said as she relieved him of his shirt and cufflinks, leaving him to address the fastening of her brassiere.

'Can you manage?'

'Do you mind? I'm considered something of a dab hand at this.' The fastening came apart, and he lifted the garment over her arms to expose modest but delightful breasts.

'They're not very imposing,' she said.

'They're wonderful; in fact, they're exquisite. I'm in love

with them already.' He proved his point by kissing each of them reverently, on and around the hardening nipples.

'I'll believe you.' There was a tremor in her voice.

'Knickers,' he reminded her, pointing to her nether garment.

'Thingies,' she said, pointing to his.

'Drawers, cellular, officers',' he corrected her, slipping his fingers inside the waistband to send them on their downward journey.

'Just a minute.' She felt beneath the sofa cushions and pulled on two concealed handles to turn the sofa into a double bed.

'That's clever.' He divested himself of his drawers, wishing they were called something more in keeping with a fashionable gentleman's wardrobe, and sat on the sofa, waiting for her to finish making a neat pile of her clothes. Eventually, in what remained of the moonlight, she finished undressing and stood naked before him.

Captivated, he rose to his feet, holding out his arms to her. They held each other and kissed slowly and luxuriously.

Presently, he interrupted the spell by whispering, 'I need something from my tunic.'

'No, you don't. That's what I was doing that Monday morning. I had an idea something like this was going to happen.'

'You're full of surprises.' He joined her on the sofa, taking her in his arms again, kissing her repeatedly and enjoying the soft smoothness of her skin. 'I love you,' he said. For some reason, he felt compelled to keep telling her.

'I love you,' she said, the final word mutating into a groan as he went on to explore her. Presently, she shuddered, clinging to him. 'You've done it... again.'

'What?'

'The... Socrates thing. You've found... part of me I didn't... know I... had,' she said between involuntary exclamations of bliss that gave way eventually to a gasp of delight as she accepted him.

⊰⊱⊰⊱⊰⊱

William opened his eyes, blinking at the midsummer sun's rays that penetrated the flat. Remembering where he was, and relishing the recollection, he felt beside him and found that Lucy was gone. When his eyes were cleared, he consulted his watch. It showed five minutes past six. It was all right; he hadn't overslept.

The sitting room door opened, prompting him to turn his head as Lucy entered in her plum-red silk dressing gown. She was carrying a tray, which she placed on the floor.

'Good morning,' she said. 'Did you sleep well?'

'Very well, thank you. Something happened last night that quite wore me out.'

She handed him a cup of tea. 'I'll run a bath soon,' she said.

'There's no hurry. Come and join me.' He patted the sofa beside him.

'You know,' she said as she joined him, 'I've changed my mind.'

'About what?'

'Men and women, mothers and fathers, what they get up to. I know, now, why people do it.'

'Ah,' he said, 'you've found the meaning of life.'

'All I know is I didn't know it could be like that.'

'It came in a love bundle,' he told her. 'That's what made it special.'

'It must have,' she agreed, sipping her tea. 'It was a new experience for me, the love bundle and... one or two other things.'

'But mainly the love bundle,' he prompted modestly. He drank half his tea, which tasted sublime. He knew it was only pusser's tea, but it was like champagne in the circumstances.

'A love bundle is such a novelty,' she said, still marvelling.

'Good, because it's all I have to offer.'

'Oh,' she said, shaking her head, 'you have much more than that to offer, and that's the most wonderful thing about you, that all you ever want to do is give.'

'In that case,' he said, 'having accepted that I've no interest in the Pendleton millions, would you consider me as a permanent fixture, the poor end of the family, as it were?'

'William,' she said ecstatically, 'if you made a church mouse look like Croesus, I'd still marry you.' She leaned over and kissed him with renewed enthusiasm.

When he was able to speak, he said, 'I thought that was a kind of paint for treating garden fences.'

221

'That's *creosote*, you barm pot.'

'I think Grandpa's been teaching you some very common expressions.'

⊕⊷⧉⊶⧉⊷⊕

Dai was waiting for them outside Room 33, demonstrably excited and incoherent. At the third attempt, he managed to say, 'Commander Challock wants to see you both. I can't tell you why. I'm sworn to secrecy.'

'Is that why you were speaking in code just now?'

Dai had no time for banter. 'Quick as you like, William. The commander's waiting.'

They accompanied the animated lieutenant to Challock's office, where they found the commander in a sunny, almost rapturous mood.

'Stamford, my dear chap,' he said, 'and Miss Pendleton too.' He shook them both by the hand. 'Hearty congratulations to you both.'

For the moment, William was silent, having no idea what could have prompted such a reception. Lucy, too, stared in incomprehension.

'Hitler has invaded Russia! After dithering, postponing and generally buggering about – forgive me, Miss Pendleton – he's finally taken your advice and turned on Stalin. We can breathe again!'

'That's excellent news, sir.'

'It's wonderful news, Commander.'

'The Prime Minister wants to see you both at four bells. That's ten o'clock, Miss Pendleton. The whole Deception Committee has been summoned.'

'Oh, Lucy,' said William, 'I'm going to enjoy the looks on a few of those faces.'

'Now, Stamford,' said Challock, 'this is no time for "I told you so", especially where senior officers are concerned.' He looked at their overjoyed faces again and changed his mind. 'Yes, it bloody-well is – forgive me again, Miss Pendleton – This is your moment. Enjoy it to the full!'

At Dai's suggestion, they called on Bea, who had already heard the news from Vice-Admiral Davies and was keen to offer her congratulations. It was a noisy celebration, and no one was surprised when Bea's intercom buzzed and the admiral's voice said, 'What's going on in there, Bea? I can't hear myself think.'

'Lieutenant-Commander Stamford and Miss Pendleton are here, sir. We're just enjoying the news about Russia.'

'Good. Send them in, will you?'

Bea opened the communicating door to let Lucy and then William into the admiral's office.

'Good morning, both of you. Stand easy, Stamford, and let me offer my warmest congratulations to you both. The Prime Minister will have plenty to say on the subject, I feel sure, but I'd like to get mine in first. You've both done a superb job. Really well done!'

❧

The Deception Committee filed into the Prime Minister's office, with William and Lucy in the rear, both managing to insert themselves behind senior officers, where they might escape the Prime Minister's notice. In that, however, they were unsuccessful, as he had already seen them enter.

'Lieutenant-Commander Stamford and Miss Pendleton, don't hide at the back. Come forward.'

Obediently, they stepped forward.

'Gentlemen.' Mr Churchill's eye fell on Lucy, and he corrected himself. '*Lady* and gentlemen. I most humbly beg your pardon, Miss Pendleton. Habit is the precursor of social clumsiness.'

William's mind was wandering. He had spotted a large tray bearing a magnum of champagne and a number of glasses.

'By this time, you will all be acquainted with the momentous news that Hitler has launched *Operation Barbarossa*. That is to say, he has unleashed his forces on Russia and the Ukraine, and I need hardly remind you of what this means to Great Britain. It comes as a momentous relief to us all.'

The door opened, and a man in short-jacket morning dress entered the office. Mr Churchill saw him immediately.

'Ah, Colville, you're here. Pour the champagne, will you? It's no good to us in the bottle.'

'Certainly, sir.' He removed the foil and cage from the bottle and, to William's secret delight, released the cork with a resounding 'funk!'

The Prime Minister resumed his address.

'It is, as I said, a relief to us all. I believe, also, that you are aware that the prime movers of the plan to influence the Nazis in this matter are with us today. I refer, of course, to Lieutenant Commander Stamford and to Miss Lucinda Pendleton, both of whom deserve our sincerest congratulations and our undying gratitude for the service they have performed for our nation.' He broke off to admonish the industrious secretary. 'Damn it, Colville, haven't you poured the champagne yet?'

'I'm just pouring the last two glasses, sir.'

'Good. Now, Miss Pendleton and Gentlemen, when Colville has finished handing round the champagne, we shall drink two toasts.' He waited with barely-contained impatience until each person present had been given a glass of champagne, and said, 'I give you "Confusion to *Operation Barbarossa*".'

The company repeated the toast and drank.

'The second toast is to the architects of the splendid artifice that made it possible. Gentlemen, I give you, "Stamford and Miss Pendleton".'

The meeting continued along less formal lines, and William was able to enjoy, in the worst possible way, the astonished reactions of certain senior officers. His gratification was interrupted, however, by the Prime Minister, who cornered Lucy and him at his first opportunity.

'Stamford and Lucinda,' he said, 'let me offer you my personal thanks and, although the nation is unaware of your services, my gratitude on its behalf. I am truly grateful. Your ruses and red herrings would be a by-word if such information were made public, which I hope it will not, at least for a very long time, because the deception we are celebrating today is your most magnificent yet.'

Momentarily bewildered by the immensity of the situation, William muttered something suitably banal, whereas Lucy, who was less in awe of the Prime Minister, said, 'Well, you know how it is, sir. "England expects" and all that sort of thing.'

Mr Churchill's face was transformed into a beaming smile. 'She does,' he agreed, 'and with people like you in her service, she is right to expect, and to know that she will not be disappointed.'

By the time the meeting broke up, William had rediscovered the power of speech. He was confronted by Colonel Loxton, who, he remembered, had been responsible for Lucy's transfer to his office.

'I confess, Stamford, I am astounded by what you've both achieved.'

'Thank you, sir.'

'You're a bright chap, of course, and Miss Pendleton clearly had hidden depths.'

'Don't we all, sir? Socrates evidently thought so.'

⊕ᛝ⊰⊱Ɛᛝ⊕

Back in Room 33, they allowed themselves a clandestine, celebratory hug.

'If you remember,' said Lucy, 'Mr Churchill referred to our "ruses and red herrings", but I prefer to think of our story so far as one of *roses* and red herrings.'

'Ah, but Mr Churchill doesn't know about that.'

'Not yet, anyway.'

William gave her a searching look. He asked, 'Are you writing your guest list already?'

'What's wrong with forward planning?' She let the thought take root and then returned to the excitement of the day, 'Isn't it wonderful? We're safe.'

'For the time being,' agreed William, 'and that's all we can ever hope for.'

'I'm so relieved, I'm going to make a sacrifice.'

'Burnt, live or abstract?'

'You've got to take this seriously, William.' She fixed him with her most serious gaze and said, 'I'm going to give up eggs for as long as the war lasts.'

'Isn't that somewhat drastic? You like eggs, as I recall.'

'I know, but I was quite affected by what you told me the night I was bombed out.'

'But, Lucy, that was nonsense.'

'It may be nonsense to you,' she said reproachfully, 'but I feel for those chickens, and it's not just that. What about all the children and pregnant women who need that protein? What right have I to accept a scarce item such as eggs when their need is greater than mine?'

'I suppose you have a point there,' he conceded.

'The worst thing, though, is when you dip a toast soldier or sailor into a soft-boiled egg, and the yolk runs down the side of the egg cup. Not only is it a shameful waste of yolk, but you have to wipe it straight away or it congeals, and then, I'm told, it's murder to wash off.'

He let out a sigh, admitting defeat.

'Gotcha!'

## THE END

# EPILOGUE

In January 1946, two entries of significance appeared in *The Times* newspaper. One was to the effect that His Majesty King George VI had been pleased to make Commander William F. Stamford, D.S.C., R.N.V.R. a Commander of the British Empire.

The other entry concerned Lucinda J. Stamford, who was made an Officer of the British Empire.

Both awards were for undisclosed services to the nation.

www.ingramcontent.com/pod-product-compliance
Lightning Source LLC
Chambersburg PA
CBHW020834260626
47169CB00003B/975